# Shadows of In

# Book One

# The Gambler's Abyss

# By David Joyce

For the wisdom of the rooms
and all those who have shared
their soul. This book is as much
theirs as mine.

# I AM ADDICTION

I start in small subtle ways promising many things,

I promise you enjoyment and pleasure beyond your wildest dreams, I deliver guilt & despair more horrible than your worst nightmare,

I promise you power and courage, I give you feelings of powerlessness and hopelessness,

I will force you to live in fear always,

I promise you relief and escape from all your daily problems, I create for you greater problems than you ever imagined,

I promise you many friends, I allow you only isolation,

I promise you happiness, I create much sorrow.

I will steal from you your dignity, your families, your friends, your children, your homes, your demons, your spirit and your life, for love, freedom & happiness are impossible to find in my presence,

So never underestimate me, I am devious and manipulating, I have no preferences as to who I pick as my victim, rich or poor, young or old, black, white, yellow or red.

I have killed men, women and children, I have no conscience.

So if you have me, always be aware if you think you can beat me that I will be gone from your life and all will go well again.

Never forget that I will always be there, waiting in the dark shadows just around the corner.

I am very patient and I will laugh in your face face if I can lure you into my evil world of hell on earth once again.          (Anonymous)

# PART ONE

December 2012

1

In the hydrotherapy pool not a ripple, not a bubble, a lifeless calm. A body limp beneath the tranquil haze. A translucent human form pickling in a warm bath of chlorinated sapphire, snuggled peacefully against the satin corner tiles, meditative, ignoring time that had started to act as a press: firstly in her throat, where her last breath had been inhaled and then down her larynx and trachea to the chambers of her lungs, which now starved had started to spasm. Beyond to her diaphragm that squeezed desperately and now to the rest of her where an intricate, vigorous and dazzling dance of blood cells responded to the lack of oxygen and build up of carbon dioxide. Her heart, no longer passive, beat faster and faster. Then the smallest movement in her right foot propelled her head above the placid surface and a crescendo of spluttering, coughing, and hollering smashed the silence and the words, recognisable only out of habit, were spewed upwards towards Michelle, her confidante and regular timekeeper.

"Did I beat it?"

"Not quite, but you weren't far away."

"Damn." Mia's disappointment concluded with another brief disappearance below the surface before quickly finding the metal steps and hauling herself off to the changing rooms.

"Stop him……..Stop him….please!!"

As Jeff turned onto 'The Ramp' he heard the cries of the two nurses moving swiftly downhill from the top of the slope but instead his attention was drawn to the recognisable traits of the man that approached him: the strained and furrowed lines on his forehead, the hair more salt than pepper, the beads of sweat tickling his brow and the blowfish cheeks gasping for air. All presented the sign of a man in the first flush of retirement and hurrying to meet his death.

Each morning, on his drive to work, 'the grave diggers,' not 'dodgers,' as he referred to them, jogged their way to early knee surgery or a stroke on the pretence of restraining the inevitable deterioration of physical decline.   They ran conservatively, barely lifting their legs above the horizontal, their pallid flesh exaggerated against the gaudy colours from which it emerged. They were uniformly adorned with white sport socks, white running shoes and head phones, battling thickened capillary walls, sagging muscles and a crumbling spine as the wind and rain battered them into submission.

Yet the similarities between 'the gravediggers' and the man gathering pace towards him stopped at the neckline. Below that, he was wearing a light green full length gown with the rear of the garment flapping outwards like a base jumping superhero, revealing his naked backside intermittently.   His steps were severely shortened; both feet tied together by the incorrect lacing of the smart black leather shoes he was wearing.  His arms were outstretched in front of him and his spread fingers pushed against air as the human obstacles parted in front of him.   Jeff's curious gaze found his eyes, which were catatonic with fear, and bloodshot around the black pin holes, ignoring everything in the periphery as he was concentrating wholly on moving forward as fast as his predicament allowed him to.

As the nurses quickened downhill they battled against the ebb and flow of the human tide and sprayed the flotsam and jetsam of shoulder bags and medical notes in their wake as they took the inevitable path of responding pursuers.

Jeff stopped and turned as the man shuffled past him but his willingness to help him was short lived. The cries had set in motion catastrophic repercussions as the patient reacted to the approaching hurly burly. Attempting to increase his pace just a little, the gentle slope showed no mercy. The man's left foot lifted, followed swiftly by his right, before the left was anywhere near planting itself. Instead the man catapulted himself forward horizontally. As he tried to adjust his body to the impending fall, he naturally turned onto one side before succumbing to gravity.

Later discussions amongst the staff disputed the event that unfolded but Jeff was convinced that the first crack he heard was that of the man's hip as it slammed and ruptured on the industrial linoleum flooring, followed quickly by his skull as his frame whiplashed with a thud and came to an abrupt halt. Knocked unconscious, the blood was already trickling by the time the throng surrounded him; the nurses pushing their way through the circle of generally well meaning but ultimately redundant onlookers. Their royal coloured uniforms of personal and private responsibility struggling to convince everyone to allow them space as they set to treat the patient. Eventually, after pushing away the crowd and castigating those who lingered too long they set to stem the blood loss that was already creating a mosaic of footprints as the onlookers peeled away en route to their various departments.

In a neutral environment Jeff would have taken a lead and directed operations but he was on their turf and his name badge prominently displayed his employer, 'Jeff

Stokes, Manager Social Services,' which, within the walls of Three Counties Hospital, was almost routinely despised. They were the clot in the bloodstream, the broken spoke in the wheel, and the road-works on the motorway. No amount of inter-professional training would change the culture of forty years and thus animosity greeted them universally within such hallowed corridors.

Jeff quickly glanced at his phone. He was late, as usual, and his responsibility to the case conference at hand allowed his conscience to move swiftly on to other concerns, in particular, the bold italicised email in his 'Inbox'. His body quickly followed as he made a rapid u-turn to collect some documents his secretary had left on his desk by marking the email urgent and writing in a large font to nudge his errant memory.

Mia Tukonen adjusted her necklace with the cross dropping in front of her and the inscribed words 'God loves me' facing outwards before vigorously drying her hair.

"I'm not sure I'm ever going to beat it."

"You will. I promise. Just give it some time. You're nearly there. I can't get anywhere close so you should count your blessings." said Michelle.

"I'm trying the divine but it doesn't seem to be getting anywhere."

"Do you think God would give up on you?"

"No. I suppose not."

"You suppose. Let me tell you. He's with you every step of the way. Are you still on for Alpha tonight?"

"Sure. I'll pick you up at seven."

"Great. Go get them."

"Who? The lost souls or the enemy?"

"There's only one enemy you need to worry about and he's not dressed in a white coat. Bye."


Michelle, the manager of the physiotherapy team, had spotted Mia on her second day and recognised Mia's increased frustration as she scoured through the hospital notes and waited for answers from medical staff that didn't seem to have time for her so she had invited her into her office for a coffee.

"So you're the new Senior at Social Services?"

"Do I look that lost?"

"No, but your badge is a big clue."

Mia looked down and smiled wryly. "I think I'm clueless sometimes."

"Of course you aren't. Jeff's been building you up for the last couple of weeks. The first lesson is no matter what you think or the pressure they throw at you everyone is working to the same aim - to enable the patient to return home safely. Once staff know you're one of the team there'll be no end to their cooperation. Please take a seat."

"I just get so frustrated when I want to help but I can't. I know it's the system and once I've figured it out it will be fine but right now I feel out of my depth, which is weird as that's the one thing I strive for."

"I'm not sure I get you."

"Oh sorry. I free-dive."

"Wow. Where do you do that? There's not much coral on the south coast."

"Actually, I'm still at the leisure centre stage. But I need to practise more. I'm trying to increase my hold time underwater."

"I may just be able to help you."

Michelle called in a favour so that they could use the hydrotherapy pool twice a week for thirty minutes in the morning before patients were diarised and it was Michelle who had pressed Mia on her philosophy and beliefs and convinced her that an Alpha course would give her more answers rather than questions if only she would give it a try. Mia feeling lost both professionally and spiritually had gripped tightly to her advocate from that moment onwards.

After Mia had applied the minimum amount of mascara and foundation she took a deep breath, threw her gym bag over her shoulder and headed off to the other end of the hospital consciously reinforcing the words 'One team, one body.' although she had become increasingly sceptical on both counts.

Jeff fidgeted with the rear of the printer and made a mental note to review the equipment in his department, despite knowing that, in essence, his hands were tied as social services were very much the lodgers in the dilapidated wing he called the 'dovecote,' due to the unwelcome but apparently invincible pigeons which resided above the suspended ceiling and whose constant pattering of feet had been accepted as part of the general hum; the tickled snare drum accompanying the background beat of everyday working life.

A whine, an orange flashing light and once more the unruly copy machine sounded the warning; he wrestled wearily with the concertinaed paper that was being digested. As he leaned further, gripping tighter, his pale blue collared shirt eased away from his trousers. His body shape was hardly uniform; legs that were sturdy oaks whilst his trunk and upper limbs resembled an immature willow prone to wavering and gesticulating, often artistically. His waist was thirty four inches at most, but as his thighs were large and his pelvis protruded he required at least a thirty six. His remedy was to punch extra holes in his leather belt with his letter spike. His shirt was always tucked in but with enough slack to hide his belt, which had started to wind its way round his midriff a second time. To his staff his concerns about his frame would have gone unnoticed as his 5 ft 10inch build was best described as slim, at worst wiry but he always arrived smartly dressed and although not handsome in a traditional sense his lightly freckled face was pleasing below foppish hair, which inaccurately gave him the look of ex public school His brow, pockmarked, now squeezed and ridged as he gently attempted to prise the offending piece of A4 from its shackles, careful not to tear the bottom of the page and leave that despairing fragment hidden in the depths of the rollers. Eventually his fingers, clumsy at the best of times and permanently bitten to the quick, smashed into the mottled wall as the printer's rolling jaws finally released its prey and he strode off to room G105.

Each meeting room had its own character and Mia had lost count of the variety of rooms that were allocated for Adult Protection Case Conferences in her career thus far. This room doubled as a small library and training room. It had comfortable seating, not the plastic buckets that had become the norm in other areas, particularly where patients and families were concerned. The side desk attached to the seating was the type you occasionally came across in annoying educational establishments and training centres. A bar protruded out to the right, immediately discriminating against left hander's whose contortions in writing no doubt contributed to their clumsiness. There was little space to write, only just enough to use a small A5 notepad, quite ill-equipped for the detailing of information about an impending investigation. Yet at least it was something; on previous occasions, in other hospitals, there had been a set of six chairs and little else.

Mia had picked up her daily mocha from the hospital cafe on route and as she entered the room, for a brief while, the room surveyed her. She was conscious that everyone else in the room was employed by the health trust and that until her lone ally and immediate supervisor arrived then she would probably be the focus of everyone else's gaze. Except this morning the throng was already preoccupied with the gossip around the hospital, centred on an unfortunate accident with a delusional patient, who had now returned to the care of the private wing. The embellishments to the story had already begun and Mia listened covertly, a little perturbed at not acquiring their attention, as the inflated description of a man hurtling down 'The Ramp' being tripped to stop him escaping. They believed he could have been one of Dr Ramesh's patients from the local Catgory C prison at HMP Coldingly, possibly for sex crimes, possibly a paedophile. The private wing and the trust had a cordial arrangement where low category prisoners could stay in discreet unoccupied individual rooms with their prison officer, more readily available in the private hospital, whilst receiving from the trust a suitable fee, and other non-contracted favours and privileges. Mia didn't bother to engage with them but smiled to herself; she too had previously been the target of such idle chit-chat, her reputation preceding her.

This was Mia's first Adult Protection Meeting in her role as a Senior Practitioner within Three Counties Hospital. She had climbed quickly amongst the rank and file in The Community Team and stood out amongst her peers. There was a spell where she had disappeared from the scene and the rumour mill was that it was linked to her prior relationship with Jeff but she had a passion for her work and was formidable in seeking the truth and flushing out the poor practice of all parties involved in the care of others.

Mia couldn't help but see her fellow participants as adversaries and regarded each meeting as a personal battle of wills. Her combat gear today was silver grey lightweight chinos with orange pumps. Her cream roll neck sweater bore no logo but a pink breast cancer badge completed the look. She wore no jewellery aside from a robust silver Celtic ring on her right hand little finger and the necklace tucked behind her sweater. Her hair was the colour of the bright enamel in her teeth, but cut short, as it had been since her entrance to secondary school in England once she had moved from her hometown of Rovaniemi, the capital of Finnish Lapland. Many of the pubescent boys had instantly been attracted to her when her tresses were longer as she stood out like a beacon against the bleak uniformity of school. But this attention was not always welcomed by those girls that missed out and their jealousy resulted in a string of name calling associated with her full length hair that dropped well down her back: "White witch", "poltergeist" "bleachy." The continual bullying not only led to her cutting her own hair, to the horror of her step mother, who immediately took her to the hairdresser to try and reshape the damage that was done, but in the years to come she experimented with colour in a number of shocking shades: pink, red, green, orange and black had all surfaced during her early teenage years often accompanied by a design more akin to a gothic horror show with hairspray as her constant companion.

As much as her hair demanded attention on any first meeting it was not her most remarkable feature. Her eyes were as blue and vibrant as the arctic skies that were her canopy in childhood with early evening stars circling randomly around her irises. Hypnotic enough, even as a child, her eyes were now fully trained. Transparent, absorbent and cheerful to her inner circle, curious and inviting to newcomers, but glacial, predatory and unhinging to those she regarded with suspicion. She could toggle from cuddly toy to polar wolf instantaneously with but a twitch in her mask.

Jeff, as usual, strolled in late in his open neck shirt, beneath his Austin Reed mohair wool suit. Mia checked her watch cheekily and said nothing; her warm smile the communicator. Jeff acknowledged her reaction with a faint embarrassed purse of the lips before warmly welcoming everybody to the Vulnerable Adult Meeting (V.A) and introducing himself to the group already assembled in a half moon facing Jeff and Mia's chairs.

Sylvia Mackay, note-taker, began the meeting on Jeff's nod. Sylvia was unique in that she had a foot in both camps; employed by the hospital but working within the domain of social services. She had trailed Jeff significantly when entering the room as though there was a desirable discernible difference between them either as Lord and servant or host and unwelcome guest despite Jeff's wish to treat everyone on an equal footing. Her professionalism, competency, timidity and silence following her opening remarks meant that even in the importance of her role most people barely registered her and the nickname 'The Sparrow' had stuck in her decade of service as each incumbent manager received a staff handover.

Apologies were received from the trainee healthcare assistant Monika; a recently employed Lithuanian agency worker who had initially taken details of the alleged theft, as well as Joanna, the Polish nurse who had opted to begin her own investigation, contrary to all good practice guidelines. Today they had been handpicked for 'emergency duty cover' on an alternative ward but had passed on a report outlining details of the initial allegation to the Ward Sister. A copy was now passed around the room and Jeff begun the meeting by reading the confidentiality statement and asking Becky to read through the initial statement made by the nurse on the ward.

Sister Becky Swaine of Hardy Ward, named like the other wards, after revered British novelists, came complete with navy blue uniform, watch-piece on left pocket, black tights and sturdy shoes. A ward sister for several years, this was Becky's umpteenth different appointment and she exuded calmness and authority through her knowledge and experience, taxiing her team through the permanent rush hour, observing and negotiating all the days' examinations and peculiarities.

It wasn't a surprise as Becky started reading that the English used in the report was poor but as Becky deciphered the statement she did so whilst consciously making editorial corrections where she knew that the meaning was in error. This meant that the statement sounded less staccato and better than it had otherwise been written and would, perhaps, negate some of the questions that were already entering the group's consciousness.

"3rd December 2012. 7.05am.    Mrs Akers in bed 5 on Hardy Ward woke at 6.30am and pressed her buzzer. She told me that her wedding ring was missing. She told me it was on her finger the night before as she kisses it every meal …..time. She became upset and started to cry and said "I don't want to live anymore. I don't want to stay here." I looked in her bed and in her drawer next to her but I couldn't find anything. There is a small cut/bruise on Mrs Aker's finger. I reported this to my supervisor. "

"Thanks Becky, have you got anything to add?" said Jeff.
"Yes...... Mrs Akers is still very distressed.   She had only been on the ward a couple of nights.   The family are also livid – a different member seems to be phoning every hour.   They reported that she's been wearing the same ring since her wedding day, 47 years ago.   The worst of it is that her anniversary is in a few days."

"Ah timing.".......Jeff didn't expect a reply. "Do we know why she kisses the ring?"

"Yes - it's an acknowledgement to her late husband, Eric. She remembers him especially when she says grace just before meals."

Jeff sighed, "What's your protocol in cases like this Angela." The question was loaded. He had predicted what her answer would be and he wasn't going to be disappointed.

"Well obviously the trust takes theft very seriously. Have we checked Becky whether the ring was listed as a valuable item on the admittance screening?"

"There is nothing recorded." Becky was as diplomatic as possible not adding that the screening process was one of the tasks that was always put on the back burner in busy periods and like most other Ward Sisters she was acutely aware of her responsibility to the Trust. "How can we have a Trust if we don't trust each other?" as Angela used to phrase it.

Angela Slinger was more than a suit with a badge. A non-executive member of the Trust, chiefly responsible for admissions and, more importantly, discharges she had completed her time addressing patient's needs. Now she was fire-fighting for the whole hospital. It was her job to ensure that the Trust not only met its four hour targets for Accident and Emergency admissions plus the 36 hour target for initial medical assessments, but she was also there to free up bed space that was currently occupied and in doing so was a frequent adversary of social services.

Angela had absolute power. She regarded adult protection investigations as an unwanted distraction from her core activities and busy schedule balancing the beds. In spite of her platitudes of concern and overtly patronising approach, the insincerity of her words was detectable by those attuned to her comportment.

Angela continued. "I don't want to play devil's advocate but is it plausible that she simply didn't bring it in with her? Many patients prefer to leave their valuables at home and sometimes are prompted by the paramedics to do so. I also believe she came in disorientated Becky didn't she." It was a statement and not a question and Mia was onto it like a shot.

"Angela!"

Mia was about to launch into her but was prompted not to do so by the smallest of covert squeezes from Jeff's foot onto hers, his brown leather briefcase concealing the gesture. She, like Jeff, was aware that Angela had perfected the look of total surprise as if this was common place and the Trust had been vindicated before. As it proved both their instincts were right in their restraint.

Regaining her composure, Mia's voice was much softer and more deliberate than she had originally intended.

"There are three points here. Firstly; do you think that Mrs Akers took off her ring for the first time in forty seven years before being admitted to hospital or that your own screening assessment wasn't completed thoroughly? Secondly, do you think someone would make this up? and thirdly, what about the bruise?" She didn't give her a chance to answer before pressing on. "I'll be meeting Mrs Akers and talking to her family later on this afternoon but from what's on our file there's no diagnosis of any mental health impairment regarding this patient and her care needs have been based almost totally around her deteriorating physical disabilities."

Angela had years of practice squeezing out of tight spots, her role demanded it.

"I believe I am right that the reason for admission was for a urinary tract infection and as everyone in this room knows confusion is a common symptom for such infections on admission."

"Well I hope that has been demonstrated - what does it state in the notes?" Mia had also done her homework, having read the notes the afternoon before and knew that the initial report was scratchy to say the least, with no definitive diagnosis to begin with.

Jeff interrupted, he didn't want a slanging match. "Thank you both for the moment." which didn't please either of them.

He turned to Selina instead. Selina Seruwagi was responsible for hospital complaints. She was dressed in civilian attire and had a manner that determined she was overwhelmed by her workload, shuffling her notes continuously and checking her mobile incessantly as though her life depended on answering the next summons.

"Selina. Have the family been in touch with the complaints department?"

"Yes they have and they're looking for compensation and a transfer. At this rate the budget for recovery will be blown before we reach Xmas."

"Why? Was it an expensive ring?" probed Jeff.

"Not really but it's the eleventh case in the last two months...." Her voice suddenly faded and her silky smooth Sri Lankan skin, blushed as though kissed by the first reddish hue of spring sunshine. She looked away.

Jeff's hand immediately went to his head and he scratched his brow. Becky's head went to the floor in embarrassment and Angela looked straight ahead with an unflinching conscientious poker face. It was Mia who broke the silence.

"Selina. Are you telling us that there have been more thefts on this ward?"

"Well...... not just Hardy Ward.    There have been more reports of jewellery disappearing on Bronte, Dickens and Austin as well."

"What?"

Jeff wanted clarification.   "Angela - why haven't social services been informed of this?" Mia shuffled upwards in her chair.

"We do inform you if your client is involved."

"I'm sure you're aware of the procedures you have signed up to Angela, *any* vulnerable client who reports *any* theft within the hospital should be reported to social services within the first four hours of the knowledge of such an event.   That is one of the basic tenets of any of our joint training sessions.   Even the newest healthcare assistant should know at least this much."

As he said this he was aware of the power of line management in the hospital, particularly to those whose first language wasn't English, and that once staff at all levels had deferred to their immediate supervisor, they could then live with themselves regarding any further action.   The chain of communication and discipline was clear.   A Sergeant Major would fit well into the hierarchy of the trust.   Others would argue that this was exactly the role that the Matrons of the ward had provided in the past but the actual picture was much darker.   Deaths in corridors, staff discontent and endless streams of government rhetoric didn't stop the love the public held for the NHS but the cracks were no longer filled in, but just papered over as the un-halting decline of the institution mirrored the changes in the political landscape where finger pointing had replaced personal responsibility.

For a split second Angela considered the argument that there wouldn't be an opportunity for any other work if all they did was spend time reporting incidents but bit her tongue on this occasion and with her attentive ear at the ready asked.

"What can we do to help, Jeff?"

The meeting concluded with a total of twenty one action points including the detailing of all thefts on every ward in the hospital over the last three months, informing the police of the need for an immediate joint investigation and further attention to the training programme for all hospital staff to understand the basic concepts of reporting.

Jeff and Mia remained behind as the others filtered off to their departments and their pressing agendas.

"Can you bloody believe this?" said Mia, as she kicked out at one of the chairs. "She's supposed to take the lead on V.A's and tells us nothing. How the hell are we supposed to protect clients when they don't even tell us what's going on?"

"They're obviously embarrassed, but I'm more worried about how long this has been going on and what evidence, if any, there is left?"

Jeff and Mia had both been long enough in the job to know that evidence, like any police investigation was the key to any prosecution. Their joint investigator training with Surrey Police at a swanky hotel in the countryside, over three days, at tax-payers expense, had provided welcome relief from the constant stream of driftwood that required rescuing, but very few of the real life investigations resulted in any police action other than a warning to the future conduct of the perpetrator at best. Despite the odd officer going the extra mile, Vulnerable Adult protection work was one of the least well-funded police departments and not a ready choice for those eager to climb up the ranks.

Unfortunately, the very criteria that enabled a client to be labelled in the Vulnerable Adult bracket was often the single most contributing factor that caused most of the investigations to stall. Any diagnosis of dementia meant that the client's testimony was likely to be regarded as unreliable, despite a change in the law and the efforts made at court to protect those most at risk of abuse. The elderly, like those with learning disabilities and children, now had an opportunity to submit earlier statements and not be open to crude questioning in an often terrifying environment. More recently allowances in their credibility as witness had been made. Despite this there were only a few prosecutions that had so far been successful.

"We'll have to wait now but I'll brief the team by email and raise it at the next team meeting. At least we can be an extra set of ears and eyes." said Jeff.
"If there's ten others that we don't know of there might be a pattern – I'll start with Becky over in Hardy– I think there's at least three more over there. I'll try and get some more info from the client and family later."
"Great – I'm on my six monthly just after lunch so I'll catch up with you at the end of the day." As he spoke Jeff tapped the top of his left breast.
 Mia laughed – she knew instantly what he meant.
"Just make sure they're long life batteries."
It wasn't the first time she'd made this remark but they both smiled just the same.

*Granddad*

*He examined the silver band under the lamp, rolling it around his fingers. What price? Was it even worth the travel? He needed the money desperately. It would mean a different pawn shop, further afield. The stones sparkled and he thought of his canny Granddad in The King's Head. The story went that he saw the sparkle of the stray coin first; it was a fifty pence piece - at least three pints worth in those days. His size 9's moved swiftly but silently across the flagstone floor and his right boot still carrying the days' toil from the local building site pressed onto the coin claiming it. The handkerchief fell from his hand as he simultaneously coughed. His weary limbs bent over slowly but with the swiftness and dexterity of a magician both the handkerchief and the coin were captured in his large hand; the same hand that earned his living as a carpenter, emigrating many years ago to earn his keep in unchartered territory. As he looked up at his envious workmate, who had witnessed the whole event and would never him hear cough again without looking to the floor, he raised a cautionary smile and winked.*
*"Same again?" as he raised his glass in victory.*

*He loved his Grandfather unconditionally. Always first to the bar, always the first to swear, always the first with a story and when he won on the fruit machine the only one to place a shiny coin in his hand and putting his index finger to his lips. "Our secret."*

Two years earlier Jeff and Mia had shared more than a meeting of minds. They had explored each other's bodies, revelling in the discoveries of every nuance, every mark that defined them. Mia's own impenetrable stamp of life had encouraged her to explore and empathise with the markings of others and Jeff had been no exception.

When Mia first scrutinised his nakedness she saw only a small scar, two inches long, slightly ridged, where stitches had once been but as she kissed and caressed his left breast and nipple the suppleness of the skin had been replaced by what felt like a tattoo in Braille. She'd paused then prodded and followed the outline of the foreign body.

"Tick tock, tick tock" Jeff whispered quietly.

Mia looked puzzled.

"A pacemaker," he continued. "You don't have to be over sixty to own one."

"I'd better be gentle then" as she went in search of another pulse.

Jeff's first signs of deficiency occurred as a child, aged eight. Standing in his smart school uniform and stomach full after a bowl of hot cereal, he would, without drama, slowly drift to the floor unaware of the irregularities occurring in the chambers of his heart. At first he had to endure the ignominy of an electric skull cap as part of electroencephalography. His own abbreviation for EEG was EGG because he felt like a boiled one and he could envisage the doctor sticking the breaded soldiers through his uncomfortable and ridiculous cap into his brain. Electrodes prodded his skull but all he could concentrate on was the graph being drawn by a rapidly shifting long thin needle attached to the shiny blue metal box to his left that spewed out reams of green and white computer paper. Other tests included those which required a sample of blood, urine and faeces that embarrassed him further. He remembered the comics placed in the small cubicle where he sat as nature took its course and the odour of TCP, a brand ubiquitous and unmistakable in 1970's households across the country, would be all pervasive in the many medical establishments that he visited that decade.

He endured the twenty-four hour tape and had taken innumerable days off school that would also lend itself to his nickname, 'Cloudy,' here one day, gone the next. The Headmaster didn't tolerate anything less than full attendance and punctuality and wasn't the least bit sympathetic with Jeff's illness, which he saw as attention seeking behaviour. Finally a consultant and a diagnosis and within three months, dozing in the theatre, the first incision had been made.

Mia expected tears, despite the generation she was serving being as tough as they come. They had survived a war, rationing and personal loss, some more harrowing than others, and she understood that memories of pain weren't shared easily and emotion was checked and stifled so when it did appear it did so quietly, politely and without drama.

Mia carefully placed her chair as close to the bedside as possible. She didn't want to promote an air of authority. She also wanted more than a yes or no, more than a nod in the direction of inevitability, more than a statistic on a government wish list. She squeezed Audrey Aker's left hand as Audrey wiped away the tears with her right. Mia wanted to get to the possible causes. Not only were their time constraints in terms of payload but Mia was worried that the patient's attentiveness was likely to wane after the first fifteen minutes, particularly in an environment that lacked the cues for memories at home, be it the sound of the kettle, the creaking of the pipes, the draft that came through a back door, the noise of neighbours returning from work. The sterility of the hospital didn't disinfect just the germs on the ward but prevented germination in the brain, anaesthetising the synapses with its blandness.

"Do you remember anything unusual about that evening?"

"Not really dear.....I don't usually eat much in the evening...Lunch is normally large enough," and Audrey painfully pushed herself slightly higher in the bed and leaned forward as she spoke without facing Mia directly.

"Did anyone help you eating or drinking?"

"Have you a tissue please?"

Mia passed a pocket packet from her left trouser pocket.

"Thank you dear" and as Audrey grappled with taking only a solitary tissue Mia could see the deep purple stain already formed just above the knuckle.

"I've tried, really I have, but I just can't remember who helped me that evening. I remember some of the nurses who came and saw me. They're all very kind. She pushed the tissue up her sleeve in her gown through habit, but the hospital gown was too big so it toppled onto the floor.

"When did you first realise it was gone?"

"As soon as I woke.... It wasn't really worth that much. It had a band full of stones.....small stones.....it was a silver ring....an eternity ring."

The irony wasn't lost on Audrey and she searched for her tissue again as the tears started once more to fall but she couldn't find it so Mia came to her rescue again with another. Composed once more she continued "My daughter has some pictures at home if that helps. It took Jim two months to get the money together."

"How was your sleep?"

"Too well for comfort.....I'm a light sleeper normally.... first up before rush hour. If my pins hadn't given up on me I'd be helping the others."


Mia believed her. The assessment on record described a woman who had brought up a family of six, lost two daughters and a son before nursing her husband through cancer to their final parting. She was a volunteer in her local community until her late seventies and despite her energy, enthusiasm and extrovert nature her hips had finally crumbled and led to her physical decline in the last year.


Mia didn't press her any further but thanked her for her time and promised she would report back the minute she heard anything. She wasn't likely to glean any further information, not about the night's events anyway, and any other discussion was only likely to place other thoughts in Audrey's mind not relative to the investigation and almost certainly a red herring.

She did though act on Audrey's concern about her sleep and requested tests to determine whether there was still anything unusual in the blood stream and despite the assurances of Angela she decided to visit security and lost property on the way back to the office.

Jeff made the same journey every six months. Despite the regularity of the appointment, he was in a part of the hospital he wouldn't otherwise visit, especially today, as another wing of the new extension had just been opened. No ward, just a dimly lit reception area at the end of a long corridor, and a small number of examination rooms on the right hand side. He didn't have any anxiety about the visits anymore as he had done as a child: the same questions, the same prodding, and the same cheery disposition from the trainee cardiologist. But he had always left disappointed that he couldn't summon the courage to ask the question. 'How long will I live for?' Instead he meditated for hours each evening through adolescence, privately weeping at his assumed abbreviated lifespan with no-one to blame but his own body. Now, since his last major replacement, he had come to see the visit as a necessary evil. He knew the tests off by heart: pulse, blood test, blood pressure and ECG. His only engagement with the procedure was to see who would be prodding him today. He'd heard earlier that week that you could go wireless nowadays and save on some of the unnecessary appointments; he was determined to raise the topic at a convenient moment.

He turned into the darkened corridor and caught sight ahead of the only bright lights that emanated from behind the desk at reception. He checked the Roman numerals on his watch face, a few minutes late as usual. He justified his lateness because of his position in the hospital and the knowledge that there was always a delay so he was surprised when he heard his name called from behind him by a young man of Indian origin, very smartly dressed in a plain dark suit, stiff white shirt and sky blue tie. His black sheen hair was perfectly groomed and he smiled warmly as he beckoned Jeff to a small room adjacent to them.

"Would you like to come straight in Jeff .........Please take a seat......How are you feeling today?"

"Good, not bad ….still ticking," his fall back line, and he patted his chest with his right hand– although he regretted it as soon as he had said it because he was conscious of how he appeared toward others and the man in front of him was intellectually alert despite looking like he was straight out of medical school; so young and eager. Jeff wondered how long before the doctor became demoralised by an ever more demanding and dispiriting career path.

"Could I have your right arm please?"
Jeff automatically rolled up his sleeve above his small bicep expecting the oversize inner tube to soon start to constrict and compress his vein and set the aorta into overdrive. As he pushed his arm forward the left hand opposite gripped his wrist tightly and whilst holding Jeff's arm secure punctured his skin with the razor sharp silver blade slowly pulling it back towards his own body and down Jeff's forearm towards his wrist.

Jeff didn't feel the blade initially, such was the precision of the scalpel but was quickly alerted to the blood that already started to drip onto the desk.
"Please don't struggle Jeff, I wouldn't want to slip and cut an artery."
*What's happening?* Jeff was screaming in his head but remained feebly silent as he switched his gaze from the point of the blade to the pupils of the assailant opposite.
"This is a warning. Keep your eyes on your own work. I've chosen your right arm because I don't want to interfere with your ability to write but the next time your limbs will be the least of your worries. There is no hiding place here. Make sure your battery is well charged."

His voice was polite, calm, controlled, and his movements were precise and minimal. His grip was vice-like and Jeff flinched and started to get a sickly feeling in the pit of his stomach as his blood pressure dropped dramatically at the sight of the blood that continued to trickle from his forearm. His brow started to sweat. It wasn't long before he started to feel himself slipping, albeit still in the grasp of the man opposite. The next thing he knew he was on the floor. As he turned on his side through the fog of consciousness, he saw a pair of shoes slip quietly out of the door before he blacked out completely.

He wasn't out long. It felt only seconds and to his surprise there wasn't a pool of blood about him but the wound was still seeping. He clutched his right forearm with his left hand but soon had to release it as he endeavoured to stand, holding onto the table as he levered himself to the vertical.

He then eyed the blue towel dispenser above the basin in the corner and for the next three minutes started to clean himself and then the furniture and the floor. Using the towelling as an improvised bandage he sat for a short while and then returned to the basin to swallow some water before splashing his face once more.

He knew he couldn't return to the office so headed straight to his car, going over the events that occurred like a slide show on the windscreen in front of him. He couldn't dare present himself at the Accident and Emergency department on site so he drove eight miles to his own local hospital and faced the ignominy of answering an extended set of questions, particularly concerning his own mental health.

The young female doctor knew that the chances of an accidental near perfect incision eight centimetres down his right forearm, delicately avoiding any major arteries or veins were non – existent and that the probable answer was that it was self-inflicted. A hazard was placed on his medical record in spite of Jeff's extravagant description of the aluminium shed side panel slipping as he adjusted carrying it. The precision of the injury aided his recovery as the decision was to glue the wound, despite its length, and the bandage was unobtrusive and easily hidden behind a clean shirt. He just needed to be careful and not place any strain on the wound.

After making his excuses at work he slumped into the sofa at home with a can of Stella in his left hand, which felt awkward because despite writing with his left hand he did everything else naturally right handed. That awkwardness resulted in a large spill on the first mouthful that Jeff ignored as he tried to remember more of his meeting earlier in the day.

The voice of his assailant was middle class, without the hint of any dialect in intonation. Neither was there any habitual head movement betraying an extended stay in foreign lands or he had eliminated it during his lifetime. He was taller than Jeff so must have been six foot but on first sight hadn't appeared so. He had a slim body, betraying his young age, but he had certainly hidden an innate strength within the figure-hugging two-piece suit. He remembered the grip – he hadn't even attempted to move his arm, conscious that he may have caused even greater damage with a struggle. He was certainly under his spell – Jeff had stared straight into his dark brown eyes, which didn't flinch as he uttered the warning.

He tried to picture any badge on his attire but he couldn't visualise one, he was sure of that. The shoes were leather, even though he only remembered seeing the back and sole of them, but the leather logo had stuck in his mind. He didn't remember aftershave but there was definitely some kind of balm. Neither was there the aroma of Indian Spices that permeated some of his neighbours' skin and clothing in his local community. Many a morning he had woken and headed to the kitchen only for a pungent dhal to float in through the extractor fan underneath his hob.

Groomed perfectly, the only blemish to the man's features was a small scar above his left eye. No moles, no dimples, no other marks of distinction. Just a gleaming set of teeth as he made his statement.

Jeff assumed he couldn't have been a Sikh as he was clean shaven, but there was a warrior in him, a trained composure unseemly in a man of his age. He was competent with a blade and had the coolness of a surgeon. He took another mouthful of his beer and said to himself *No way you bastards. I'm right on it now.*

'Oreo' pushed upwards and gently nuzzled the neck of Mia finding the spot where he'd become most comfortable before Mia had turned her page. Mia reciprocated the tenderness and stroked the protrusive spine of the black and white Cardigan Welsh Corgi. Battersea Dog and Cat Home had been the matchmaker and despite a shocking loss of weight, half a left earlobe and a left foreleg operational only as a symmetrical crutch the relationship had flourished from the second they had met.

Oreo, named after the biscuit, was an instant interrogator of any invader of their privacy. He was a house dog, petrified of the outside but a proud, affectionate and confident companion within the home.

Mia had decided on her new flat-mate a month or so after her break up from Jeff. Whilst they had worked in the community team together their relationship had blossomed on the foundation of a mutual professional regard. He to her was the steady tug pilot of her bruised and precarious vessel battling through choppy waters. She to him was the lone yachtswoman, determined, persistent, driven, unshaken and battling above the unfathomable surges of the political and bureaucratic nature of the waters they sailed in.

Five months later and Mia had ended it. His warmth, boyish charm, humour, cynical diligence of the world around him, and compassion for others were still there in abundance but in crept lateness, forgetfulness, irritability, inability to listen, apathy to her needs. In essence he'd lost the sparkle in his eyes and despite his meek protestations and request that she should be able to point out explicitly what she wanted from him they separated. Neither knew if the other was speeding off to the horizon in a catamaran or floating on a rudderless craft carried by the tide on a course the shapeless waters controlled.

At home, Mia's evenings were now taken up with reading, Film 4, the Discovery Channel, and keeping the flat tidy. Her attendance at a free diving club and a bike club maintained her physical fitness and retained a youthful feel to her thirty years accentuated by her choice of adolescent clothing.

She kept her road bike in the flat with her, which was enticing to Oreo who pawed the foot straps and used the attached grated metal as a cleaning mechanism. The bike club met a couple of times a month, and early mornings was the time she liked to be outside, pushing against the battering wind, sweating in the burning sun, drinking in the raindrops. No weather deterred her.

Several years earlier, at the local leisure centre, Mia had joined the free diving club after she'd caught a programme on the Discovery Channel about the extreme sport and one particular experience had been reawakened. Her personal growth had been forged the months she had travelled independently around Europe and North Africa; a quickening, moulded by the extraordinary, the beguiling, the perplexing, and the infuriating against a compendium of colours, smells, noise, tastes and feelings that rocked her to her core. Mia had finished her travels with a week on the beach in the Sinai. Like most pilgrims, persuaded by the constant encouragement of cafe owners pursuing a piece of the tourist pie, as well as by the glassy-eyed accounts of intoxicated tourists themselves, Mia visited the The Blue Hole near Dahab. In an utterly compelling drama she had stepped timidly off the rocky shore, easing herself gingerly into the gentle lapping waters and dipping her head into the murkiness before snorkelling amongst the phenomenal luminescence. Mia's world view had been washed away for she had entered a gate to another world: a world of inward peace, a world of infinite beauty, a world of glorious possibilities, a world of freedom.

Thirty minutes later and the ticking of the second hand was the only sound in the flat. Oreo was banished behind the kitchen door and Mia focused solely on the black plastic rimmed clock sited directly above her on the ceiling as she took her place on the yoga mat in the centre of her living room. She breathed normally for a minute and a half watching each second pass. After ninety seconds she drew in her last breath and held it for two minutes her focus remaining on the red second hand which seemed to dwindle between each passing second. She tried to focus on a favourite view, looking out from Charles Bridge in Prague towards the castle as the light dazzled across the water but her mind wandered to less desirable memories. She was now underwater but dreamlike and all she could see in the blur of the rippling undercurrent was her outstretched arm, straining with all her might but to no avail. The beguiling scene caused her momentarily to lose her grip on time before she returned to the second hand which loitered between each mark before gathering her focus once again and returning to the programme she had set herself.

Mia repeated the exercise, only this time she reduced the time she breathed normally by ten seconds and did so with each subsequent repetition assisting her to build up resistance. A quarter of an hour later and she was ready to move from the carbon dioxide training, the accumulation of which was the trigger for her to breathe, and not the lack of oxygen as often mistakenly believed. Yet this exercise was quickly followed by her focus on oxygen, specifically building up tolerance to low oxygen levels and whilst her normal breathing held for ninety second intervals her breath hold steadily increased, fifteen seconds at a time, until she had safely reached five and a half minutes. She stayed motionless for a further five minutes, relaxing, smiling to herself, contemplating her first dive and the further training required, specifically in the water. She was determined to break the six minute barrier. She accompanied her regimented breathing exercises with other recommended training included working on her rib cage and her diaphragm to encourage the elasticity and enlargement of the organs that allowed her to hold her breath for longer. The calming of her mind had been an ongoing battle but meditation had given her some solace, although she had moved through different techniques as fads came and went. She had lived in the past, chanted mantras, remembered the unremarkable, lived in the moment and now was praying to Jesus, yet peace still hadn't come.

There wasn't much on a security level that got past Mark and Jeff respected him for his work ethic but not for the almost endless stream of misogynistic and racist comments that Jeff ignored rather than tackle but if he was going to have to trust anyone regarding recent events then it would have to be Mark. They used to sit together on monthly board meetings in their respective managerial roles and Jeff knew Mark had his finger on the pulse, so it was to Mark, from home, he made his first call that morning.

Mark had oversight of all the staff passes in the hospital and knew the majority of staff, especially those who had a habit of losing them.   His daily 'adherence' rounds meant he went through every department so Jeff hoped that he may have an idea about an impeccably dressed Indian man that walked round with a scalpel in his inside jacket pocket.

"Hi Jeff.  Your boys took a hammering the other day.  You might as well give me the £20 now."  Mark, as usual, was quick on the draw.

"Ten games left yet and you've messed it up before. Perhaps I'll hold on a little while."

"Yeah. Right."

Jeff knew his chances were slim and their annual bet about who would finish higher in the Premiership between West Ham and Spurs would end up in Mark's hands again.

"There was a man here the other day trying to pass himself off as a consultant. He's an Indian man in appearance about 6ft 2, young and slim in a sharp suit. Have you heard or seen anything?"

"There's a lot of their sort here, seem to be taking over the place."

"He doesn't wear a doctor's badge or gown.  If you ask me he was wearing a made to measure.  Seems educated but might be taking advantage."

"When did you see him last?"

"The new block, second floor, where the reception for cardiology is. He was only here yesterday afternoon. You can't find him on any camera can you? I'm just trying to work out how he got in here or where he came from."

"The new block is not online yet but he must have come in from somewhere. I'll check the entrance. If there's anyone meeting his description I'll give you a tinkle. What time did you say again?"

"Just after 2pm." as Jeff placed his left hand on the bandage, just to confirm he wasn't hallucinating.

"O.K –will do."

"Cheers Mark – I owe you one."

"Don't forget to get saving. It will be a Guinness – the next time I see you out and about."

Fear and confusion continued to attack Jeff mercilessly that morning. The new hazardous levels caused a panic, a desire to fight the foe, and what he couldn't wrestle with he would detail, download and disguise. To avoid detection and preparing for the real possibility that his life was in danger Jeff had begun to assemble a plan. Firstly he opened an electronic diary, deliberately plain, and with three more passwords to deter any random user if stolen. He had also taken to hiding his I-Pad. The usual suspects had already been considered: The lining at the bottom of the sofa, the gap behind the ill fitted wardrobes, behind the oven with the collection of broad but safe electrical wiring, in the small cupboard where the sink outlet waste pipe was accessible, in the chimney of the now defunct fire-place. All these were rejected until that morning a chance occurrence presented itself.

In the smallest of downstairs hallways; a five foot by three foot reception allowing only enough space to hang a coat and admire the fuse box before either proceeding immediately up the stairs or turning ninety degrees to the left, a small stone had caught at the bottom of the internal door to the lounge. As Jeff hurried to leave late for work the outcome was inevitable. Not only did the stone leave a scratch on the mottled tiles but, as he assessed the damage to the door, he saw an opportunity. The door was like every other in the property: hollow, lightweight, fitted just on the right side of adequate but with lock mechanisms so poorly constructed that Jeff was forced to remove them after several houseguests in the early days had to be rescued with various implements following the failure of the lock to undo. The door leading to the lounge was the only one that had been modified. It had a large glass panel inserted with a mermaid design that covered the majority of the door. The wood below the glass was the part of the door that received most damage as feet scuffed and banged into it as visitors squeezed to enter the house. In the winter the door enlarged and scraped against the lock and the floor and it was this weathering near the floor that caught Jeff's attention.

As he wrenched the door free from the stone the paucity of the constructed veneer had been exposed. Four small pins that secured the ply covering flew off the door and left a flap of the veneer hanging loosely at the bottom. Jeff didn't have time to fix it there and then, but returning from work later that day he crouched before falling to his knees and then finally lying prostrate on the floor he discovered the hollow gap behind. He was simply going to return the pins to the holes from whence they came by tapping them onto the wood but instead he took out his tablet from his shoulder bag and found it fitted neatly into the shelf at the bottom of the hollow where it could be sealed when the flap was secured. It was a tight fit but the cosiness was an advantage as the tablet wasn't able to move once secured from the outside.

He couldn't remember the film he had seen but he was convinced that the best hiding place was the one that was looking straight at you and he decided that this small but perfectly fit alcove, although well hidden, would remain easily accessible by prying out the screws and preserving what little security he had left.

The design of the glass frame above the door had, over time, melted into Jeff's consciousness but to those that entered the property for the first time it was an instant conversation starter. The panel was partly frosted and the design was mirrored either side. At the bottom of the glass was a rolling seascape, gentle waves lapping against the door ready to fall onto the tiled floor below. Rising from the waves was a tail that, without attachment, could have represented the grand tail of a bottlenose dolphin, about to slide into the waves as it played in the ocean. Instead an enchanting mermaid rose above the curtain of water, with her face turned slightly facing the onlooker, her eye lids tentatively lowered in embarrassment whilst her left arm dropped to the waters and her left hand played with the overflowing essence of her being.  Her small breasts were slightly exposed but the viewer was drawn to her mouth where the tip of her right hand wiped what looked like blood dripping from her chin.  The enigmatic smile left the viewer in no doubt that as beautiful as she was there was something sinister about her, some unobtainable secret that would not be revealed to mere mortal minds. A lazy moon in the background completed the print and provided glimmering light across the sea and shone through the tresses of her hair that blew lightly in the breeze, strands of which concealed her forehead and her shoulders.

The hiding place, whilst adept, also provided the strongest memories of his relationship with Mia.  Every morning, during their cohabitation, Mia blew one side of the glass panel causing the glass to condensate and with Jeff looking directly at her from the other side as she was about to leave to work, normally a half hour earlier, she wrote him a message by drawing on the glass with her index finger; sometimes a few words of comfort, sometimes a symbol - a love heart, sometimes a number, occasionally sexual.  She would then kiss the panel and exit through the front door whilst Jeff sat contemplating her message.

Mia had been able to write in a mirror image without any effort at all.  Jeff had always struggled with such a task and found it ridiculously hard to even cut his sideburns in a shaving mirror with a pair of scissors, particularly when completing it with his right hand.  He assumed that her years of practice in front of a mirror adjusting her minimal make up, trimming eyebrows and inventing hairstyles had enabled her deftness at such a skill.

For Jeff too the panel had special significance; Mia was his mermaid, the free diver, who captured his heart more than anyone else before.  He rubbished the term soul-mate but Mia was as close as it came to an immortal ally, not that he would ever tell her so.  He took her for granted until the day came for her to leave and then with one of the few times she hadn't breathed on the other side of the panel and with a flick of the front door lever she was gone and Jeff sat abject against the pane dwelling on his departed mermaid and ocean of despair.

The elderly man who had fallen on 'The Ramp' heard the birdsong but couldn't identify it. As he tried to gather his thoughts the sweet music became a throb and the pain in his skull started to increase as he became more sensitised to his environment. He went to move his arms but couldn't, his eyes opened with a startle but closed just as quickly as the brightness of the lights above him burnt them. And just as soon as he had woken he drifted off again.

Just a few minutes later during his next attempt to enter the land of consciousness he was aware of movement. He couldn't see her eyes but could feel the gentle breeze of speech across his face and a whiff of citrus. He imagined lemon groves and Mediterranean warmth. He gradually opened his eyes again and all was dusk around him, no moon, no clouds, just a jolt in his side. As the tingling began to sharpen he was aware of others near him, murmuring, saying something to him. He tried to lean forward and could not do so and all he could imagine was sinking slowly.

He did what he thought he needed to do in discovering his predicament, he screamed. At first his attempts were "Help!!!" but soon with no seeming response from those around them he just shouted anything, anything to rid him of his destiny. He was on the move but not moving himself and then he entered a room producing much cooler air than the predecessor. He shut his eyes and started to weep and shudder and as he did so, unknowingly, a small scratch took him away from his battle and soothed his journey to peace.

A list finally arrived on Jeff's desk detailing the eleven alleged cases of theft from hospital wards over the past three months. Jeff was aware that nothing had been achieved up to this point, nor yet passed over to the police. Only Angela had the whole picture and, no doubt, there was a certain amount of pressure from the powers that be about any adverse publicity.

As he returned to the list of names, his phone rang and Sally, a member of the admin team, who you could set your clock by, reported that a member of X-ray wanted to speak to 'The Manager' with concerns about a member of staff. This wouldn't be the first or last such call that Jeff would receive and normally it was in relation to the lack of progress about a certain discharge but Jeff did wonder *why from x-ray*. Sometimes in his mind he would agree with the complainants in the knowledge that social work did attract a certain amount of saviours and survivors and whilst they had noble intentions, they would occasionally use any number of excuses to deflect the stress they felt in completing assessments and care plans by not allowing the patient to be discharged. Spurious claims of incomplete medical investigations or distracting information provided by others, notably the family, delayed the process. A model to address such prolonged stays was being introduced but when there was a dispute about finance the hospital was the one that bore the brunt by retaining a medially fit patient and the term 'bed blocker' was banded.

"Hi it's Jeff, Team Manager, Can I help you?"
"Well I hope you can." replied the confident voice on the other end. "My name is Kath and I work in x-ray records – the wing opposite yours. Actually if you look outside your rear window you can probably see me waving at you."

Jeff extended the curled phone line to its zenith and turned towards the windows that were obscured by a set of grubby stone beige blinds with all manner of stains on them. He pulled one of the cords nearby to only find that the end nearest to him lifted quite sharply so that any further it would have started to give the look of a rhombus. He let go and then reattempted with both cords and transferred the phone to his shoulder/neck. This worked well enough so that he was able to raise the blinds but on reaching their summit, a foot below the top of the window, he realised there was no place to tie the cords so that the whole blind came down again. Becoming frustrated he lifted the blind behind himself, knocking the phone on the floor at the same time. He then reached for the phone directing it under the blind so that he could stand, a little ruffled, looking straight out of the window with his nose just a centimetre or two away from the pane of glass. As instructed he could see Kath not ten yards away with her left arm raised and a grin and a chuckle as she witnessed the show.

"Having trouble with your equipment?" she asked cheekily.

"Not for the first time."

"Sorry to disturb you.....I wasn't sure if this was some kind of 'in joke' in your department but five minutes ago a member of your team was walking up and down on the grass between our wings and she suddenly collapsed. I ran out of our office but by the time I got round to the fire-exit off The Ramp she was gone.

"Oh – God, can you tell me what she looks like?"

"About late twenties with blonde hair. I only knew she was one of yours as I remembered her on an induction tour. There's not many with such striking hair. I just wanted to check she was O.K."

"That's very kind, I think I know who it is but I'm not sure what's happened. Let me catch up with her and I'll come back to you. Can you just give me your extension number and I'll ring as soon as I know."

"Yes…It's 542 and my name is Kath.... Kath Priddy".

"Thanks very much Kath, I'll be in touch soon."

He was about to wander out of the office and go looking for Mia but as he struggled to escape from his temporary cage he was looking straight at her as she strode purposefully towards him.

"Picking a fight again?" she said, with no justification because she knew that there wasn't any man who was less likely to, although he would stand his corner and was never afraid to back his staff even in the most disadvantageous circumstances.

"According to reports I've just received it's you who's the one who's picking the fights. This time with invisible strangers who knock you out whilst walking on the grass in-between the wings."

"Sorry I overstretched" and she looked at the floor for a moment as her voiced faded.

"Someone just rang in with their concerns."

"I'll be more careful next time."

"I think you need to walk round with a health warning."

It had happened only twice before and only once when Jeff was present but because of her concerns the first time around, when there was no-one with her, she preferred to complete her walking and breathing exercises in the view of others, just in case. She always chose soft grassy ground but knew that if she held her breath for too long and she blacked-out that in turn her very black-out would cause her to breathe again. It was only a serious problem in water where she never trained alone.

"How far did you manage this time?"

"Two hundred steps but I was pushing it. Trouble was it was new ground and I just overdid it a little. The grass was so lush. I knew it would break any fall. I half expected you to come out running."

"Well X-Ray did but by the time they got there you were gone."

"You should get some fresh air yourself – dust of the cobwebs."

He knew she wasn't just talking about the state of the room and hoped it was a small concession back into her life. At this point she went and raised the blind then tucked the loop around the plastic tray at the top of the blind and pressed open the window ajar. Jeff chuckled to himself and fantasised for a second – he knew she was adept with her hands.

"Have you got a key to the door?"

"Top drawer."

She retrieved it and as she turned the lock it squeaked so she manipulated the door towards and away from herself several times before the door gave way and the fresh air came pouring in.


For the next thirty minutes Mia and Jeff went through the list. Those who were still in the hospital were marked with their current ward number. Those who were discharged had a date. One had died in the hospital so that would remain their responsibility. The unusual amount of cases would require more than the bog-standard one or two meetings. If it had happened in the community then a major senior strategy meeting would have taken place with representation from various bodies including senior management from almost every interested partner. But as it was a hospital there was an unwritten rule from above. If social services don't tread on the trust too much then the trust wouldn't press too hard on the lack of timely discharges; as they both knew there was a financial penalty to pay when they did so but politically for both sides it would have created more unnecessary tension between departments.

The two divisions were expected to be working in tandem, although in practical terms the independence, stature and power of the social work teams had long been eroded and the general expectancy, particularly from health staff, as prescribed in memos from the highest echelons, was that an independent social work team would, in the fullness of time, become another subsection of the growing metropolis.

Mia's first e-mail was to the head of the council's vulnerable adults department. It listed the clients who had reported theft and stressed the importance of reviews that would need to take place across the whole of the area for those who had been hospitalised in Three Counties recently. The question that needing asking urgently was whether any hospital visit had raised any concerns about their general treatment whilst receiving care.

Whilst taking hold of the ongoing investigation Mia remained perturbed about the process: all investigations in any social care or hospital domain remained confidential. Only the select few had a right to know and only the select fewer had an overall picture of the amount of abuse that was currently being experienced in the sector and the severe lack of tools and punishments that were available to be dispensed where any wrong doing was clearly evidenced. The victims almost always had the smallest voice and those that even made it to an investigation were only the tip of the iceberg. Mia wanted to dig deeper and spread the news further and despite feeling handcuffed there was a part of her that relished the challenge ahead.

## 16

*The Victor?*

*He froze, in the most glorious moment at the age of 11, when the reels had fallen into place, all he felt was guilt. The machine was ablaze with flashing lights and waves of high pitched melodic sounds before the hailstone of coins clattered into the metal tray. The biggest jackpot available in any pub and club fruit machine across the county was now falling into his lap. He tried to replay in his mind the fall of the reels into place but there had been no drama, the last reel not even exaggerating its' spin to add to the tension. The reels had simply just aligned themselves; click, click, click, click, click. All five gold bars lined perfectly in a row creating a cacophony all around him but he stood silent as he felt the gaze from the public bar fall upon him.*

*Eventually a regular of the working men's club sitting up at the bar had called the manager who had replaced the coins with notes because there simply wasn't enough coins in the machine to pay out. Sensing the mood of the room the manager had reminded him of the minimum age limit and escorted him back to the family bar where his bemused parents, grandparents, auntie, uncle, and siblings wondered what all the fuss was about until they learnt of his success and then the celebrations began. Out of £100 he had ended up with £24.60. £50 went to his grandfather, who had given him the 50p in the first place. A round of drinks and crisps galore for the family followed by a round of drinks for the bar staff and lastly a small share for his brothers. He had seen the beaming smiles and jubilant faces and he had pleased them all. He felt their warmth; the condoning paws of men on his shoulders, the embarrassing hugs from his grandmother and aunty. He felt their joy, and revelled in their happiness not realising he might never again feel the moment where he was the hero of the hour; where love was so inexhaustible.   Before he fell asleep and overwhelmed with words of kindness and wonder his thoughts were singular; when can I play again?*

## 17

The private hospital was only a fraction of the size of the main hospital but the private clientele expected and received more. Carpets covered the linoleum; a subtle tangerine with a check pattern. There were no bays only a series of single rooms, some with extra beds for relatives to stay close to their loved ones during their hours of need. Yet, for most, their stay was not an emergency. Elective surgery, yearly check-ups, knees, hips, breasts, slips and trips, nips and tucks, were the mainstay. There was a separate department, as the sister used to decry, 'for those who were at the wrong end of life.' These were the private equivalent of the local hospice, or severe dementia patients, who following investigation, or a tinkering with medication, would be found a requisite comfortable local residential or nursing home.

The rooms were all ensuite, with a non-chargeable t.v, but not extending to cable stations. There was a welcome pack of tea, coffee and biscuits, a bowl of fruit and for the most part a room with a view even if it was the hospital car park. The curtains were clean, the room smelled pine fresh and the staff knocked before entering. They also worked quietly and efficiently, and had neither the banter nor the chaos of the NHS, at least not on the ward or in front of the paying customers.

The staff wore purple uniforms whilst the sister was resplendent in gold with a navy blue pin-stripe. All wore the company logo, an overblown octopus body with four tentacles protruding from each side curved round to meet each other gripping the company name Octocare.

The private hospital contract had been won by Octocare following the demise of one of Britains larger healthcare organisations whose rapid expansion had resulted in a thinning of resources, staffing and most importantly financial savvy. Octocare had its headquarters in Delhi and a sub office in London but to the ignorant was a distinctly British Operation. This was one of two private hospitals run by the group and both were stationed in the South East commuter belts, prime location for those who fit the bill for private health-care.

Both hospitals were the flagships when it came to providing services for its customers amongst the well manicured lawns of Surrey, Hampshire and Berkshire. They were supported by a fleet of residential and nursing homes with a private bed starting at a cost of £1000 per week, several rehabilitation studios, beds at numerous specialist units across the south east and a flotilla of qualified consultants, nurses, auxiliaries and qualified mental health and psychiatric nurses, predominantly born outside the UK from the Indian sub-continent and South East Asia.

At the head of the organisation was Dr Ramesh Raja, C.B.E who had come across the government radar for his efforts in providing logistical and ground support in many humanitarian disasters in Bangladesh as a result of flooding caused by cyclones in the Bay of Bengal. The Bangladeshi government and British government noticed his outstanding philanthropic efforts in the face of adversity and a British Passport was a formality twenty years ago.

Concerns about the expansion of his group in impoverished areas of India and claims by some human rights organisation over the concern of certain practises were quickly washed over. There was always going to be collateral damage was the foreign office view in any move towards a new world India, the prime example of free enterprise in a rapidly developing economy reliant on the importation of billions of pounds of British Manufacturing from lasers to prosthetics.

Dr Ramesh tapped the flashing red light on his phone in his London residence as he spoke to his overseer in Three Counties and didn't waste time with greetings.

"Be careful not to let the noxious weeds grow in the garden Sue. They have a habit of contaminating the whole crop. I trust you have the pesticides I sent you."

"Yes Sir. I'm confident we have everything under control."

"Confidence implies faith Sue. I'd prefer it if the results spoke clearly and definitively, even if we lost the odd bunch of roses. Keep me updated now."

## 18

*The Warning*

*He was never going to be a sporting hero at school, despite his efforts. Hour upon hour upon hour he spent in the street, in the local park, in the playground. If it was round he would play with it and he needed only his own company and a brick wall, garage door or open field. His imagination was his greatest asset. He could be Michael Holding the cricketer, Socrates the footballer, Bjorg the tennis player or anyone of their peers. His attempts at assimilation drove him to practice more and more yet despite his unlimited energy his anatomy would often let him down, particularly when he had to prove himself amongst others. He didn't find strength in his gangly frame. Tall but as skinny as a rake his nickname at comprehensive school was 'Cambi' a reference to the then humanitarian crisis in Cambodia where in a tragedy of immense proportions boys and girls of his age were no longer defined by their skin moulding around their bones but where their bones had moulded around their skin; eyes became sockets, chests became ribs, and their stomachs ballooned.*

*So in the playground games he couldn't and wouldn't compete against other boys who would brush him aside physically and would torment him psychologically. Instead he would wait for the those rare moments in a game when he would have time and space on the periphery and the ball would come his way but such was the pressure that he would fluff his lines despite auditioning himself for the role a thousand times.*

*Perhaps because he offered no threat in either physical or mental aptitude he was wholly accepted but forgotten. He would take part in all those activities that those boys who ran the year would govern were in the spirit of the time. He was on the fringes of the sporting group, attached to the group of troublemakers and regular absentees, a member of the small clique that smuggled Martini's in plastic syringes to imbibe during breaks in the toilets, at home in another group that laughed their way through the day at everyone else's expense as well as the amateur card sharks. He was the shadow in all their footsteps, missteps and misdemeanours but no-one singled him out as a part of any core.*

*He remembered one event clearly. It was a beautiful summers' morning, with not a cloud in the sky nor a care in his heart. Three-card brag was the game of choice and there was a group of eight of them, blazers strewn all over the floor as they huddled beneath an oak tree that sat in the corner of the large school playing field. In the years before the card school it was 'penny up the wall.' His dinner money gambled during morning break. It didn't matter that he had no food for the rest of the day; there would be ample at home.*

*The cards moved through their hands quickly. There was little time to celebrate each win as the bell rang in fifteen minutes so they continued hand after hand stopping only occasionally for the richer or more deceitful schoolboy to light up a cigarette and offer it clockwise to all those who chose to draw on nicotine as well as the monies they had pilfered, borrowed, and misused on the chance that there would be greater rewards. So absorbed were they in their game that they failed to notice the Assistant Headmaster driving his chocolate brown Ford Granada hurriedly across the sun parched field where not enough rain and too many children had left mainly bare patches of hardened soil. The dust flew up from the wheels and it was only when the imposter was forty yards away that they looked up and noticed the mirage, too late. The cigarette was thrown, the cards tucked into pockets but all of them stood motionless as Mr Lyon thrust open his door, stumbled out and with his face red with rage ordered, in his broad Newcastle accent, the lot of them to meet him outside his office immediately or face the consequences.*

*As they stood in a bedraggled line leaning against the wall that was stained with the marks of their predecessors, whose oiled hair, soiled clothes and muddy soles had blemished the magnolia backdrop, the key decisions had been made. No-one was gambling, no-one was smoking and the cards should now be held by the person least likely to be suspected, the most inconspicuous member of the gang, who would hold the cards until break-time. One by one they were ushered in one door and dismissed through another until only he remained, with the cards tucked in the back of his socks beneath the purple stay-press trousers. As he waited he wondered whether the others had been searched and, if he was, then what the consequences might be .*

*Each introductory question was answered truthfully until Mr Lyon removed his glasses looked him straight in the eye and asked*

*"Anything you want to tell me?"*

*"No sir"*

*"Nothing at all?"*

*"No sir."*

*"Were you gambling laddy?"*

*"No sir."*

*"Smoking?"*

*"No sir."*

*"I haven't seen your face before."*

*"No sir."*

*"Well here's a little advice pal. Stay away from this crew. They're nothing but trouble.....that is unless you want our next meeting to be with your parents."*

*"Yes sir..... I mean..."*

*"You can go."*

*"Yes sir."*

*As he was leaving by the alternate door with his heart accelerating he was still in a state of fear that was about to worsen.*

*"One more thing laddy."*

*He turned his head back over his left shoulder to face Mr Lyon who looked like he was staring at the floor.*

*"Yes."*

*"Give me your hand."*

*"Yes sir."*

*Three strikes later with the whiplash of a cane, the last of which clipped his nails and remained painful and swollen until break, he guessed his ordeal was over.*

*"You won't forget now laddy."*

*"No sir." As he looked down at his reddened palm."*

*But that was not the concern of the brutal man opposite him.*

*"Lying......Lying gets you nowhere fast."*

*"Yes sir."*

*Mr Lyon's dejected gaze returned to his desk and the mountains of paperwork in front of him.*

*"Beat it."*

*He left the office timidly but with each step he took further away from Mr Lyon's office he couldn't disagree more. Lying not only gets you out of trouble but actually it was easy, easier than he could possible imagined. It wasn't until four years later when he was sacked from his first job that he recalled their meeting and wondered whether Mr Lyon was fully aware of the indentation of the pack of playing cards from his tapered trousers as he left the room.*

## 19

It was rare to be invited to Angela's office and as a consequence Jeff was disorientated even more than usual. It was easy for him to roam amongst the wards and wings where he was a regular visitor advising in disputes, assisting weary staff and helping the conveyer belt move but the only other two times he had been to Angela's office during his two year tenure he had been accompanied and as such he was like a passenger in a car with the licence to mentally roam where he liked, taking in the unusual as well as the unremarkable yet without an ultimate goal; expanding his consciousness of the environment and visual anomalies as a discussion point rather than as a landmark for future use.

Jeff knew it was on the third floor - the view had been great. The main trunk road could be viewed in the distance. To the right was an abandoned warehouse that the financial executive had her eyes fixed on for years as the former green space in the hospital had given way to new accommodation buildings for nurses and doctors; an enticement to work in a crumbling system with excessive demands in extraordinary circumstances.

In the foreground were the car-parks, extortionate in their rates and enforced regimentally for all those who dared infringe the rules. The trust defended it on monetary grounds, the local council on parking dispersal but the end result was that the local community, a sleepy hollow ordinarily, suddenly looked like an approach to a car boot sale with cars parked on all verges and in any spaces that hadn't been lucky enough to receive a council go-ahead for a single yellow line.

Even though the porter had described exactly where Angela's room was located he walked aimlessly up and down the naturally light corridor, starting to feel uneasy again, rubbing his right forearm above the wrist and looking for signs of life. Not a footstep, not a squeak, not a murmur. His heart-rate increased and he remembered their first meeting.

Jeff had been introduced to Angela as part of his induction. She had been dressed in her usual attire: a navy blue two-piece with a silk shirt complete with bow, black shoes and her jet black hair tied gently at the nape of her neck. All smiles and politeness she had personally escorted him, keen as always to show the best side of the Trust. Jeff in return asked the same four questions whenever he met someone for the first time on a professional level. What's wrong? What's right? What can be fixed? How can I help fix it?

Jeff was convinced that getting a description of what was wrong can often reveal more about anyone's motivation for doing their job, reveal more about their character, the micro as well as the macro, the gripes that would ordinarily go unnoticed and the principles of their work that often became entangled in a net of rules and regulations, health and safety, and political correctness. Jeff could also gauge with which mindset they viewed the job: the disillusioned, the perfectionist, the jobs-worth, the agitator, the professional climber, the satisfied, the for the sake of it, the passionate, the calling, the idealist, the divisive, the learner, the naive, the working beneath themselves, the money only, the motivated. He had seen them all.

He didn't cram anyone into any single box but these questions got to the heart of why someone was working there, without asking them directly. Some would take any chance to drop the professional veil, whilst others were initially more guarded with their responses. Others closed shop, perhaps due to the bitter experience of working with social services or had a personal dislike for Jeff's predecessor. Some also had personal experience which didn't help but taint their view of the opposition.

Angela was smart, she toed the party line when she had to but threw in the odd vignette, the softener, which had its desired effect and Jeff was very conscious of the words that Angela had upon him, a noticeable relaxing in his body, more expression in his gestures and a twinge, born out of insecurity, those deeply human moments, more often with a stranger, where he felt he could just reach out with his arm and wait for their hands to merge together.

He was suddenly startled when a door opened behind him and a slim brunette with the Octocare badge of honour, smiled gently. The fact that he was motionless in the middle of the hall indicated his quandary.

"Third on the right if you're after Angela….She won't have a light on and normally locks the door."

## 20

Angela was used to people searching for her, if there was a problem she was the master key to unlock the solution. Everyone wanted a piece of her. The lock to her own door was purposeful - she was busy. Only the light tapping of her laptop, oblivious to the movement outside betrayed her. She could even set her pager to vibrate and place it on her second mouse-mat, a useful sound buff. She rarely had the light on preferring the natural light that leapt through her large window.

When Jeff knocked rhythmically on the oak veneer Angela, uncharacteristically, leapt like a jack-in-the-box. She let him in and his apologies for his lateness were soon rebuffed.

"Don't worry…I'm still waiting for Richard - he's on his way."

The conversation proceeded as many others between them. The state of play on the days' discharges, offers of equal support to assist in the processing of such delays, and lastly, and for Jeff's ears only, a discreet enquiry into the actions of a social worker in a particular case concerning the lack of action or obstacles that seemed to have presented themselves. Angela had a pulse on everything and information was her ally. "Of course I'll look into it."

Detective Sergeant Richard Matthews knocked but didn't wait for an answer and walked straight in, having already been briefed by Angela earlier that morning. His position as lead Detective in the Vulnerable Adult division in the police force of Surrey was now cemented and seemingly a coast to retirement following a turbulent career with the Metropolitan Police, not least because of his belligerence against the discrimination and prejudice he received as a result of the colour of his skin. Born in Streatham but adopted by white parents at the age of two he had received a grammar school education but unlike most of his peers refused the opportunity to go to University to pursue his first love; that of being a British Police Officer.

His place at hooker in the school rugby team was a perfect fit as he added the arts of battle alongside his natural combativeness, and was adept in the role as focal point for war on any playing field. He wore his suits, like his school uniform, ready to burst from it at the seams and his lack of hair, broken nose and cauliflower ears did little to diminish his reputation as 'a bruiser' during working hours but to those who knew him well there was a softer side that looked more pragmatically and humorously on life and when he laughed, which was rare, he took the whole room with him.

They all sat away from her desk in a trio of soft chairs with a small coffee table between them. Richard and Jeff had politely refused the hospitality offered and Angela wasn't going to waste time and abandon them to make herself a cup of coffee so she quickly moved onto the pressing matter before them.

"It appears that one member of staff, more than any other, has had the opportunity to take advantage of the patients around him. He works days and nights and is known to have been working on the wards that have been targeted at least two thirds of the time. He may also have had access to the other wards and it is quite possible that he may have even assisted on these wards without any formal notification or registration."

This must have rankled with Angela, Jeff thought, but on one hand this was typical Angela; trying to convince you before you had even the smallest piece of factual information at hand.

"What's his name?" Jeff enquired.

"And his motive?" said Richard.

"David." and she shuffled through paperwork. "He's an agency worker and has only been with the trust for six months before the spate of thefts started." She smiled smugly. "Here it is...Lewis."

"Are you talking about 'Marley'? You must be joking he wouldn't harm a fly."

Jeff knew the suspect. And those that did know David knew he worked at his own pace and moved about the ward silently. His tall, slim, muscular build, anchored by a pair of legs no wider than most peoples' arms, but comely grin, tufts of facial hair and dreadlocks tied in a bun, often referred to as 'Marley' after the Rastafarian songwriter Bob, was also one of the kindest and politest men they had ever met. His smile was enough to lighten the hearts of all those patients he cared for. It was as if he was made to serve, not as a man deprived of his pride but as a man who was glad with all his heart to make that day, that hour, that second, the best, sometimes in direct battle with the elements of fragility and frailty opposing him. His touch was gentle, even with his buckets for hands, and he always kept his word.

Richard couldn't wait any longer as he sifted through some of the records Angela had brought to the meeting and was itching to bring Angela back in line.

"Well even with the records you have described there is no evidence at all and we certainly wouldn't be questioning him alone. But I do have an idea."

"I'll have to stop you there Richard as I've got some CCTV footage that might help."

"Really?" said Richard.

"Let me play you this and see how you feel afterwards."

She tapped the screen and went to the file section. As she tapped again the view of Austen Ward filled the laptop.

This was not the first time Angela had used technology during an investigation and the number of CCTV cameras had quadrupled in the last couple of years, not only to protect the staff but the trust as well. Any element of scandal could ruin a hospitals reputation in the blink of an eye. The picture was a little grainy as Richard and Jeff leaned forward to take a closer look but the form of David was undeniable.

He walked down the main ward and stood by the nurse's station for a brief moment.

"Now watch this."

He then entered a six bed side ward immediately opposite the nurse's station and the camera switches to the one above the station and follows his movements.

"This was only yesterday evening, but by this stage we had formulated our own ideas so we were keeping an eye on him."

"Is this legal?" Jeff announced.

"Quite .....and quiet now." replied Angela

This bemused Jeff because there was no sound to the image that was being produced but Angela wanted their full attention.


David stepped towards the first bed on the right, he gently pulled the curtain around the patients bed and then as he stood behind the curtain his shadow could be clearly seen and then disappear as he crouched and then as he rose up holding what looked like a small tumbler gently leaning it over and bringing it to the patients lips, before, like a magician squeezing it in his hand and placing it in his pocket. At this point there appeared to be a lighting issue as the picture blinked several times before catching David gently pull aside the curtain again and walk straight out of the ward and down the corridor elsewhere as the camera followed him as far as it could.

"Hold on that's part one."

"I hope so." said Richard – "I don't think giving someone a drink is against the law."

The time on the camera elapsed forward another thirty minutes and the event appeared to be repeating itself. David moved behind the curtain again, only this time he didn't crouch. Instead he stood next to the bed for twenty seconds and as he did so leant over the body of the patient. As he started to withdraw and draw erect the right hand of David, lifted the left hand of the patient until it was nearly full vertical and held it for a few seconds before suddenly releasing it and letting it fall from the vertical to the bed side. It flopped and as soon as it did David moved quickly away from the patient, pulled open the curtain and walked much faster than normal, as fast as anyone could ever remembering him doing so.

"Just in case you want to know he spent the next 10 minutes in the staff toilet on Dickens Wing."

"I'm still not sure that gives us anything." remarked Richard but Angela was on him like a shot.

"Hold on, there's more."

On the next stop David returned to the ward and straight to the patient's bed side and leant over her once again. This time he appeared to take something out of his pocket and place it over the face over the patient who moved rapidly onto her side. David then cleared the curtain and back to his usual pace walked slowly away from the patient.

"Back to the toilets again I'm afraid. Can we arrest him now?" asked Angela.

"No there's not enough evidence." replied Richard.

"How about searching his flat? I know we'll find what we need."

"No" said Richard "We're going to need more than a grainy CCTV image especially behind a curtain."

"He doesn't fit the type." said Jeff. "Not Marley, there's no-one I would put more trust in."

"And what type is that Jeff? He's just drugged a patient and robbed them!" We're focusing on Mar….David, that's why we had the camera trained on him. He's the one that fits the profile."

"What profile is that?" demanded Jeff. He wanted to say young and black but knew it wasn't appropriate.

"What about any other suspects?" asked Richard.

"We aren't able to identify any and we can't have five staff monitoring every nurse in the hospital. We had to reduce to the probables from the possibles. You both know how many people come and go in this hospital."

"What about in relation to the other dates. Is there any other evidence, video or otherwise to support your theory? He would surely be on some camera footage each time a theft had taken place."

"We do have the cameras but the ward gets so busy and some of the wards have entrances and exits not covered by cameras because they're for staff. To be honest it would probably take at least a month's work for two staff to even start to unravel it. But I believe he'll crack under any kind of pressure. At the very least I should suspend him."

"No – not yet." said Richard "I think in terms of what you have said that you should continue just to keep an eye on him, because if it is him he's likely to re-offend. At present I don't want to alert any other staff that anyone is under suspicion. What I will need though is the names, dates of birth and addresses of all the staff on this particular ward as well as the night staff to run through the computer to see what we come up with. Does he have any time off soon?"

"Hold on" Angela tapped away at a screen typing David's name. "He's off for a couple of days at the end of this week and the start of next but going by his recent attendance he is equally likely to be called in."

"Well please make sure that doesn't happen. Keep the two days clear and then if we have any further evidence we can interview the other staff before questioning David on his return. If he's our culprit then we mustn't alert him in any way shape or form just yet. You're trained as a joint-investigator aren't you Jeff?"

"I am but I'm absolutely loaded at the moment. Mia, my Senior Prac can probably help you, she's also trained, and reasonably fresh, looking to get involved a bit more."

"O.K – we might use her as a silent witness as there may be some expertise she has in social care that would help us glean more information from the staff. Don't tell her just yet but I'll let you know by the end of the week if I intend to go ahead."

"Anything more I can do?" requested Angela, agitated but eager to support in any way possible.

"I'd be researching more of that video evidence if I were you." replied Richard.

## 21

The three parted and returned to the day job, and whilst all of them had a heightened interest in the events that were unfolding each believed the others were flawed in their assessment of the situation.

Angela could see no other suspect. She wanted an immediate update on anything suspicious and her last half hour of the day was consumed with scanning some of David's actions in the hospital on disc. He was caring, there was no doubt, but he was also careful, too slow and pedantic for Angela, as though he was considering his every move.

Angela had taken David as part of a group that moved from Birmingham and he had shone at the beginning. His deep West Indian lilt was soothing and his rapport with patients was excellent, but now she considered this just a cover to ensnare his victims. She was convinced his head was turning towards the camera pods more than necessary and she was also convinced that they had just missed their best opportunity.

Richard was concerned that the investigation was already compromised. He was aware after reading the conference notes that the trust had avoided all protocol and broken every rule in the book and now Angela was on a personal crusade collecting inadmissible evidence.

Jeff struggled with the race issue. As far as he was concerned he was inherently racist. He believed you couldn't have been brought up in the 70's in a conservative borough in South East England without being so. For a start, deliberately or not, the culture of Britain at that time was racist. The T.V and media portrayal of anyone who was black was a caricature of idiocy, ridicule and untrustworthiness.

Where the Irish had signified the lower working class with the butt of all jokes it was the immigrants who replaced them at the bottom of the rung. It was the immigrants who seeped into their communities and the immigrants who were needed to bolster the work force especially in the care sector.

The stain of inter-race marriage would have shocked any community in south London but in the suburbs it was unheard of. His family were like any other, prejudicial through ignorance and that was their defence. The ruling classes were racist and the empire wasn't relinquishing the role of paternal educator.

As a child he remembered the only African person he used to see in the neighbourhood, and it was the only person. The Chinese, Vietnamese, or the Bangladeshi's he didn't see much outside of their business ventures, takeaways or, even rarer, restaurants visits that most families struggled to afford in the 1970's.

The school playground was the same and the general prevailing wind was that the different Asian kid could be accepted, up to a point, but even if he was good at sport he wasn't part of the team and in the playground games he was never allowed to win. As for practical jokes there was only one person to test out the theory on.

The social work course Jeff had taken had pounded him with the prevalence of racism in society and the need for a dramatic redressing of the cultural experience and the values of those who had been downtrodden as a result and become a second class citizen in every sense. He had to fight himself continuously as he was also aware that every time he walked down the street, every time he considered a staffing issue, every time he saw a crime or misdemeanour and every time he placed his trust with a person from a different culture his creeping thoughts would be worry, expectation of failure and condemnation and he wondered many times whether non-racist thought was an achievable goal with his upbringing or was it just lip service to the need for the current climate of political correctness. To him it was the fourth dimension - a dimension he had inadvertently inherited, a nurtured form that was shackled to his soul, at least for this lifetime, so much so that he loathed himself for it.

## 22

*The Bookmaker*

*Each morning he would rise afresh, with no consideration of the previous days'*
*calamities that had resulted in another series of bets on the horses that failed to*
*provide any return by the end of the day. Quite simply he lost, he lost every day*
*but it wouldn't stop him. He would tweak the betting system he had already*
*created. He would scour the horse results to see how his system could have*
*worked. And then he would return to the smoke filled betting shop tucked away in*
*an inconspicuous part of town. It had two doors from two different alleys so that*
*your secret was never revealed if you didn't want it to be. The gambling premises*
*itself was divided into two, separated by a few steps, with the cash desk in the*
*middle and a glass barrier between punter and cashier.*

*All male life was here. Discrimination and prejudice were left at the door. From*
*judge to road-sweeper, retired hunchbacked man with a cane in his right hand and*
*an extinguished roll-up permanently hanging from his lip to young buck in a shiny*
*suit who strode around the place in a hurry with perhaps only a lunch-hour to*
*throw away his money, to the Chinese men sitting quietly, their faces pressed*
*against the newspaper form guide displayed on every board, on every wall, taking*
*in every detail. Yet there was rivalry. One man's winnings was another man's*
*losses. One man's 'sure thing' was another man's 'donkey.' But they shared a*
*passion, a moment in life as addictive as any high from a drug, any euphoria in a*
*drink, any climax in sex. It was those moments when the heart began to beat faster,*
*the senses became more alert and the outcome more perilous. Where even the*
*shirt you're wearing is hanging by a thread. Bedazzled by the screen, the*
*crackling in the commentary, or the cheers and groans of those around them it was*
*the unknowing, the moment where life had no certainty, no divine plan.*
*"That's why we're here. To tempt her." Regaled one punter.*

*"To tempt who?" he had replied.*

*"Fate. Fate of course."*

*Winning or losing was a by-product. If he won or lost the result was the same. He needed to meet her again in whatever form that took. It could the spinning of a wheel, the turn of a card, the roll of a dice, the hooves of a horse, a ball hitting the back of the net, but he wanted her embrace because then it wasn't his fault and he wouldn't have to make choices and ultimately avoid responsibility altogether.*

## 23

Jeff didn't normally work late but the investigation had left little time for his regular review of his in tray so he had stayed on. The silence around him was interrupted by a tap on the window and for a second he felt guilty simply for not having given full attention to his work as his mind had wandered.

"Sorry to disturb you, I thought I was the only one burning the candle."

Sensing that Jeff didn't immediately recognise her but not taking it personally. "I'm Kath from X-ray…. I rang earlier…. about your member of staff."

"Please…sorry" as he hurriedly opened the door and cleared some papers from the chair nearby, "I only had a silhouette of you in the first instance, come in and have a seat."

As she entered he threw out an arm "I'm Jeff, Team Manager, social services." regretting immediately that he had added a professional title after his name.

"I know…..I was just checking how she was."

"God, I'm sorry, I didn't get back to you."

"You don't need to explain. Everyone is overloaded; I'm surprised anyone gets to talk to anyone round here."


He was already measuring her, the shoulder length dark hair, with a hint of grey, 5ft 7 inches or thereabouts, curvaceous. Her complexion was pale and her hazelnut eyes seemed to hide deep into her sockets. She wore a cream sweater below a red jacket above a plain skirt and dark brown leather shoes. Her body language and expression was one of openness. If he'd had to hazard a guess she would have been of Irish descent, but she was definitely Home Counties now and whilst there were several rings on both hands, the wedding band was conspicuous by its absence. He saw no make-up other than some foundation but trimmed eyebrows and a hint of white musk. He would always recognise it. It had been the perfume of choice for a couple of his girlfriends in his mid twenties and he would admit under the most stringent of questioning or during an alcohol induced state to close friends that he had chosen to wear it himself for the best part of a year. Her hand was warm and light and he felt a bond instantaneously.

"Would you like a tea?"

"No caffeine after 5pm, thanks. So what happened?"

"Ah. That was Mia and her exercises. There's no stopping her when it comes to her free-diving training. She holds her breath for minutes at a time and walks as far as she can only this time she went too far and blacked out temporarily. I can't blame her. Her tenacity is admirable. You'll never change her mind once she's set. Have you got any outrageous hobbies?"

"Only if you count skiing, but this time I'm determined to get on a snow board and give it a go."

"Sounds like you're off soon. I hope you've been doing your exercises."

"I found my old gym card from the start of the year. It's about time I used it."

"Where are you heading off to?"

"Igles......Austria.......with some girlfriends."

"Oh wow! I've just heard I'm off to Rovaniemi soon. Not for skiing. It's a once in a lifetime Christmas trip for my young cousins. Twenty four hours of madness. Can't wait though. Have you been here a while? The hospital I mean?"

"Five years too long."

"Two years for me. It's non-stop. It feels like I'm on one big conveyer belt but the small victories make it worthwhile.......not that I feel I'm in a battle though." and he smiled and raised his eyebrows in a gesture that didn't go unnoticed.

"It can be crazy sometimes can't it."

"Do you ever see the real bodies over the images that pass through your department?"

"Rarely. It's all going digital nowadays unfortunately. I do go on a wander now and again and occasionally we're invited."

Jeff's mind wandered and for a split second he wondered what an x-ray of himself would look like before his thoughts slipped to thinking the same of Kath before he was shaken from his reverie with Kath's words.

"Well I'm glad she's O.K. I just couldn't understand it; there one minute gone the next. A bit like life really just slips through your fingers. Fancy a bite to eat?"

"Er......ok. Why not? I've got another thirty minutes work though."

"Me too. Give me a call when you're finished.......542 if you've forgotten."

Jeff didn't work at all instead he spent the time going over in his head about which restaurant he should choose: The open plan Italian restaurant on the main road, dimly lit but with a view of passing traffic and pedestrians that might stimulate conversation if it didn't go well. Or the small and intimate modern French café with a limited menu but great food or the expensive Japanese basement restaurant, the latter, pretentious as it was, served dishes that were greatly enjoyed by those that were romantically inclined because of the procession of quaint and theatrical concoctions, served by waiters that took you to another continent, another time, another religion, the religion of service.

Kath rejected them all for a large drink and nibbles in a country pub near her home and their conversation flowed all the way to her king size in a two bedroom semi in a faceless modern estate. Their passion untainted by either expectation or consideration was raw, the chemistry latent with no time for pondering the anomalies of each other's bodies although before he left in the morning Kath had stripped, kissed and replaced the bandage covering the wound on his forearm promising to "make you better." Her sensitivity and touch were enough for both to know that the weekend would be theirs and more than once later that next day Jeff was caught peering out though the blinds in his office, where he hoped to catch her eye. But she didn't dwell or signal, just looked up and smiled and returned to her work at hand, which, as she had intimated, had been replaced by the digital world and therefore she spent extended times staring at the screen in front of her.

## 24

The next morning Jeff delivered the agenda items of the team meeting with his thoughts elsewhere. His experience of team meetings was that half of the time would have been taken up by higher management rhetoric. The core of the meeting, to him, was discussion around practice in hospital. This was the only chance he could actually seek to find out more about the base-line of his staff. Their voice was the only one he hoped to influence, albeit with support of the other stronger characters around the table.

He had in the past offered the chair to each member of the team, but the staff-turnover even within a relatively small team meant there were always new faces less able or less willing to take up the mantle. Only on rare occasions did staff wish to remain in the hospital environment. The pace of the work was ferocious, the rewards low, the perks minimal, the pay no higher and the division between health and social services as wide as it could be. Salmon swimming upstream to lay their eggs was the analogy most often used by him and the stream was never ending. There were no breaks and only training courses offered the odd day's respite. Those who enjoyed the challenge often moved up the career path, those who didn't were either crushed or forced to consider alternatives, or worse, played the system rather than seeing the client.

There is a fine balance between acting in a clients or a professional's best interest. Some became so politically charged they forgot to see the client in front of them and the impact on them. Staying for an extended stay in hospital, unless for medical or rehabilitative purposes was simply not advantageous but some took it as a personal battle or worse still a battle of who should fit the bill for ongoing care. As a result the elderly patient would sit there, gradually dissipating and shrivelling away like dishevelled prunes having the life sucked out of them.

The team sat in a semi-circle alert and eager to know more about the current investigation. Back at her desk Mia had sworn aloud about the perpetrator on several occasions as she had sifted through the wreckage of testimonies that started to come back from other departments and community teams. Anyone in a five yard radius had heard her but for the most part it was only Jeff and Mia who were up to speed on the investigation.

"Morning everyone....we have a series of incidences in the hospital. As you may be aware I have asked Mia to lead the investigation from our end and she will be working directly with Detective Sergeant Richard Matthews. Mia."

Jeff was aware that Mia's thirst for knowledge was greater than his ever was, she had a better memory, she hadn't lost her appetite for the cause, her spirits not dampened by what she considered the underwhelming achievements of others. She had the brightness and energy of any star in the constellation.

As with anyone whose aspirations were higher in practice, her reputation had preceded her and she knew she would have to make some accommodation for those who didn't trust her and saw her as an adversary initially, particularly with the rumour mill on her arrival, but she was not going to let anyone comment against her principals. Everyone who listened to her now could feel the passion in her voice.

"We all know that clients with mental health problems and learning disabilities are frequently discriminated against in a hospital environment not only with the management of their treatment but with the general attitude shown towards them as clients of services but believe me older people are not far behind in the lack of dignity and care they receive on the wards. Unfortunately it is human nature to neglect those who are most vulnerable. Those who don't complain, argue, or know their rights, have a hard time. It is often their carers, most of who are nearly retired themselves who act as their voice. It's not just about money. A lack of staff is an issue, there's barely time to deliver their medication but there is certainly not enough time to ensure that their backside is clean and dry, that their throat isn't parched. You pick up any fluid chart in this hospital and if fifty percent are getting enough water then the hospital is outstanding. It is our job, our vocation, our duty to protect the elderly whilst they are here. Those with dementia receive the poorest treatment; medicated to the hilt it isn't a surprise that when any lucidity remains they call out. They're shipped out to homes like cattle, left to graze in a bed until the sores on their heels or their buttocks eat away all the soft tissue and muscle until all is left is bone and septicaemia takes them to a better place. We have an opportunity, all of us, to educate everyone here in principles of dignity, love, companionship, freedom, emancipation, independence, diversity, tolerance, the moral good.... So look around you... and react... and report. We have a duty to support them because no-one else will. Keep on the lookout. There's a thief roaming the wards and we're going to catch him or her. Don't let anything unusual go. I want to know all of your suspicions, however ridiculous they may sound. This thief is a slippery eel so believe what your clients are saying to you and make a note of what jewellery they have on them. We simply don't know the extent of the problem at the moment. It could be a whole lot worse than we think. Let's make sure we catch this bastard and let's make sure we're protecting those who have given so much of themselves for us."

## 25

The police interviews at the hospital took place on Tuesday and were held in the comfortable video suite in the security block with adjoining room. It was arranged as an internal investigation by the Trust and like most things you didn't question it. From a legal standpoint there was justification for a lawyer or at the very least a friend or advocate to be present but the interview was couched in preliminary terms.

Detective Sergeant Richard Matthews had completed his initial screening and unravelled a few potentials and decided to concentrate on those who spent most of their time on the wards that were at the forefront of the investigation. He was long enough in the tooth to know that a caution at aged fourteen for shoplifting or a charge for drunk and disorderly at nineteen wasn't the precursor of a career with the criminal fraternity but nevertheless the occasional charge sheet did give rise to suspicions.

Richard had invited PC Rebecca Halliday, one of the new breed of police constables to assist him in his investigation. Bright, tall, athletic, physically strong and despite the outward appearance of naivety and openness, a Rottweiler once blood was smelt. Rebecca was also blond and attractive and she was never quite sure whether her physical looks were a blessing or a hindrance in her role. For Richard they were most definitely an advantage. Even the toughest witnesses would not be moved to say something to her, albeit a throw away chat up line, and she had the ability to allow the uniform to disappear to suspects during discussion.

Mia was placed in the adjoining room, and was able to witness the whole series of questions and answer sessions. She was invited to make some rough notes of each interview as part of the enquiry and could interrupt if she needed Richard's attention. She was also an extra pair of eyes, and Richard knew that the eyes of another could well provide some additional material whilst confident enough in his own abilities to defer to his judgement.

Each interview followed the same line of enquiry. The interviewee was made clear that this was a voluntary interview, whilst hinting politely that the police could request the attendance in more formal circumstances if they refused to co-operate. A gentle introduction followed stating the aims of the enquiry, and understanding of each and everyone's role and movements within the hospital, which could be verified with the use of CCTV currently available. There would follow a dialogue examining the potential loopholes in the system, and potential suspects, although this was never a leading question and was framed as 'Have you noticed anything or anyone recently that has given you cause for concern?'

Richard also had the staff files made available to his team, although never revealed to the interviewees, and they remained on the desk next to Mia but Richard had spent three hours the previous evening cross matching the employees against any record they had on file. Richard understood that those who were the most innocent were often those that were most nervous and one way of deflecting their nerves was by becoming amateur detectives themselves. The opportunity to ask questions at the end was severely limited in its scope but the two officers were always very polite as they finished the process and thanked everyone for their time and patience during this unsettling period.

Richard had deliberately chosen Sally, a long standing auxiliary nurse as his first interviewee. He was conscious of two things prior to the interview: Firstly, she had no record whatsoever and was generally happy with her lot at the hospital and evidently part of the furniture. Secondly, and more importantly, according to Angela "Sally has enough gossip to fill a warehouse on a daily basis."

Sally didn't disappoint and had a view on everything and Richard was meticulous in his own recording of notes. She knew every door in and out of every ward in the hospital and had a number of theories about the actions of the thief, how to sedate a patient, what time staff were likely to be on their own, the possibility of working as part of a team of thieves, which Richard made a small mental note of because he hadn't really considered it as a viable option, but as Sally reported "Flying in nurses from across the globe was a sure way to attract the unsavoury element." Sally had a high regard for the Filipino's, despite smiling too much but she raised concerns about the "cold ill wind from the East," and "the lazy dark cloud from the West."
Mia couldn't help but smash her feet against the wall in the adjoining room.
*She's even bloody rehearsed these lines.*
Richard didn't flinch or even raise an eyebrow but offered exceptional gratitude for her time and support whilst Mia continued to swear under her breath.

Richard having completed the interview expected that the word on the ward, according to Sally, would be that the Police couldn't find sugar in a chocolate factory, that she had put them on the right path and that despite their stupidity they were kind and there was nothing to worry about, just as he had hoped.

Bryan was next. Aged 32, five foot eleven, a little overweight, softly spoken with cropped, spiky dyed blond hair that was in need of another application. A nurse for 4 years, he had not yet fulfilled the potential initially identified in his early career. According to Angela, a series of catastrophic relationships with his male partners had a debilitating effect on his confidence and tasks that should have been regarded as routine for one so experienced still required the occasional helping hand. Whilst on his good days he could be the life and soul of the party there were as many others where he would loiter, head down, saying barely the minimum. His patient communication skills had suffered and on more than one occasion he had needed a quiet word in relation to his abrupt, frosty responses, which weren't in keeping with 'the agenda of the Trust.' Richard's own background check had revealed that Bryan had been the victim in a domestic related incident on more than one occasion and wondered whether he would get a word out of him at all.

The interview started promisingly, Bryan was in good spirits, and Richard let Rebecca take the lead. As the discussion moved to the victims of crime, particularly as Rebecca noted the physical, psychological and emotional abuse suffered by the clients who had been financially abused Bryan lost his energy and enthusiasm and started to drift in his mind before wilting before them.

"I'm innocent you know. Well no doubt the files have been whipped out I can't imagine what it says about me. You make one mistake here and you're tarnished for life. They have you over a barrel. I threatened to resign once. They said 'You know we will have to be honest with our references Bryan.......what does that mean?

Bryan was beginning to slump in his chair.

"I know what it's like to be a victim," he added with a tear in his eye, I couldn't put anyone else through the same."

"We're not saying you did," said Rebecca "but do you think you can give us any pointers to possible suspects?"

He was trying to hold out and Rebecca could sense it.

"Come on Bryan, as you've just said, you, more than anyone, must empathise with the trauma they're suffering."

"It's not easy for me."

"What's not easy?"

"It's just that David has been helping me out recently. He doesn't like the paperwork and sometimes I don't have good days with the patients. Please......can you keep this from management? I don't want to lose my job... I've been having a tough time of it recently."

"Go on. You can be assured of our discretion; this isn't about judging people at work. It's about stopping a thief cruelly taking the little dignity that patients have left in their lives and if we don't stop it soon we're worried it will escalate even further."

"What do you mean escalate?"

"Well one day someone is going to try and stop our thief or he is going to get his sums wrong and whatever he does to help himself to their belongings could have a longer lasting effect on the client than he may have anticipated.......So you were saying......David?"

"Nothing really... I just let him get on with the patients but I do notice that he's on and off the ward a lot. You're not allowed a phone in the hospital but if you're going to use one anywhere then it's in the toilets, not the staff area, as we all have access to that and you only need the wrong person to walk in to get a severe dressing down. He's well liked you see."

Rebecca didn't interrupt just sat and looked him patiently in the eye.

"I do his paperwork - he manages the ward. We have a little meet up every day so he can pass on the details......The thing is .... He sort of knows people outside."

"What sort of people?"

"The sort that can get you drugs.....recreational only.....but I do think that sometimes he isn't all quite there and wonder if anything is getting on top of him."

"Do you buy drugs from him?" interrupted Rebecca

"No...I'm on enough medication."

Three of the next five interviewees were Filipinos nurses drafted initially from the same agency and were about halfway through probation before having an opportunity to acquire a full contract with the trust. Richard knew their dates of work didn't tally exactly and unless there had been a conspiracy of an immense size with the three of them in cahoots then there was little to suspect them. When Richard threw out questions about other members of staff they had very little to say. He didn't make an example of David but when the name cropped up he did notice that a couple of them blushed and squeezed in their shoulders ever so slightly but he didn't pursue it, although it didn't bypass Rebecca either.

Richard took the unusual step with Eva and Ava, sisters from Lithuania, to be interviewed together. Eva, the eldest was slimmer, with bright red dyed hair, sylvan looks, chiselled features and a vulnerability about her; where her diet in life had not quite enriched enough, the childhood perhaps not as gentle. Her sister was younger and larger in frame but was more comfortable talking and spoke with a less pronounced accent. They lived together on site accommodation and gave more thorough answers than the Filipino nurses, elaborating where they could on every occasion, light-heartedly skipping through the interview.

In terms of thefts the girls didn't have any knowledge and as per trust policy wore no jewellery at work but the holes piercing their skin in their eyebrows, nose, ears and lips and indentations on their fingers meant they enjoyed wearing it.

Rebecca took their good spirits to press further and whilst David was described as 'nice' by both of them, Rebecca was determined to probe even if meant making them uncomfortable. They confirmed that David also lived in the staff accommodation and was obviously popular, a regular caller at the flats of other nurses, and she knew that by nurses they meant females. He was always at any party they ended up at and was barely in his room. He had a reputation as a considerate man, a gentle man.

"Does he smoke?"

"Yes at parties"

"What does he smoke?"

"What do you mean?"

"What I mean is does he smoke drugs?"

"I don't know."

Rebecca couldn't hold herself back.

"Has he offered you any drugs?

"No"

"Do you find him attractive?"

And they both laughed. And then a bit of pressure

"You do know that the trust has a zero tolerance approach to drug taking on their premises.......What about hard drugs ..... crack, speed, acid, heroin, Charlie."

The girls looked at each other and became more and more defensive and suddenly seemed to know him less and less. Richard brought them back to the main issue and asked them to keep an eye on the wards for any suspicious activity but Rebecca pressed on and in the end the picture became obscure. He may have smoked but didn't give them anything. The parties were frequent and alcohol was plentiful. They hadn't entered a personal relationship but were pretty sure he was popular and there were rumours that the moans from his bedroom weren't those that required intervention but he never spoke of what happened behind closed doors to anyone.

After they had exited Rebecca turned to Richard.

"How would you like to play this? You know the word will be out there and he's been on the ward an hour."

"I want him to be nervous and I want him to know that he's the focus of attention." replied Richard.

He subconsciously hoped that David wouldn't arrive, that he was already running from the situation. He never let it slip to Angela but after reviewing the CCTV evidence it was pretty damning, enough to get him the sack.

"Let's be prepared to find the holes in his story."

## 26

It was 3.00 pm and the interviews were running to schedule. There was the slightest tap at the door before David appeared head first.

"Come in David – please have a seat...My name is Detective Sergeant Richard Matthews and this is Police Constable Rebecca Halliday. In the side room is Mia from social services, who is helping us. Say hi Mia."

Mia leant round the doorway and waved.

David was a giant of a man in the flesh. Fully 6ft 7in he had bowed his head as he entered the room and the regular blue cloth desk chair on black steel legs looked like that of a primary school chair against his frame. His knees were high above his waist line so as the interview progressed he began to gradually slip them forwards until they couldn't be seen anymore and on more than one occasion David accidentally knocked his legs against Richard as he adjusted his chair. His uniform was ill-fitting both in length from the neck to the navel and even more distorted in the length of the arms. In fact beneath the rectangular apparel was disguised an upper body that was muscularly formed and well proportioned apart from his small neck that was just a servant to a large glorious smile with teeth that glowed, below a regular nose and dark brown eyes, with eyebrows that were short and pugilistic. Above there was a large brow below tightly tied long black dreadlocks. His hands were enormous but soft to the touch as Richard lost his amongst David's in the customary handshake but his voice was a paradox to the man, soothing and whisperingly quiet, and both Richard and Rebecca had to strain to hear his answers as the interview began.

"Could you tell me how long you have been working in the hospital?" Richard knew the details but wanted to check David's memory.

"About six months. I first started via the agency in May..... after my birthday."

"And how do you feel you've settled in?"

"Yeah – well really. I seem to be getting on with everyone."

"How about your relationship with patients? How do you feel you have been getting along there?"

"Good, I do what I can."

Richard was getting tired of the generalisations, so became more direct.

"What exactly is can?"

"What do you mean?"

"What I mean...David, is, what exactly is your role in your professional support to patients?"

David picked up the change in tone and the nuance and suddenly became more alert. His answers took on the form that he would give if interviewing for the job he already had, detailing the types of support he offered. Richard let him finish but he wasn't listening after just a few sentences, instead already formulating his next questions.

"Do you understand why you have been called here David?"

"Some rings have been stolen?"

"Yes that's right. How do you think they may have been stolen?"

"I don't know."

Rebecca intervened

"Apparently you have a very good rapport with the patients on the ward David?"

"I try my best."

Rebecca took off her jacket as she asked her next question, never taking her eyes off David as she did so.

"Do you have any suspicions who it may be or any member of staff you feel may be struggling in terms of completing their role at the current time?"

This was Rebecca's loyalty test and to see whether there was any mileage in the interview that had been carried out with Bryan.

"No I don't think so."

"You don't think so or you don't like to say?"

Perhaps it was nerves, perhaps it was just the pressure but David became self conscious of his nails, which he bit routinely, so he moved them under the table.

"We all help each other out and everyone pulls their weight."

"What if several staff members had pointed their fingers at you. How would you react to that?" pressed Rebecca.

"I'd be surprised. I do a good job round here."

"David, how many of the thefts have you heard about?" said Richard.

"According to Sister there's eleven."

"Yes that's right. Can I read some names to you?" said Rebecca

"Of course."

She read the list and there were some vague recollections that returned to David. At one point he even raised a wry smile; *that one kept everyone up all night the short time she was here.*

"I certainly recognise some of them."

"Well according to the medical records on the wards – you've probably worked with all of them."

David was not expecting this interjection from Rebecca and shuffled a little bit in his seat.

Richard grabbed the reins again. "The thing is David, there is a lot of record keeping and surveillance on the wards. I mean there are cameras everywhere for starters and with the current use of technology the entire hospital is not only filmed but available digitally nowadays."

"Do you think that I'm capable of robbing patients and getting away with it, do you? There's eleven of them. More often than not we're picking up things they claim to have lost, only they forgot that they'd left it on their sheet, or tucked under one of their pillows. Go and check your records carefully and you'll find

I report more items of lost property than anyone else in the hospital." David didn't know that for sure but he felt backed into a corner.

"Do you work lots of night shifts David?" Rebecca knew he put more hours in than any other nurse.

"I do my fair share."

"And what do you do most of the night?"

"Catch up with paperwork, regular checks, deal with any emergency calls from the patients' alarms."

"Tell me about your paperwork. If you're not on a night shift can you manage it yourself?"

David hesitated significantly before answering. "O.K, me and Bryan have a little arrangement sometimes, but he's been going through a tough time at the moment and he's lost some confidence."

David pulled his hands from beneath the desk and spread eagled them, looking like he could scoop up the whole room.

"He's offered to help me with paperwork if I deal with more of the hands on."

Yet as David said it he started to rephrase it in his head but whatever he started to come up with he realised that to adjust it might make them believe he was being deceptive so he clarified the statement with what made most sense, the truth.

"Look I have the most contact with patients but I enjoy it. I'm not the quickest with paperwork and Bryan can fly through it but I still give him the details.....and I initial everything to say that it's my account. It's accepted by those on the ward. They all know what a state he's in."

Rebecca wanted more "Who asked who to do what...Wasn't it your idea?"

David put his head in his hands

"I haven't done anything wrong."

"Do you want us to take you down the station on a more formal charge or are you going to start telling the truth?" said Rebecca.

"The truth about what?" he pleaded, again with his arms outstretched.

"O.K David. Let's talk about anything that might be in your memory. Did you complete any late shifts last week?" said Richard.

"No!" was his first response before he even started to think but as he did so he changed his answer "Yes... I mean yes. I was working the Tuesday and Thursday night, I did the 7 to 7 shift."

"And what wards did you cover?"

"The usual."

"Which ones?"

"I cover a number of wards."

"Can you remember what time you visited Austen ward?"

"It's normally the last one before I go central."

"And what does going central mean?"

"It means I take a desk on Dickens' wing, which acts as the central hub for a few wards and I go basically where I'm requested."

"So what time would you get up to Austen Ward then?" Rebecca interjected.

"Well if things are running smoothly anytime between 10.15 – 10.45pm. Most of the patients are asleep by then, but for those who aren't it is a reminder to turn off the T.V or radio and to get some rest...if they can."

Rebecca scribbled on a piece of paper which said 10:18pm and passed it to Richard, which unnerved David.

Rebecca continued "Do you remember any of the patients you assisted that evening?"

"There was probably only Mrs Priddy awake."

"And why is that?"

"I don't know why she was awake, you'd have to ask her."

"Oh don't worry, we already have." Rebecca was lying and David sighed but she wasn't stopping.

"Would you like to tell us exactly what you were doing round Mrs Priddy's bed on that evening given that we have her testimony on record and we had the camera pointing straight at you the entire time."

This was too much for David.

"Am I under arrest?"

"Not yet."

"Well I'm not saying another word unless I have a solicitor in front of me. In fact I'm not even going to stay here. If you want to take me in under caution then that's fine but I've done nothing wrong. As he stood up he pushed the desk forward like it was a matchbox and uncharacteristically raised his voice that boomed as far as Mia. "And what sort of Kangaroo Court is this anyway?"

"Please sit down David." Richard pleaded.

But nothing was stopping David as he brushed aside the chair and left the room.


Mia appeared from the back room.

"Can he do that?"

"I'm afraid he can – the only way we can get him down the station is to arrest him – and he clearly isn't going to play ball without a brief. No we're going to need more than just a camera angle. We've got no witnesses and no testimony from Mrs Priddy and are unlikely to do so."

"Well what now?"

"A hunch.......and you can help Mia but no-one and I mean no-one is going to say anything outside these four walls, and that includes Angela and Jeff. I'm afraid there will be too much red tape. Let's meet again tomorrow and I'll go through it to explain the details."


As Mia left she considered further the request that Richard was making, particularly regarding the withholding of information. She was smart, smart enough to know that not everything was gilded in truth during the assessment process and on occasion's exaggerating or overlooking certain information in the right place assisted the funding application and Jeff would trust her implicitly. The advent of new computer software meant that it had almost become a tick-box exercise with an embellishment of emotionally laden phrases yet the social work training was at the essence of all their work before them and the client's best needs was the fuel for the fire inside them.

What Mia didn't know was that Richard had long suspected that Angela and Jeff had a brief affair when Jeff first moved into the hospital and that this mutual regard meant if any information went to one party he was pretty sure it would end up in the ears of the other, which would only lead to delay and after the events today he knew he was running out of time.

## 27

The Bank

*They were blind and therefore vulnerable, that was her first mistake. Her second mistake was ignorance. A confident young cashier straight from university had tried to steal the blind couples' money because she had an eating disorder and felt compelled to prove to her family that she was eating more than she said but somehow had missed the fact that blind people have statements in Braille and it was only a matter of time before the statements were read and her plan was uncovered. She left her job in the bank overnight and that was that. Like the blossom on a cherry tree all trace of her had simply vanished after the storm had blown through.*

*How could anyone have made such a mistake? His deceit would be better by design with planning, skill and bravery. He was already in debt, which was frowned upon for a career in banking, and on a daily basis he would outspend his income. His lunchtimes were spent in the pub with his work colleagues. Two pints of lager guaranteed an afternoon of leisure and daydreaming; there was never enough work on the clerical side to keep you busy.*

*He was in a room that was only three metres square but the walls were three foot thick and the vault door was solid steel. A collection of ledgers were on the shelves and he started to flick through them as he rested after pulling the trolley of coin, dutifully dropped off by the security firm at the bank's entrance, so that he had to wrestle with the enormous weight all the way through several doors and corridors to the rear of the building.*

*The statement in the ledger had the name of a Saudi Prince. £40,000 left just sitting in an account for year on year. Not a soul touching it and almost certainly forgotten. His own annual salary was a little over £3,000. Justification was a key motive. What a waste of idle money. If only he the funds to follow through with his systems then he could prove that he could overcome fate and forge not only his own future but that of his family and friends as well.*

*His plan was hatched. Whenever he needed it he transferred a small amount of money from the Prince's account to his, so there was never any chance of them questioning his own balance. There was technology but primarily transactions were a paperwork process and he could destroy evidence and alter accounts as he needed to. Even as the three yearly external audits took place he continued to forge documents literally under their noses still fighting for his chance to prove his abilities. Whatever was amiss through his childhood would find solace in the scramble for attention but only when he had proved himself and his system. All he had proved thus far was that he was a formidable liar, a calculating thief, a desperate man with a vacuum of morals. He had given himself over to all the dark shadows that inhabited his soul, which were gladly tearing him to shreds.*

*He walked home along the riverbank the evening the bank suspended him before he was duly sacked following further investigation. His tears flowed freely; the last time he would allow emotion to rule. A process had now begun, a process that eliminated pain from his life by ignoring the degradation and consequently diminishing the goodness within him. He had become a spy of humanity and no longer a participant in the greater good.*

## 28

Angela, as was her way, didn't knock but walked straight into the security office and upon noticing Mark with his hands clasped behind his head, leaning as far back as he could manage in one of the new fangled office chairs, asked politely

"May I have a moment?"

"Of course."

"Outside."

"Sure. Hold the fort Steve."

Mark knew his place but he was one of the few lower ranked colleagues who wasn't afraid of Angela. He ran a tight team who worked hard when they needed to and relaxed when they didn't. Most of the difficulties they ran into were dealt without needing outside intervention. And for this the Trust was happy for him just to get on with the job. There had been complaints, there always was when security does their job properly, but his loyalty to the trust was unquestionable.

Most of the incidences were with alcohol or drug fuelled patients and relatives and even when they weren't Mark had a knack of simmering any confrontation. His portly build, shaven head and large beard that reached the top of his sternum carried an air of authority but this he coupled with a sense of humour and a professional disarming manner that defused even the toughest combatants.

"What's the problem?" he knew there must be one and he preferred to get straight to the point.

"It's David."

"Arrested him have they. Need a hand?"

"On the contrary, they have let him go."

"What.....really?"

"I need your help."

"You've got it."

"I want some eyes on him permanently, whatever it costs."

"I'll get someone on it straight away."

"We'll leave Richard to carry on his own investigation but we can't allow this to continue."

"Not on my watch we won't."

"Go the extra mile if you have to and regular updates please."

"You've got it."

"Is there anything we can do around the accommodation block?"

"I'll look into it."

"Thanks."

And she was gone.

## 29

As Richard entered the cosy office where Mia and Rebecca sat patiently he deliberately put down his brown leather briefcase on top of the desk facing them both. This was his opening statement; he meant business.

Richard had never forgotten his brief but mesmerising turn as an eighteen year old juror in a rank and file drug dealing case that lit the fuse for his application to join the police force.   The majority of his fellow jurors had remained stoically unconvinced that a stash of money in the flower pot; drugs on the premises, scales under the sofa, described by the defence as being used to weigh baby food, and thousands of packets of small clear plastic pouches used to supply the drugs, were enough evidence for a conviction. Instead their deliberations tediously went into a second day.  Overnight Richard had a crisis of conscience and conceded that the defendants were guilty as charged. The next morning sitting alongside his fellow jurors the lead foreman had picked up his own leather case and emptied the contents onto the table in front of them all.  Falling all around them were nails and screws of every description clattering and clinking as they dispersed themselves, some inevitably falling to the floor as they poured forward.

The older conservative foreman then stated.

"See how many of this assortment can go in the plastic pouches."

The defendant had sworn that this was the purpose of so many pouches, simply to bag his fixings that were normally kept in the shed.

"Go on. Don't be shy." he urged.

It didn't take the jurors long to accept that only a few of the several hundred that he had furnished would fit in the pouches and less than an hour later a unanimous guilty verdict was returned. To this day Richard didn't have a clue how the foreman had eased the case past security but the performance was indelible and it was now his time to educate.

"Good morning. There was a man walking along the bank of a river and he was walking downstream. It was a beautiful sunny day and he was lost in his thoughts when he suddenly heard cries of help. Just at that moment he saw in the corner of his eye someone struggling in the water. He picked up his pace as the river started to take the drowning person away from him. Then with no regard for his own safety he ran ahead and jumped into the water, swimming to where he imagined the person would flow past. He was a little out of square but caught hold of them anyway and using most of the techniques he had learnt when younger he turned himself and the person onto their backs and kicking ferociously made it to the riverbank before hauling the young woman out of the river. Exhausted he checked she was well, warm and led her to the nearest place of safety where others took over her care.

He returned to the riverbank determined to finish his walk only to hear another cry and unbelievably another person had fallen into the river. Aware of the repetition of the event, once more he ran forward, jumped into the river, and saved another from drowning. Unfortunately, this wasn't to be the last and no sooner had he returned to the river bank then another person yelled from the fast flowing river.

The question is at what point does he forgo trying to save the victims in the river and go back and search the root cause of the problem so people aren't falling into the river in the first place?

It appears to me that all we are doing is jumping into the river to placate the victims of our criminal's behaviour. The only way we're going to catch the criminal is by going back to the root cause and catching him in the act in the first place."

"If the root cause is David how are we going to stop him?" asked Rebecca, more interested in action than analogies.

"David may be the perpetrator but what is causing all these people to be falling into the river? David may be taking advantage of their tricky situation but what do they have that others may not?"

"Isn't it their vulnerability, their poor memory, their ability to be conned?" urged Mia.

Richard smiled. Mia had given a wonderful professional driven answer but not the one he had hoped for so he served it up on a plate for them.

"They're all areas that our thief is taking advantage of to a lesser or higher degree but what I'm thinking of is something more obvious......What is our thief after? What do they have that he doesn't?"

"Jewellery." bemoaned Rebecca who thought the whole performance was for Mia's benefit and in a quiet place between them Richard wouldn't have denied it.

"Exactly, and if we are going to catch a thief then we have to play them at their own game and what our criminal has that we don't is an insatiable appetite to steal someone else's valuables. If he was a murderer then we'd be calling him 'a serial killer'. Well, he is a serial thief and to catch him then we need to go fishing. I can provide the bait but I need you Mia to think how we are going to catch his eye in hospital."

Richard opened his briefcase in front of them.

"Modern technology - you just can't beat it." and he pincered the two rings between his thumb and forefinger. "The rings meet all the requirements. They are, of course, reasonably good copies, there has to be some precious metal, even if it is gold plate. But Zirconia is good enough and I don't imagine the thief being too picky."

Richard was determined have something concrete to orchestrate an arrest especially if he was to justify tactics that were likely to bring pressure from several quarters if the operation went awry.

"This is 'Operation Precious.' We're hunting a Gollum. Whoever it is they can't stop themselves. They're probably harbouring an addiction but that doesn't allow them any sympathy. They had the choice and they chose the wrong option. It's payback time."

There was nothing more satisfying for Richard than seeing payback; the moment a perpetrator was led downstairs from the dock. It wasn't the looks on their faces; the majority knew it was coming. Many criminals in the Crown Courts were prepared, already wearing a pair of fashionable jogging bottoms and trainers, items that would be more comfortable 'in nick.' Some wouldn't care and would shout there last two penneth in before being led away. Others would be happy and compliant - any reduction in sentence would be a bonus of course. The virgins, who were in the minority, were the most likely to be affected emotionally, and their families. Many relatives didn't know that not all viewing galleries in Crown Courts afforded sight of the prisoner and they were unlikely to see or hear their loved ones again unless there was a tirade. Otherwise the last words they would hear would be the length of sentence and 'Take him down'. And it was always down - down to the dungeon below, the single cell with no comfort cushion, no shoulder to cry on, just the scratched remarks and barbs of the other detainees who had passed through the justice system. That is what drove Richard; the equalisation.

The rings Richard chose were engagement and wedding rings of an era gone by. The former was gold plate with a cluster of Zirconia diamonds, but he added another, a slim piece of gold metal plate that would act as the old wedding band.

"The reason for two rings is to entice the thief on monetary value alone. Even if he or she is aware they are being watched this might just be too great a prize to ignore. If the thief is as brazen as we think they are then two for the price of one would signify their power and the inability of those around them to stop them. This is where you come in Mia. I need a less conspicuous helper and I don't want any other member of health or social care staff in on the operation. Jeff highly recommended you."

"I'll try."

## 30

*Friendship*

*His shame was so great from the sacking of the bank that he had devised an elaborate alibi for his parents and friends. His life become absurd. For the first three weeks after his sobering walk on the riverbank he told no-one he had lost his job except his best friend and on the pretence of leaving for work donned his suit and walked the streets until he felt it was safe to knock on his friend's door with whatever he could plunder from the freezer so they could at least eat. Neither his friend nor he had money or motivation to seek employment. They lived in a bubble of idleness. The stealing from his parents continued unabated, small amounts that he hoped weren't noticed. Even a single £1 coin found in the sofa lining was enough to buy a packet of tobacco and would gladden their hearts and retrieve the day.*

*It was on such a day and time that on exiting the newsagent with the prized tobacco in hand that he had bumped into his mother and the pretence came crashing down but still he allowed only half the story to be revealed, the full truth laid hidden deep within him. His family bought the story; he had lost his temper and hit a work colleague, a story so perverse that it had worked. He was an anti-hero of sorts, although no-one could understand it because he was the gentlest of creatures, a weakling, a chick yearning to be accepted, scrawny, ugly, weather beaten, scruffy. Now he had some sort of closure and he started the climb to leaving his parent's nest.*

*The bank didn't prosecute; publicity of in-house embezzlement wouldn't encourage the investors. They asked for the monies stolen to be repaid in the form of an interest free loan and reported 'We will be frank with our references.' So when he sat holding a letter addressed from the very bank he had just been sacked from on the fourth day of his new employment; a clerical position in an office of a major carpet chain, he had another choice to make, choices that thus far had lost him his dignity, his employment, his self worth. Honesty and freedom come as a choice and sometimes at a cost. He stuffed the letter in his pocket and later that evening wrote his own reference carefully embellishing his skills as he saw them; a mind that had lost reference to reality and had started to orchestrate a grand symphony of illusion.*

## 31

Mia stood in her kitchen watching the rice simmer and reflected on her relationship with Jeff.

"You know you're the one with all the passion." Jeff had whispered as he kissed her tenderly as they lay naked under the sheets "You've got more oomph than me and you're great with the clients."

"Thank you but your compliments only seem to flow once your feet have left the floor."

"I'm sorry. If only I had your natural drive and empathy, I've had to learn mine. You come as the hunter.....I come as the scavenger picking up the scraps along the way."

"So I'm a scrap now. Did you pick me up?"

"No." but Mia was already silencing him with a kiss.

"Do you think it's just females that have a natural tendency to support those more vulnerable, an empathy with the downtrodden, an independent mind, not afraid to take sides in the debate and argue with vigour or is it just me?"

Mia looked vacantly at the wooden spoon she was stirring and became worried about Richard's words. *How can I withhold any information about the investigation from Jeff? What if it all went wrong? I'm just beginning to make an impression in the hospital. Was the gentle giant really the thief?* She didn't really know Richard and Rebecca but felt that Rebecca had pushed far too hard even if the evidence was overwhelming. *Why hadn't they just arrested him in the first place?* And as far as some of the questioning, it was very leading. Oreo clawed her for attention and received a meal that cost more than hers, followed by an extended cuddling session for them both but her thoughts kept returning to Jeff and being dishonest to him. *How will this stack up against my willingness to be more honest about myself and others? Was it for the greater good? Would God understand?*

In the early part of their relationship there had been some rival banter between Mia and Jeff. Jeff had studied in Glasgow, 'The natural home of social work' he eschewed whilst Mia had made Royal Holloway, in Surrey her learning experience. They had read some of each other's old essays and dissertations and Jeff was struck by how militant and rebellious Mia was.

"I tried to think outside the box but you tear the bloody thing apart."

They had laughed about some of the joint training with the Police, each profession battling for the most hated in the public eye. They remembered the professional actors who stepped in as clients when the video interviews took place. Respect for the actors assimilating skills was cemented the afternoon they became six year olds harbouring sexual abuse secrets, or teenagers with a learning disability beaten by their carers' or older people neglected in their own home.

Jeff would often tease Mia with an ethical dilemma.

"A group of holidaymakers was on a coach tour of Mexico when their coach was stopped and ordered off the road by a group of bandits. Everyone was asked to get off the bus and stand in a circle. As they gathered around the head of the gang ordered his men to take valuables from them, so they cleared the bus of all its valuables, handbags and searched other large bags for items of worth. Once all the passengers were checked they stood semi-naked. The group leader invited the coach driver into the middle of the circle with him. He then put a gun to the driver's head and shot him through the brain, killing him instantly. He then pulls another person out of the group who is you. He explains very simply that you have to decide what to do next. You must choose another person in the group not yourself or him, nor any other member of his gang but one of the tourists, who isn't a volunteer. If you shoot them dead you save the lives of the other forty eight left in the group. If you don't do this he would order his men to kill everyone. What would you do?"

"Are you in the group?" joked Mia and he was on her, tickling her. Mia thought about it for a minute and mumbled "The oldest, most frail person I suppose but I'm not happy with it. I don't know if I would have the guts."

"Is the oldest always the frailest? I know ninety year olds that are fitter than some fifty year olds."

"That's true. Maybe someone would volunteer, give me some sort of signal. I guess we all have an idea of where we are along life's line. It's too difficult. Who knows. What about you?"

"I was thinking I might shoot a baby on the basis that the baby would be the only one that wouldn't be affected psychologically prior to its death."

"What about the mother!?"

"Mmm I knew there was a problem I'd missed....what about you being a mother?"

"Not a chance."


There were some subjects that were taboo and children was one of them. But for those dreamlike shared moments in bed they thought they could change the world with their ideals before sealing their commitment with their bodies. Yet, even now, as Mia thought of the equal partnership they had shared before Jeff ceased to see her and his mind had wandered she considered her betrayal of him. She wouldn't do it as a form of retribution, although for many months she had wanted some despite being the one to leave. She was now part of Richard's operation and according to him was the key to the successful implementation of the trap he was setting. She would do it because she didn't want to see the pain on another victims' face, the tears that drained every bit of hope from their lives. They had experienced enough. They didn't deserve another lesson in the fragility of morals of those they had fought for.

## 32

Whistle blowing wasn't acceptable in the NHS and Richard always felt there was a culture of bullying by higher management to those in lower positions. He had seen it before in his own profession and had hoped naively that the biggest employer in Britain may have bucked the trend but they had their own positive image to maintain and anyone who thought that the gradual crossover to privatisation would assist the antiquated system improve its self regularity was sorely disappointed.

Targets became tougher, the squeeze on staffing became tighter. The profession relied heavily on the input of labour from all parts of the globe and these who felt most vulnerable and easily replaceable in their jobs weren't going to the front of the queue when they saw and delivered some practices that they knew were shameful. They saw only one option; to toe the party line.

Richard never had and he had paid the penalty. His chances of promotion in the Met had been sealed over a decade and a half before. The man in the flat was black and he'd taken one hell of a beating. This wasn't unusual in itself. Drug wars on the street were commonplace and treading on another man's turf often bought ramifications but his injuries were off the scale. A fractured jaw, dislocated shoulder, two broken ribs and a body riddled with bruising. As the interview had progressed it wasn't another gang member but two of Richard's work colleagues who were implicated. He'd believed the helpless man; why would he make it up? From that moment onwards he had pursued his colleagues with a ferocity that remained unabated even though the internal investigation found nothing to answer for. His reputation was sullied, his colleagues' trust lost and any chance of promotion destroyed. He had quickly become disillusioned but loath to throw it all away had steadfastly remained in his role despite the barrage of attempts to remove him.    In Mia he saw a soul in the same mode; someone who had the gumption to stand against inequality in whatever form it took.

## 33

Mia sat at her desk oblivious to some of the pressing cases that lay in the tray on the right hand side. She had come to the inevitable conclusion that she couldn't actively involve any of the hospital patients or social services clients. She would need to try and take as much responsibility as she could herself. She spent the afternoon, identifying some patients who were likely to remain on the ward for the next few days. The task was made easier by her regular meeting on the Medical Assessment Ward (MAW), which was the first step for a patient after being admitted to the hospital, although for purely political and technical reasons they weren't being admitted, simply assessed. The MAW provided a larger and more investigative screening unit to predict how long a patient would need to stay. If it was less than forty eight to seventy two hours then they would remain on the ward without being transferred and not regarded as a full admission before returning to wherever they came from with a reinstatement of the same services. This made sure that any care packages provided privately or by social services would remain in place whilst 'the assessment' was ongoing. If there was a clear need for a longer term stay in hospital then there was the expectation that, beds allowing, they could transfer the patient onto a long stay ward and it was there that our thief was roaming. The longer term wards specialised in the care of the frail and elderly and included those that had mental health issues like dementia. It also harboured those with slips, trips, falls, surgical fractures and temporary states of confusion.

Mia made an effort to quickly pop her head in to see five clients that had been identified as requiring a longer stay and of the five patients two were lucid, one had a very large supportive network who were visiting daily, another had dementia but her husband, who was her carer, and entitled to some respite himself, instead, continued to visit every day, much to the relief of the ward staff. That left one and in an effort to get noticed she spotted Dr Batt outside the same bay.

There are many reasons to attend the A&E department and whilst almost every one of the eventual admissions are genuine, there are those young and old, who burdened by psychological trauma see hospital as a haven, a safety net from the endurance of day to day existence. From the 25 year old with Munchhausen syndrome who will weave a story of staggering complexity and undetectability to the ninety two year old admitted for a warm-up, feed-up and a bit of company to the 52 year old shaggy and haggard drug addict, detoxing for the umpteenth time to the 38 year road crash victim, whose life has unravelled before him in hospital leaving his partner dealing with a  tangled web of lies and deceit and the very notion of a return home to face his demons is avoided at all costs.

For each and every one of these 'patients' there will be a consultant tearing their hair out to effect discharge, to clear the bed for those who have needs that require immediate and prolonged care that will require careful management and a lexicon of knowledge beyond any general medicine education  They will need to nod to the new disciples in medical management, have an awareness of alternative and complimentary therapies, a tome of reflecting upon actual experiences, the successes, the failures, the warrants for new investigations, the sharing of information with colleagues, the desire to improve the system and the self sacrifices of time and cost to their own family.

And for every group of consultants there will be one devoid of compassion for his fellow kind, who will enforce their own will, own ideology, own philosophy, own desires. A practitioner who sees only a never ending queue of 'lab rats', never wrong, never to be questioned, and the drive and determination to see off any who would appear to disagree with their judgement. Dr Batt was that man and Mia had recognised in her short tenure that his word was the 'word of God incarnate' in the hospital trust.

"Good morning Dr Batt. What's the story with Mrs Kelly?"

Dr Batt looked up and down at Mia and made no effort to address her but went straight into the kind of diatribe that Mia had come to expect.

"Mrs Kelly is just another in a long line of preventable admissions. She fell out of bed in her nursing home, the same nursing home that is supposed to be protecting her. With a diagnosis of Alzheimer's and generalised frailty the home didn't think it would be in her best interest to have protective barriers around her, the consequence being that in a rare moment of lucidity she tried to walk to the bathroom herself and now has a broken hip.

"Perhaps it was the first occasion."

"I don't care if it was the first or the last she is now a drain on services when there are others with more pressing needs. Broken hip or not I would have sent her straight back to where she came from but some bright surgeon thinks he can operate. I personally give her a week."

"Are there any family?"

But Dr Batt had already started to walk off down the ward.

"It's not quite as black and white as that." said Michelle who appeared from behind a curtain in the next bay. "Unfortunately as she fell she put out her arm in front of her and fractured her right wrist as well. None of the staff at the home seem to know how long she had been on the floor but eventually she was found lying quietly where she had fell, accepting her fate, like many do, not a struggle, not a last defiant grip on life. Luckily there does not appear to be any head injury and even though she was on a trolley for three hours in a corridor, they managed to whip her to X-ray and the cast for the wrist has been dressed whilst she was on the holding bay. The hip's going to further assessed by an orthopaedic consultant in a couple of days and a decision about whether to operate or not will be calculated."

"Sorry, but what sort of calculation is that? When is it more advisable not to be able to walk free from pain, turn in bed without pain? What percentage of death from surgery would suffice, 5%, 10% 20% 50% 95%?"

"Who knows but she's going to need some tender loving care and our prayers for the time being."

"Ok. I'll keep an eye of her."

Michelle left Mia to see another patient and Mia started to think about possibilities.

*If the patient was being placed on an orthopaedic ward then she was in the domain for the thief and even if they didn't decide to operate they would at least monitor her for a few days before sending her back to her nursing home. The home would, of course, keep the bed open for her and may also need to come in and reassess her needs before any discharge could be confirmed. The chance of getting a reassessment of her needs before any discharge depreciated significantly the further you got into the working week and knowing the workings of most homes there'd be no chance of getting one out on a Friday for a weekend discharge.*

She was going through Pat Kelly's charts at the end of the bedside when a voice behind her said.

"You won't need to worry about this one. She's off to Hardy."

Mia was now able to hatch her plan. The broken wrist in this case was an added bonus. Now Mia had an excuse as to why the rings were off her hands. She waited in anticipation for the meeting with Richard later that afternoon.

## 34

*The Decision*

*He looked at the box of credit card slips abandoned in a cardboard box outside the back door alongside the remnants of an empty store; another victim of the boom and bust generation at the end of the 1980's. These were the days of a credit card imprinter that swiped the details of the card onto a triplicate form; one for the customer, one for the business and a last for the bank and piles of them lay tied with rubber bands a testament to the free spending days of the past decade. The discarded forms had the purchasers names and addresses; their credit card details and with little guesswork their bank, all the tools required to set up a fraudulent account elsewhere. The processes in his mind went into overdrive; neural networks firing off in every direction, premeditating every counter move against his devious plan.*

*He had moved on from his clerical work, via labourer, failed carpet fitter, milkman, barman, agency worker but the result remained the same. Money gambled as soon as it had arrived in his account, the odd win enough for a flurry down the shops but in general day after day of devastating losses so much so that he was in debt again, a debt this time he had no funds to repay. He'd used his parent's before and his lies about store card repayments, overspending on a holiday, and losing his wallet had been enough for them to part with her money, but he couldn't do the same again, not now that his father had died.*

*It was another crossroads. This time he could see the chasm below him. He knew where it would end but there was an almost insatiable appetite to get there. Yet in that hour a seed of goodness remained in him, a seed that could grow if only his mind could feed it but planted so deep that in the moments where decisions are made he could scarcely recognise it. Hesitation was his only ally and at that moment a set of footsteps approaching the alley removed him from his train of thoughts to oblivion.*

*That evening as he wrestled with the decision making process time became his healer. From the deepest well of his spirit, like the air that escapes from a fissure in the earth and rises in a pool, small bubbles of clarity began to form. By the morning he had decided to tell his mother and he needed to prove that he was serious; he knew she would be shocked. But first he had a call to make. Before the helpline was answered he had hung up. It was on his third attempt that he finally heard the answer to his call for help. "Hi this is John from Gamblers Anonymous."*

# PART TWO

## November 2012

### 35

"How the hell did this happen?" said Mia as she sat next to Jeff in his car flicking through the notes of a Senior Strategy Meeting.

"Unfortunately we're not entirely blameless on this one. We've been using The Orchard extensively as a hospital resource simply because they are one of the few homes that accept our rates, which you know as well as I are completely out of touch with the general cost of care. Therefore the home has to cut the costs somewhere and if I'm completely honest they never had the best reputation in the first place."

"So what do we do about it?"

"Well nutrition is the basis of any care regime."

"You are joking."

"I'm afraid I'm not."

"What....we've got to make sure they eat."

"Yep."

"No"...and she looked around her "but we've only got half a packet of stale ginger nuts and two Mars Bars."

"That will do."


When Jeff first received the news he sighed because he knew in some ways both he and social services were culpable. It was a call from the visiting nurse assessor who had first raised serious concerns about 'The Orchard' and triggered a safeguarding alert. A routine visit and review of several of their patients to consider whether they needed any nursing component was the brief. Instead the nurse had found that the majority of residents, placed in the main by social services, probably met the very highest level of care. That alone was unusual enough but the additional concern was the lack of staff on site, totally inadequate to the needs of the 48 frail residents, with a range of complex and intense care needs and as a consequence the home was failing even to meet their basic requirements.

Several frantic calls later and discussion amongst the highest representatives of safeguarding in both health and social care a swift action plan was brokered. Firstly, the management of the home would need to increase staffing levels immediately, which they reported they would endeavour to do by the end of day. Secondly, an entire review of every patient in the care home who hadn't received one in the last three months. This was to be a joint review by health and social care to look at the appropriate funding stream and their care needs. Thirdly, a senior strategy investigation of the home as a provider to ascertain whether it was capable of meeting those with the highest nursing needs, particularly in regards to their mental health. Lastly, social services staff to monitor every meal time over the first weekend when staffing was normally stretched.

It was this last action point that had affected Jeff, and the staff in his hospital. They would be providing two senior members of staff to focus on the delivery of meals, the cleanliness of the establishment and the general welfare of residents. Jeff and Mia took up the mantle as neither had anything seriously planned for the weekend, they both lived fairly local, they were both trained investigators and if anything was going to get worse then it was likely to be this weekend.

On entering the premises Jeff encouraged Mia to wander the rooms as she hadn't visited the home before whilst Jeff stayed on one side of the main lounge, which doubled as 'The Restaurant' for those who could get out of bed and had been provided the opportunity to do so.

As Mia started to climb the stairs and head down a narrow corridor the unmistakable stench of urine wafted in the air despite the home's best efforts to disguise with carpet detergent, air freshener, window cleaner or anything else they could spray in the air or on the floor to diminish the smell.  Many of the rooms were small and pokey and being an old Victorian building there were plenty of tight staircases and corridors, presumably where the staff of yesteryear used to scurry around in their roles of service.  It was easy to get lost and very easy to miss people out so she systematically listed the rooms as she passed them; she was determined to make a difference.

Mia was thorough in her time with the clients during the lunch period; typically the largest meal of the day. She used the opportunity to check through their belongings in rooms that suffered from the same odour as the corridor and explained the need for the windows to be open during the mild and windy autumnal morning, that blew the leaves like whirling dervishes in the courtyard below her.  When Mia picked through their wardrobes and drawers she couldn't help but think *Where do their lives go? Surely their life's worth had not been reduced to a few rags, already spoilt in size, colour and shape by the laundry team.*  There was the odd photo on a shelf but other knick-knacks were small in number and size and jewellery was nowhere to be seen; apparently locked up in the safe. As for the residents, as reliable witnesses to the general condition and care of the home, there were only a handful who were able to voice their opinion in any coherent manner.

There were other obvious shortcomings; dirty toilets, dirty bed-sheets, dust everywhere.  In fact, she even requested and took a Hoover to one room to make a statement.

"I want them all looking the same and I'll be back to check."

The food was barely palatable although she was reassured that at least, on this occasion, the food was being provided and eaten, delivered via a spoon to the mouth right in front of her eyes. She demanded a minimum of a litre of water in a jug and a full cup of water in every room, as well as a supply of straws. Although she wasn't medically trained the over prescription of drugs was another of her philosophical bug bears, particularly in a nursing environment, where she felt that unless there was a strong relative monitoring the situation the likelihood of abuse was high.

It was embarrassing watching people being fed so Jeff looked at other opportunities to bide his time whilst he was in the general vicinity. He looked at the resident checklists and recognised some of the names and the background to some cases. When clients moved straight from the hospital into residential and nursing care the funding could only be authorised initially by himself in the hospital, so many of his staff would be presenting the cases in front of him in an attempt to secure funding and both had pressures: the care manager from the hospital, to get the client out and Jeff from his line management who viewed placement, rightly, as a last resort and often had financial projections which severely limited the number of placements that could be made.

Jeff was fair and didn't use his position to deliberately halt the process, but those who were not thorough did inevitably have to go back to gather the correct information or follow the correct procedures to make the case. Jeff understood that those who ended up in nursing care, for the short-term or for respite or rehabilitation, rarely came out. Care was a business after all and there was an enormous number of fail-safes and support required for real rehabilitation to prosper and act as a revolving door by getting older people back to their own homes, where most were comfortable. Quite simply there wasn't the resources.

For families, sometimes the merest fall or unexpected admission immediately raised alarm bells and their focus shifted to getting their relatives into care. But more than a few had soon realised that if they wanted any type of residential setting that all  avenues would have to be exhausted before this was even a consideration. When families heard "Yes, your loved one can go into care if you want them to but they don't meet our criteria so you'll going to have to pay eight hundred pounds a week yourself." then most would withdraw their earnest gaze and try to work with social services to create a package of care at home.

But strip away the professional guise and you wouldn't always find in Jeff a man of principals. He was easily swayed by the prevailing argument of the hour. He could identify with both protagonists in any argument but rarely took sides instead justified his life by the most recent decision he had made not by any incisive consideration of any argument or way of being.  He had in essence become driftwood floating atop the prevailing current, prone to the swells and obstacles around him. Only Mia's re-emergence had reignited the embers of passion for his work and his heart.

## 36

On Sunday Mia and Jeff swapped roles. Jeff took the upstairs and back rooms whilst Mia went on the hunt for poor practice in the dining room. Jeff's first stop was Mr Harper, who, as he entered the room was just returning in a crotchety fashion from the toilet. He looked young for a resident with a full head of dark grey hair combed back over his ears past his neckline and a boyish face not weathered by outside work yet below the neck he was disordered. His pyjamas were round his ankles and his netting for holding up his incontinence pad was hanging from his left hip, clinging onto him with the barest of tape. His crimson slippers were on the wrong feet and his pyjama top was held open by one button that wasn't linked to the corresponding eye and therefore hung at an awkward angle. Around the room his duvet was flung open and there was a wet patch on his bed sheet. If he was to surmise the situation Jeff would have said that the incontinence pad had come lose sometime earlier and after urinating in his own bed the client had then been prompted by his own brain to go to the toilet and was returning to bed and the patch that was soon to welcome him. This was the perfect breeding ground for a bed sore, because if he had succeeded back to bed seconds earlier, then it was unlikely that anyone would have noticed the trail of humiliation and desecration of the human body and spirit.

Mr Harper didn't even seem startled by Jeff's appearance but stood patiently in the centre of the room looking downwards possibly expecting some kind of intervention. Jeff scanned the room and found what he was looking for on a bookshelf now doubling as an incontinence store. He pulled on a set of rubber gloves guided the man to sit on the edge of the bed, laying a towel on the side. He firstly removed the man's slippers, which were also sopping wet. He started to remove the man's pyjamas and netting before collecting a bone dry flannel from the basin in the toilet, soaking it in warm water, and gave the man a wipe down all over his lower body. In reality there was no need for Jeff to complete such a task, he could have gone back to reception and asked for a member of staff. As repugnant as this task might seem to others, Jeff missed being in the field, and even in this humble role he felt he was giving something back to society.

After drying him and finding him another set of pyjamas he removed the gentleman's top. For the first time he noticed a very small bruise above Mr Harper's waist on the right hand side, more like a bump and thought there must be a story to come with that one, but Mr Harper wasn't responding to any of Jeff's questions.

The gentleman hadn't shaved for several weeks, or to be more precise, hadn't been assisted to, and his hairs protruded from his nose and ears like lightning bolts. He had no teeth but there were two blue beakers on top of the wardrobe and Jeff guessed that one would contain his dentures. Just as he was doing up the buttons on his shirt, a thirty something Asian woman, without knocking, entered the room. She was dark skinned and Jeff believed probably from the Indian subcontinent and as she approached he was able to read her surname, Sue Thilakarathne, that he correctly assumed was Sri-Lankan.
"I'm afraid we've had an accident here."
"I'm so sorry." With that she was gone, out of the door hollering in a language he didn't understand. Within just a few seconds two older ladies in purple carer uniforms bustled in and, after making sure Mr Harper was comfortable, mopped the bathroom floor, changed the bedding and started to serve Mr Harper his lunch.

Before Sue left and no doubt rushed around every other room, it was with excitement that Jeff found out her birthplace was Kandy because he too had visited the beautiful plateau, walked among the tea plantations that covered the hillside around the city and roamed the botanical gardens with its enhanced collection of orchids. He was also mindful that she was born on another continent and now served those children of ancestors that ruled her families ancestors with an iron rod, bullets and a claw to grab everything it could out of the beautiful country.

Jeff accepted the ubiquitous weak and milky cup of tea and felt he had an ally in Sue.

"What caused the bruise?"

"Oh it's just a graze he picked up at the day centre. He's a private client of Dr Patel's. We're doing the utmost to make sure that Mr Harper's stay with us is a comfortable one."

"What's his diagnosis?" he whispered as they moved to the far end of the room so that Mr Harper couldn't hear.

"He's got multi-infarct dementia, following a stroke. After a brief spell on the specialist ward at the hospital he returned home with a package of care. Unfortunately the package of care broke down and he came to us to meet his 24 hour care needs."

"He doesn't seem to have much – what about his family?"

"I'm afraid Mr Harper doesn't have any surviving family members. His wife died two years ago and they had no children. He was a bit of a recluse even before his death. The neighbours reported knowing her but not really him."

*His reclusiveness was probably been because of his dementia,* Jeff thought. *So many couples hide their partners deteriorating mental health until the last resort, or, in this case, until the partner dies.*

He continued through another six bedrooms, popping his head in, hoping to get a better general feel for the service the clients were receiving. Three of them had eaten, two of them were being encouraged to do so. Sue had made sure she was in the vicinity but Jeff had asked her to leave on a couple of occasions so that he could talk privately when he thought he had a chance of a response.

When he came to the last random room he slipped in quietly, after knocking gently, without Sue on his tail. Many older people enjoyed a siesta after lunch and as he entered he immediately recognised the lady sat upright but dozing before him with her head turned to one side. Miss Powell was her name and Miss P was her pet name, coincidentally the name of his physics tutor at comprehensive school, which was far and away Jeff's worse subject, but he never forgot the teachers bowed legs and shrieking voice. Miss Powell was altogether different. She looked like a throwback to the 60's. Mousey grey-brown hair tied in a bun, with reading glasses attached to a gold necklace, above a silk chemise, with a patterned cardigan that had dulled through washing. Her skirt was tartan and fell to her ankles and her black stockings were barely visible above a set of 'proper black shoes'. A retired schoolmistress would suit and he was surprised that she presented as well today as when he had first met her some four years earlier, as a Senior Care Manager in the community.

Then it was her co-habitee, a woman who was about ten years older who was struggling with her mental health and came with a diagnosis of first Parkinson's and eventually dementia. Throughout the assessment process Jeff had thought highly of Miss Powell's determination to support her friend. He was witness to her tears and her stories. For many carers this would be the first opportunity to discuss openly with someone the relentless examination of their own personal strength as friends and loved ones tested their patience and stamina to the limit, often leaving them exasperated, and sometimes even denied, before finally having the trauma of losing them physically after the mental loss was at its widest aperture.

He had discussed all these trials and tribulations and then had to leave the client with a set of finance forms to fill out on her friend's behalf; *how galling this must appear*. Whilst he was writing up his assessment back in the community his mind passed over the rooms he had been shown round and he suddenly started to understand the relationship that Miss Powell had been desperate to impart but her fifty years of secrecy had dared not reveal. The two elderly spinsters, as neighbours knew them, in Miss Powell's words, had met each other shortly after the Second World War, working in the town's library. Miss Powell reported that her skill set was mainly in her art but she had taken up a part-time role, as the friendship had flourished. They had moved several times but always together and their individual family ties had gradually collapsed though their faith in each other had never wavered. He checked notes and realised that the words that Miss Powell was using was not that of a friend but of a lover and that is why she had gone to extraordinary lengths to help her to remain at home for so long. Her lover was dying before her very eyes and she still couldn't even tell the social worker that her whole life was being ripped apart by the deterioration in the woman who had shared everything with her.

Jeff then thought of all 'the spinsters' that lived with other companions and concluded that, like out of marriage pregnancy, a woman loving another woman was just something that wasn't talked about. He'd rarely ever discussed sexuality in old age with his clients despite its presence in the assessment pro-forma. Then he felt appalled and ashamed and he spent an inordinate amount of time considering and expressing in his assessment the depth of support that Miss

Powell had provided whilst still retaining her right to privacy regarding her sexuality and the gaping hole that she was now facing in her life.

So as he walked over to her now and pulled up a spare chair beside her, lightly squeezing her hand and gently speaking her name he felt an enormous sense of duty to support her as his mind had been changed forever by the dutiful lady in front of him. She woke slowly and he wondered whether her memory was as good as his. Initially he thought so because she expressed delight with first her eyes and then her voice that she was pleased to see him. In an accent that flowed like a calm brook over polished pebbles she asked him

"Have I taken my medication dear? "

"I think you have but I'll check in a minute."

"Is my kitty around?"

"I haven't seen a cat since I arrived."

"Not a cat dear – my kitty – Kate."

It was then he felt a fool as it dawned on him that she was remembering her partner, now deceased, and still in her mind keeping an eye on her as she had done all her life.

Jeff talked to her for a few minutes but the responses he was getting were only consistent with her confusion. He wondered if there was a friend or neighbour. He doubted the home, on his investigation thus far, had the acumen or the endeavour to support Miss Powell as she wanted to be seen.

As he made his way to say goodbye her cardigan lifted and fell away as she tried to rise from her chair and Jeff caught a glimpse of crimson for the second time in the day, this time the blood on her chemise. He returned to her and asked if he could have a look at her side.

"Oh, it's nothing dear."

He was persistent and she agreed to him looking as she turned slightly to the left. Lifting her chemise he saw a bandage with a small trickle of blood leaking onto her side in the same place he had noticed Mr Harper's. As if guilty of a crime himself he covered the evidence quickly, told Miss Powell to relax, placed some water beside her and told her he would send one of the nurses in as soon as he had located one.

Jeff's curiosity was aroused. He headed back down to the main lounge where the nurses' station was situated. There he requested the file for both Mr Harper and Miss Powell and asked for someone to attend to her bandage. He waved to Mia as she moved past him quickly followed by a member of the staff. Sitting in an easy armchair in the corner of the lounge, away from residents and members of staff, he opened the files.

Jeff wasn't really sure what he was looking for but his instincts told him that something was definitely wrong. The daily diary notes were his starting point. Jeff hadn't questioned the day centre visit it at the time but attendances at such a resource were unusual when a client was in residential or nursing care as the home has a duty to provide stimulation and activities as part of its remit. Unfortunately for the most part an activities co-ordinator was normally a part-time role and for some reason throwing a red ball around the room as clients sat in a horseshoe seemed to provide as much jocularity for staff members, but not as much for the residents who if they weren't humiliated or disinterested would occasionally spark into life and hurl the foam ball as far as they could. He had seen some areas of really good practice: support with painting, both indoors and outdoors in the summer, walks outside in the grounds for those who were fit enough, and even opportunities to assist in the kitchen to take away the tedium and boredom of the very long days, but for the most part it was television, simple puzzles that remained incomplete and background radio. Occasionally outside entertainment was ordered in. There could be Carol singing at Xmas from local schools, a troubadour who was happy to reel out the tunes of the 40's, 50's and 60's. He imagined for a second what it would be like by the time he needed care and whether the punk era at the end of the 70's or the New Romantic movement of the 80's would get the same treatment.

There was just a short entry about Mr Harper's return from the centre; nothing to report that he had an accident and nothing at all in the activities section or health plan. He decided to cross check with Miss Powell. She too had a diary entry for the day centre that day. But once again aside from a remark noting that she hadn't eaten much supper that evening but returned to bed early there was nothing out of the ordinary so they had both gone to the day centre and returned with minor injuries to their right side. But there was not a jot on any of their records.

"Do you have a list of clients that attend the day centre please?" asked Jeff to the nurse on reception but before she had a chance of responding Sue, as if by magic, appeared from the office directly behind the station.

"We don't Jeff. There is no definitive day for clients to attend but we do write it in their diary and it will be in the care plan under the activities section."

"So how many residents go to the day centre?"

"Oh, not that many really – we try to book a few people at a time but we try to give them as much support in the home here as we can."

"And what do they do at the day centre?"

"I think it's more one to one therapy really. At the centre they have more staff and can engage the client and assess more of their interests. We then add it to the care plan and try to meet those needs in the home."

"Thanks."

Jeff immediately returned to his chair and scrupulously scoured the care plan for Mr Harper and Miss Powell. His memory of the latter expected a report about her skills as an artist and a keen knitter, he remembered the copious balls of wool dotted all over the lounge when he struggled to find a seat. He was particularly taken by a picture of Arundel Cathedral, which he had served in as an altar boy, holding the Roman Catholic Bishop's 'Mitre'. He wondered about the impact of their religion on their relationship and what decisions they had to make to accommodate both.

Yet there was nothing, only a small note that puzzles – aged 10-14 – might be to her advantage. As for Mr Harper, reminiscing using photos was the only entry, although unsurprisingly he had deteriorated in recent days as he flicked through the notes.

"Well. That's about it for this session. Fancy a late lunch and we can update each other?"
"Not for me, I'm checking on Oreo." replied Mia to Jeff's invitation, a refusal which disappointed him. He decided to skip lunch and concentrate on the home instead.

Sue was now on reception and he requested the opportunity to look through all the residents' files.
"Any particular reason? Perhaps I can make your task easier - anything we can do to improve our client's records we'll gladly take on board?"
"Not really – I'm just trying to get a feel for the clients here. I'll make a few notes if you don't mind."

"No sure – please go ahead.  Who would you like to start with first?"

"It doesn't matter I'll take them as you file them."

"Well we try to keep them filed in wing and floor order.  Let's say we start downstairs."

"Have you got a private space I can use?"

"Yes there's an empty room just at the end of the corridor – with a table.  Sit yourself in there and I'll get someone to bring them in for you."

He had required the space to keep away from the gaze of prying eyes and surreptitiously make recordings.  No-one knew of his library of private recordings at home.  He had bought the pen several years earlier and then, unbeknown to his staff, he would use the device for supervisory meetings as well as for important meetings with families of individual clients, particularly when he knew he was going to be in for a rough ride.  The recorder was voice activated and the recording easily transferable to his computer at home.

When Mia arrived an hour later he had already been through the ground floor and was working his way through the upper floor.  There were four entries that included trips to the day centre but the records only went back to the beginning of the year.

"The rest are filed away according to data protection standards." said Sue.  "We're hoping to bring in a complete electronic system before the end of the year but the transfer of information will require a lot of work and time."

Of the three clients he found only one, Miss Powell was known to social services.  The other clients Mr Reece and Mr Sharma, like Miss Powell and Mr Harper were private funders. There was once again nothing in the general activity plan.  He checked with daily notes and Mr Reece had been prone to falls for the last few days. None of them had required hospital admission. He went back to Sue for more answers.

"What happened to Mr Reece after his day centre visit?"

"We're not sure if he over exerted himself whilst out, but we've found him on the floor a couple of times. He's better now, and when he's out of his room we always keep an eye on him."

"I'd like to see him."

"Room 22, 1st Floor."

"Thanks" although he'd already noted it on the front of the resident file.

Mr Reece was sitting in a large blue comfy chair. The room smelt more neutral than many of the others and the window was open letting in a light breeze. Based towards the front of the building the traffic hummed in the background and even small children could be heard from a nearby neighbour's garden.

Mr Reece sat with his hand on the adjustable over-bed table and was facing Jeff as he entered but didn't say anything. Jeff was drawn immediately to the large white bandage covering his left eye with small strips of tape holding it onto his cheek. Mr Reece gingerly moved his hand found towards the plastic cup in front of him and eventually located it and placed it to his lips. He choked a little as he did so and very carefully returned the cup to its position.

When Jeff spoke Mr Reece glanced up but didn't say anything. Jeff knew that his mental health issues could have acted upon him in a myriad of ways upon his general health and he was never quite sure of what type of conversation he was about to enter into.

"How are you Mr Reece?"

Mr Reece stood up quickly but his calf muscles remained tight against his seat. "It's a lovely day today. Please don't get up I like just a little word. I'm just going to take a seat next to you if I may?"

Jeff moved to his bedside and as he placed himself on the bed Mr Reece just stood there and looked straight ahead until Jeff gently squeezed his hand at which point Mr Reece turned his head sharply, without moving his torso.  Jeff asked him straight away. "Do you mind if I take a look a look at your hip this morning?"

Mr Reece didn't move so Jeff decided to be more proactive.

"Can I adjust your shirt as you seem to have it in a little mess?"

The left side of the blue cotton shirt hang outside his trousers, which had slipped down a few inches as he stood.  He wasn't wearing a belt and weight loss was one of the standard features of dementia.  The mental triggers for eating and drinking were simply forgotten and unless a very careful dietary regime was imposed the likelihood was that a person on their own would simply starve themselves to death.

Jeff started pulling the rest of Mr Reece's shirt out of his trousers when with considerable force Mr Reece's right arm swung across Jeff, striking him in the chest before latching onto his wrist and squeezing tightly.  As he did so his long nails scraped across the top of Jeff's hand digging into the skin and caused it to bleed.

"Ah…shit!"as Jeff's hand, in turn, gripped Mr Reece's.  "It's O.K. I'm not going to hurt you."

He held it for 5-10 seconds before slowly starting to return it to the side of Mr Reece and wiped his own hand with some nearby toilet roll.  Jeff gently resumed pulling open his shirt and then hurriedly looked about Mr Reece for possible bruises or injuries that he may have obtained whilst at the day centre. He was sure there would be some mark or disfigurement that tallied with other residents but there was nothing other than a few moles, some with long single hairs hanging from them.

Mr Reece didn't raise his arms when asked so Jeff guided him to do so but didn't go any further as the ridiculousness of the situation he was constructing became apparent; if anyone was to enter right now it could easily be misinterpreted. Disappointed he assisted Mr Reece to return to his chair and left just as a nurse flew round the corner and acknowledged him as he headed towards the stairs.

Jeff returned to the nurse's station and started to question himself again, maybe he had been a little hasty and paranoid in condemning the place. There was certainly no smoke without fire but it was easy to define a home on the basis of an investigation, as strong as it was. He knew that there were other forces at work, outside of their control and he almost smiled to himself to think that there was any other great conspiracy. He picked up the folder of Mr Sharma, Room 4, which was on the ground floor, a short distance from the main entrance and as he passed reception he noticed a blue light shining outside. He walked round the corner and saw the doorway he was looking for on the right hand side next to the kitchen.

The door to Room 4 was a remnant of the original part of the building. Large oak panelling with a brass knob and lead inlays. He tapped lightly on the door, no answer, so he tweaked the handle purposefully only there was no movement. He turned the opposite direction and pulled then pushed becoming more energetic. He even leant his weight against the door but not a budge. He knocked louder but still no response.

"I'm afraid you've just missed him." said Sue

It was a remark that was said so nonchalantly that to Jeff it sounded like an appointment missed with a busier line manager but this was the highest need nursing home – you don't just miss somebody.

"What do you mean I've just missed him?"

"He's just been admitted to hospital."

"Why?"

"His markers were very low this morning and the consultant has asked him to come in."

"On a Sunday?"

"Health waits for no-one."

"Was that him outside?"

"Yes."

"Well can I look in the room anyway?"

"If you insist."

"Just a quick look if you don't mind…. And have you got his medical notes?"

"I'm afraid that they went with him."

"Did they!....Is that normal?"

"Well it gives the best information to the hospital. They'll have a record of his vitals and his behaviour. We can request them back if you need them…. Let me just get the key for you."

Whatever credence Jeff had given the home had just dissipated.


Sue returned with the key, but there was nothing in the room, no pictures or memorabilia. Clothes were piled neatly away in draws, the bed was made, the windows were shut, the curtains were drawn, the table was clear, the carpet was clean. The room was sterile as though Mr Sharma had been wiped clean from it.

"Which hospital is he being taken to Sue?"

"I'm not sure" said Sue

"Didn't the paramedics say?"

"No they were waiting for confirmation before they left?"

Jeff couldn't argue. It wasn't unusual for ambulances to be redirected even whilst on route, such was the shifting sands of A&E admissions. Dunes could be built in just a couple of hours; a glut of admissions and the whole process could be blown off course. A Sunday was always a testing examination, families seeing older relatives, a reduction in the support network for older people, the reduction in staff at hospital and almost a complete lack of movement from Thursday night to Monday morning for people who needed packages of care.

"Has he got any family members that need updating?"

"Not this gentleman I'm afraid. He has no-one."

"Do you only accept waifs and strays?" Jeff regretted it as soon as he had asked.

"As you know Jeff we don't discriminate against anyone here in terms of admission and many a time we have had to bail out social services from the little hole they have dug themselves."

"I'm sorry Sue. It must be the weekend working – it's getting to me. Thanks for your help. I've got a few more files to look over and then Mia and I will be off. There don't appear to be any major issues this weekend." And as he said it he knew he was lying.

## 37

*The Room*

"*My name's Mike and I'm a compulsive gambler. It was Peter Bromley's commentary for me. 'There's only one horse in it. You need a telescope to see the rest!!' I had Shergar at evens in the 81 Derby and from that moment I was programmed to destroy everything I had ever loved. I lost my wife, my children, my house, my self-respect. There was literally nothing left until these guys saved me. They're right when they tell you that you'll end up in one of three places; it's prison, the gutter or the grave. Well I was well on my way to being six foot under. I'd left the suicide note and I was standing on the fifth floor balcony and I got a call you know from one of these guys. I wouldn't be here if I hadn't. There must an angel looking out for me. I'm grateful for the small things now, smelling the flowers, seeing my grandkids growing up. How selfish I was. I used to get up at 4.30 in the morning to go to the newsagent so I could bag a copy of the Sporting Life so I could study the form before wasting all my money. There is nothing I wouldn't do to get money for a bet and I mean nothing. You learn to take the small steps here to get back on track. So if you're serious about getting better then keep coming back here and stay with the programme. I'm not alone these guys will tell you the same thing. The best of luck to you.*"

*He had listened attentively. It hadn't been easy climbing the steps to his first Gamblers Anonymous meeting. There were six of them and each one exaggerated the drudgery of his life thus far so that by the time he reached the door he barely had the strength to push it open.*

*He'd received some relief from his mother the week before. She took his honesty and baggage, as much as he had allowed her to know, and carried it on her own shoulders, as though she had been waiting at the side of the railway carriage ready for him to disembark and offload.   Perhaps she had seen it coming but hadn't told him.   It was a given, she would pay the debt and support him in his recovery. This act raised him from the ground and gave him what he craved - hope.*

*But hope is a doubled edged sword for a gambler.   It is hope that drives a delusional gambler forward on the pretext that they can find a way to beat the system, that each new dawn is the start of a change in their fortune.  It is hope that enables the gambler to make the small adjustments on a daily basis that he believes, wrongly, will define his superiority against the odds.   It is hope that obscures that the act of gambling is just part of the problem.   And if this wasn't enough even when hope is realised for what it really is; a freedom to start to make the right choices in life, a freedom from the warped mind that would rather be in a bookmakers than by the side of a sick child, then hope, without solid foundation, provides the fastest road to complacency and a subsequent return to gambling in any form.*

*He looked round the room, a little in awe, a little in fear.   The stories were the same.  Tales of misery, tales of deceit, tales of horror, tales of regret and, for those that kept to the narrow path, tales of the wisdom of the room.  Whoever he heard, there was a key word, 'Yet'.  He may have been a small time gambler and he may have only rippled the surface as he dropped into the ocean of addiction but there were depths to this ocean that no-one else would wish him to discover where the light fades and murkiness reigns, where if you continue to fall you become so deeply embedded within the silt that there is no light, no hope, no means of escape. It wasn't a matter of 'if,' it was a matter of 'when.' Compulsion is a vice that moves only clockwise, tightening its grip on its prey until it has squeezed every bit of life out of them.*

*The sons and daughters of God in the room may have spoken but there was no disciple in him. It took only two meetings before he thought that he had heard enough; that despite the evidence and the testimony articulated before him that his plight was not the same as theirs. He rejected religion, rejected God, and rejected the spiritual programme. He was young enough at twenty one to overcome these obstacles with his own mind, his own strength. He had heard where it could take you and he sure wasn't going to go to those places.*

*He left with a skip in his stride and a beat in his heart. He felt like his hero, the champ, 'Scurlogue Champ' a greyhound like no other. The beast was left forlorn and labouring at the start of any long distance race before his size and stamina came to the fore. As his heart rate steadily grew so did the hearts of the spectators who adored him and put their livelihoods on him. The whispering of encouragement in the packed stands would crescendo as he started to reel in the competitors before erupting when, in an astonishing turn of pace, he destroyed all those before him before stretching away.*

*He, like the champ, may have been at the back of the pack, he may have been lost, but to find a way to succeed was his goal and when he had accomplished it the world would love him for it.*

## 38

For a change Jeff was early. His sleep was interrupted, racing with concerns about the mysterious day centre. It took only one member of staff, one hand, one pinch, one punch. He tried to picture the attacker and amused himself with his ridiculous caricatures; male; female, bald head, overweight, scruffy, highlights, lowlights, straight, gay, tall, short. The memories flooded in from bullies at school. He wondered whether he would recognise them anymore. He wasn't directly affected very often but he understood the victims' fear and he was on the outside looking in, witness to the damage they received.

The terrifying look on the faces of the bullied, their hunched shoulders, head to the tarmac, reconnaissance glances, dread in their eyes, awaiting the inevitable: name calling, shoving, pushing, human pin-ball against the machine. Never entering a toilet during break-time, nor a classroom alone, finding any group to shield him from the assailants. Eating alone, studying afar, last into class, first off the bus, impressions to last a lifetime. And all the time he stood and did nothing. He might laugh. He might sympathise. He might pity, but he always denied them. It was this reminder of his cowardice that drove him forward now.

He rang reception at the hospital who passed him onto admissions at 8.05 am.
"I'm trying to check whether Mr Deepak Sharma was admitted last evening." He had made several calls like this in the past from the duty desk in the community team where he traced those who had simply disappeared overnight from their homes and the care assistants finding no-one had moved onto the next client. Ordinarily no information was ever provided to 'an outsider' under the data protection act, yet his name and position and the patients name and date of birth was enough to secure the information.

"Just one minute please." – the tired voice replied as he heard the keys tapping away. "Hello…Can I ask what it is in connection with?"

"He's a client of social services." He lied

"Well Mr Sharma was admitted last night directly to the private hospital but I'm afraid he passed away that same evening."

Jeff paused, bewildered.

"Can you tell me what he died of?"

"I'm afraid that's not recorded here. If you need any further information you'll need to go through the private hospital or medical records but there will probably be a delay because of certification."

"Can you tell me the consultant?"

"Yes.....he's under the care of Dr Patel."

"Thank you."


He had no affinity with the client, no knowledge of who he was apart from the grainy picture on file at the home. He had no family and for all intents and purposes was just one more statistic but Jeff now felt responsible for him. Jeff slammed his fist on the desk and his metallic red coffee canister toppled off the back of the desk and spilled it's contents onto the flooring denting it's base as it did so.

"Fuck!" and the fist went down again.

He wasn't upset about the spillage nor specifically that the resident had died. But within himself he started to feel ineffectual, unable to counter anything that may have caused this event. He resolved the day centre would be next.

## 39

Mr Sharma's funeral took place within two days, as was common practice for Hindu cremations, and it was fortunate that the town's cemetery had a spot available at such short notice. There had been no need for an autopsy. Mr Sharma had been on a well documented downward trend in recent months, and this wasn't his only hospital admission, although on this occasion the private hospital had accepted him directly from the home.

If you didn't know the crematorium it would have been easy to pass it by. Set opposite a school it sat just outside one of the many villages that gave character to the mundane larger town nearby. Each village had its own identity and this one was very small, with a dainty high street, a canal crossing and a sense of community. This didn't allow it to remain free from the expansion that was in the name of progress, pushing the property prices in the ever populous suburban high rise town, but driving through the village now its history became increasingly invisible.

Jeff had attended several funerals in the community. It was always pitiful that a chapel should be so empty, but this service, like many others, was on a tight schedule. Revealing very little Jeff had invited Mia along to keep an eye on those who attended the service on the basis that there may be some information he could gather about the nursing home and there was likely to be more honesty at a funeral than at any other time; there was no more neutral ground than a crematorium chapel. Even without a visit in the last couple of months of the man's life Jeff believed in the mysterious vine of communication when it came to the death of a person. The residents of the home were still a generation away from using and understanding social media so Jeff was relying on telephone and the word of mouth and hoped to see some faces. The crematorium chapel acted for all faiths and a representative of the Hindu faith had been summoned accordingly; a small, bearded man with several layers poking their collars above his vestments.

The morning was bitterly cold and the chapel had barely risen above freezing. It was the first service of the day and no-one was about to remove their jackets or coats. Other than the priest, Mia and Jeff there were only four others. Sue and another member of staff from 'The Orchard' Jeff recognised and acknowledged as he walked into the chapel. Of the two others, one was a petite older woman and the other a younger woman, too young to be her daughter but possibly her carer Jeff decided. They were both of Indian origin, and Jeff was immediately drawn to the younger, who was much taller than her companion. Mia didn't miss it either. She knew Jeff had a wandering eye and whilst, as far as she knew, he hadn't been unfaithful during their time together that hadn't stopped him flirting with those he met both professionally and socially.

It was natural enough at the end of the service that all who attended should meet up. Jeff made sure that Mia and he were out first and whilst Mia, under instruction, went straight to her car Jeff waited in the archway that offered some protection from the icy breeze. Sue and the other staff member quickly followed.
"It's not often that you get a member of social services, let alone two at the funeral of any of our residents. What's so important about Mr Sharma?" said Sue.
"I felt we ought to bolster the numbers, particularly as he was on our watch." said Jeff. "It's such a shame there weren't more here to celebrate his life. Do you know the others?"
"I can't say I recognise them."
"Do you know why he died?" Asked Jeff, eager to squeeze out the last bit of information.

"I think it was pneumonia in the end. He kept getting infection after infection. We tried to keep him comfortable."

Jeff had heard that line before and was starting to get irritated.

"How's the home holding up. Still busy?"

But as he talked a silver Mercedes, which could have passed as a funeral family vehicle, pulled up not 10 ft away and Sue and her colleague quickly turned and then turned again to wave their goodbyes as they popped into the back seat, with tinted glass hiding all the passengers and driver, glass that Jeff was convinced was way above the legal limits.

The Hindu priest stayed inside readily prepping himself for the next service and one or two had already begun to arrive in their cars as the last two churchgoers, gripping each other's arms, took precautionary steps as they exited through the arch with the smaller lady leaning on her taller younger compatriot.

"Hi I'm Jeff from Social Services. Are you a member of the family?"

"Oh.....no. We used to work together. I'm Mrs Latif and this is my granddaughter Sajani."

Jeff didn't shove out a hand as he usually did, instead he just raised his right hand in acknowledgement and was happy to receive the same as a return. Now much closer he could see how attractive she was.

"I think the best way to describe it is that I was his shop assistant. He had a store in Walton Road before they decided they needed ten take-aways in the same street. Sajani's studying at university – you've just finished your second year exams haven't you? She's just finished for Xmas and if I hadn't seen her yesterday I would never have known."

Sajani was deeply embarrassed and chose not to answer.

"I know it's a bit late in the day but could I ask a few questions about Mr Sharma?"

"Yes but this isn't the place to talk, please come back to my flat. I don't live far."

The flat was on the ground floor "But only after a fight with the council." she acknowledged. The smell was of sandalwood and he could see the incense burners in each room as she lit one in the front lounge.

"There's a terrible smell of damp in these flats. Would you mind making chai Sajani whilst I talk to the gentleman?"

Jeff's ear pricked up at the sound of chai. He'd got used to it during his phase buying authentic Indian food from a supermarket not far from where the linen and clothing store used to be and just a little further down the road he'd enjoyed ciabatta, tallegio, parma and san daniele from the Italian deli.

"Now let me see I have a couple of articles here."

She dug out a folder from an ottoman next to her own comfy chair, whilst Jeff sat on extra large dark leather sofa.

"Here we are." and she showed him several old newspaper cuttings with five or six Indian's, in their best jackets and dhoti's standing outside 'Sharma's Couture.'

"We were very proud, and very busy I might add. People came as far away as North London to visit the store. I worked with him for 24 years and we were just starting to consider the celebrations for the 25th anniversary when he had his stroke. He was just so young; sixty four and everything he had worked for gone in a flash." as she moved her arms together and then out as if stretching like a flowering bud in super fast motion.

"It wasn't the same after he left. A couple of local businessmen said they would provide a 'fair price,' but I knew the store wouldn't remain the same and instead the shop closed and a chicken takeaway was up and running before the year was out."

"What a shame."

"Nonetheless he was a prudent man and had been wise to provide for his future. He had a good insurance package that made his move to nursing care smooth, with one of the largest rooms on the ground floor as well. I was a regular visitor, the only one in the end. Physically he rehabilitated well but his mind, well it went quickly the other way. I was the next one to end up in hospital with a tumour scare that knocked the stuffing out of me. I used to go on the bus and walk and then it was community transport, but now I have to pay for a taxi or get the occasional lift from my family, but they all live so far away. In the end he didn't recognise me and it was very tough. The last time I went was a month or two ago."

"Did he ever attend a day centre?"

"Oh no – he wouldn't be one to sit in a group. When his shop was closed for the night he was a very private man. He worked in the evening with his accounts. In the home he stayed in his room. He was scrupulous with money. I guess it's all gone to the birds now."

"I don't understand."

"He had one passion outside his work in the shop - birds. He used to spend his Sunday's travelling to all parts of the country with his binoculars. I prefer people myself. Well he used to joke and tell me that if he ever went first he'd leave me something.... 'a little bird seed' he called it. The rest would go to the Royal Society."

"For the protection of birds?"

"Yes that's right."

"Did he live above the shop?"

"Yes it was very small and cramped. All his stock was up there."

"Is that why he chose the home – I guess it's pretty local?"

"No it was that nice consultant who helped. Said he knew one in the local area that would cater for his needs both culturally and spiritually. Some of the staff speak Hindi, which helps......but not always. They asked him what he wanted to eat in the early days and when I came in one lunchtime he was being fed roast chicken and peas."

"Sounds lovely."

"I guess it does but not to a vegetarian. He had asked for chickpeas."

Jeff laughed. He had come across the occasional residential establishment that leant heavily towards the cultural needs of Hindi's but they were few and far between and based nearer London.

"Did he have any problems during his stay?"

"He did become very yellow, jaundice once. I was worried he would need some kind of transplant. He became more and more confused. The last time I was there he'd had several falls I remember. They had to move all the furniture for him."

"Ah. Here we are. Thank you Sajani."

Jeff just started to enjoy the sweet taste of Chai when his phone rang. Within one minute he had made his excuses, promised to be in touch and hurriedly tapped away at his phone trying to get back in touch with Mia.

## 40

*The Trigger to Hell*

*His only remaining parent, his mother, died when he was thirty, a pulmonary embolism that took her life away in an instant. It would easy to attribute that event to be the trigger of his woes but that would be an injustice as undeniably his life was already a shambles. He continued to work furiously to pay the bills and transferred from one agency to another in an effort to maximise his income. He worked as hard as anyone else, but he had to, it was the only way to fuel the fire; you cannot gamble with nothing.*

*At her funeral he was already bereft of emotion. Each passing year had seen a gradual decline in his ability to connect with anyone. He withdrew from the concerns of the heart finding neither joy, sadness, laughter or tears in daily life. Growth and maturity was no longer an achievable aim. He lived, instead, in a perpetual world of nothingness and naturally bereft of the natural beats of life that fed his soul he had begun to withdraw, wither and die. Not that anyone who had met him would attest to this disintegration. His relationship with others was based routinely on spouting what they wished to hear. His life was wholly concerned with his next bet and the moment he'd identified his mother's body at the mortuary he was already devising a plan to use his inheritance, a two bedded detached cottage, to his own ends. This was the break he needed. This was the opportunity to ply his trade with the big boys. He had already spent all his income and racked up several credit cards and personal loans, playing each one against the other paradoxically tripling his debts but increasing his credit rating at the same time so that each month he would apply for a higher credit limit on any given card.*

*He couldn't even put a number to the different strategies he had used against a spinning ball. For a year he'd lived and breathed roulette, both when he was awake and in his slumber. There was no respite for him. Every second passed was another moment wasted unless his eyes were on the prize. Despite every book he'd ever read reporting there was no way to overcome the house edge unless the table or croupier was crooked he was adamant he could find the answer to the conundrum. Weekly he would print off another random ten thousand numbers and every day compile another system that fitted the numbers, and if it didn't then he would move onto the next until he was convinced that his new system could work. Following the practice run he would then go online and play. Occasionally he would win, temporarily, and sometimes for several weeks he would still be using the same system but eventually, without exception, it would fail. His thoughts then switched to the reasons why. What small error had he made? How did he miss it? How could it be rectified? Where would he tinker? There was never anything other than a deluded belief that he could overcome all barriers because he was unique, above all his peers, above all those who had failed before him.*

## 41

It had 'one careful owner' according to the advertisement and it had been Mia's only foray into the car market. The light blue Ford Fiesta did show signs of wear and tear: it was rusting beneath the door welds and across the wheel arches, it had a few bumps and bruises at the rear, and required much more oil than would usually be expected. The stereo was tinny and the screen-wash on the front and rear windscreen never worked so she always had bottled water, glass cleaner and a variety of sponges alongside the toys she kept in the car for Oreo whenever they went out for picnics.

Jeff had been sketchy on the details but had asked Mia to follow Sue at the end of the service just to see where the journey took her, "don't put yourself at risk" - although she wasn't sure what that meant, "and keep in touch."

Mia was inconspicuous as she kept several car lengths away after exiting the crematorium. She was a careful but competent driver and even though Jeff couldn't believe how close her seat was to the windscreen he would openly admit she was better behind the wheel than he ever was. When Jeff drove his mind would wander aimlessly both at the environment around him and the dreamy thoughts in his head and the car would often drift across the road causing him to rapidly correct the steering as it did so.

Mia loved the freedom in her little blue 'Basil,' as she nicknamed it, because it was 'Fawlty' but adorable. She was determined not to be shaken off by any bruising Mercedes and as she kept an eye she imitated Janis Joplin as she tried to relieve any tension. "Oh Lord won't you buy me...." Mia guessed the journey was going to be highly uneventful but then the Mercedes had turned left at the first roundabout and not straight on, which was the shortest route to the nursing home.

Fortunately for her the road continued without endless sets of traffic lights. Instead more roundabouts and pedestrian crossings linked the route towards the town centre.

As they continued out the other side of the town to the six-cross roundabout the Mercedes indicated right, and Mia maintained her distance and kept two cars between them. Mia was blind to the other side of the roundabout due to the large tree and hedgerow in the middle so she kept indicating right as she checked the third, fourth and fifth exits but there was no sign of any Mercedes anywhere. There was no car in front of her now so she continued to indicate right and was about to indicate left guessing the driver had u-turned back on the road from whence they came but still she saw no sign.

Now believing she had managed to lose them she began to swear. Bewildered she ran it through her mind again. *Had the car turned left at the first few exits and I was just too preoccupied? Was there a quick turning off any of the exits? Have I finally lost it?* In her confusion she carried on round continuing to hug the roundabout and checking again every exit gradually slowing and almost in embarrassment leaning even further forward and twisting her neck left and right in search of any clues whilst at the same time physically indicating to other drivers that that she was in fact lost or had missed her turning the first time around. As she did so two high beam headlights suddenly loomed in her mirror and for a second she was blinded by them. Mia had now travelled nearly twice around the roundabout and as she continued turning she could clearly see the side mirror and the the silver bonnet of the Mercedes. She panicked and swerved violently into what would have been the last exit but was now her twelfth. Basil lurched as it did so and violently jerked her but she wasn't worried about anything other than the two beams that stayed firmly in her rear mirror and caused her gaze to avert; firstly to her side mirrors and then to the road ahead.

The half mile straight they were on now was one of the few that didn't have any restrictions. Mia was waiting for something calamitous to happen, and checked her wing mirrors relentlessly, but the Mercedes travelled at the same distance away from her steadfastly in the centre of the road with two beams continuing to point directly through her rear window.

As she approached the next roundabout she became flustered. *What the hell should I do? What has Jeff got me into?* She decided to indicate right, heading back towards the general direction of the crematorium as it was Jeff's fault that had got her into this mess. As she indicated she heard the screech of tires and the Mercedes flew past her on the left at the first exit.

She started to tense up and and a mile further on she had started to hyperventilate as she pulled quickly over into a parking bay reserved for recycling. She opened the car door and struggling to breathe tears began to well in her eyes, more upset with herself for agreeing to do what Jeff had asked. She grabbed her phone and held down number 2. It didn't take long to answer. "What the.......what the fuck.......... have you got me into?"

When Jeff swung into the lay-by Mia was sitting on the kerbside with an old newspaper wrapped around her face in the shape of a cone.
"What's happened to you? Are you O.K?"
Mia removed the cone
"I didn't expect to be followed?"
"Are you sure?"

Mia didn't even have to answer that question – the look told Jeff the story.

In fits and bursts Mia went on to explain how the tables were turned.

"Is there something we need to discuss?" She asked

Jeff remained calm "No it was just a hunch about the dual relationship with the day centre. I've no idea why they would chase you..... But I guess we'd better go through the usual channels. I'll talk to Richard."

"No you won't. What are you going say? 'I was followed by someone I was following.'"

"O.K. O.K."

"What about the others at the funeral?"

"Mrs Latif doesn't know too much about the home. Good Indian hospitality though. A beautiful cup of chai and some real Indian sweets. I don't think I'll need any more sugar for the rest of the month." Mia forced a smile.

"What about the younger girl?"

"She knows nothing."

"Attractive though?"

"She's off to see the rest of the family in Brentford later today."

"Do we need to go back in the home?"

"No – unless you have any other concerns, but health and the local community teams will be reviewing cases for the next few weeks so I think we've got enough people going in to keep an eye on the thing.........Did you ever get any view of the driver or any other passenger?"

"I wish...... I could barely see anything. The only thing I did notice was that both males in the front appeared to have shades on and dark hair but I don't think this will give you very many clues to their identity. Why, do you know who it might be?"

"I haven't a clue but I'm going to visit the day centre tomorrow. I'm hoping to get more answers there – some things just don't add up. I think someone might be getting conned and I don't think there's enough money in the public purse to allow anyone to take the piss."

*Idle Hands.*

*His soul starved of goodness caused any radiance of the fledgling star as a child to collapse inward upon itself plundering all humanity out of him. He had become idle in his mind and the enemy was happy to fill the void. In came laziness, crassness, an addiction to pornography and the degradation of women as sexual objects. His spirit crushed and his moral compass awry his inner self crawled towards places he had never known exist. He wasn't even a shadow of himself anymore; the metamorphosis into a monster was complete, he was detestable. If only he was able see through the fog of addiction, so dense that he was almost completely blind.*

As a manager of social services Jeff had unprecedented access to a range of services. He had visited many day centres before and they came in many guises but most were either built for purpose or located in community centres or church halls. There was a huge variety of services on offer and practice now dictated they were less generic and specialisms sprouted in a number of areas. Carers groups, dementia services, physical disabilities, learning disabilities, mental-health services, over 60's to name but a few.

The Orange Tree Day Centre was set in its own landscaped grounds and the display board was prominent with its colour scheme and design in a flower bed full of pansies. Despite booking only an hour earlier and arriving at the end of the day near closing, Jeff was warmly welcomed and led straight into the manager's office which looked onto the rear garden, again manicured to perfection. Anwar, wearing his name and status on his badge attached to his grey sweater, arrived at the same time as a silver tray of tea, coffee and biscuits, placed on a side table between them. Jeff plumped for black coffee and couldn't resist a couple of Garibaldis.

It wasn't long before he was cajoled into accepting a tour of the premises and the numerous amounts of technological advancements made to assist people with dementia. He was given a demonstration of some of the latest dementia orientated gadgets used for a wide range of groups that accessed the facilities at very competitive rates, which troubled Jeff as it was clear it was a thoroughly modern building, well furnished, well staffed and well provisioned, which would ordinarily come at a premium.

On return towards the central hub a member of staff acknowledged Anwar and reported "the ops room is clean now."

"What you have a theatre here, whatever for?"

"Oh really it's just a private consultation room for Dr Patel that doubles as a first aid facility when required. A client cut his head today and there was a lot of blood so we gave him some first aid and rest in the room. It just needed a clean up afterwards."

"Do you have a lot of falls here?"

"Not especially so."

As they approached Anwar's office Jeff saw a figure emerge from a side corridor and exit quickly. He partly recognised the diminutive frame and bustling stride but chose to ignore the implications.

"Would you mind if I asked a couple of questions about a client?"

"Of course but client files are held in another room. What's their name and I'll have a look for their folder."

"It's Mr Deepak Sharma born 8th August 1942."

"Give me a minute." As he left the office his mobile began to ring, "I'll just take this."


Jeff waited patiently but as the minutes passed he knew the longer it took the less likely it was going to go according to plan. He munched on another couple of biscuits and sitting quietly with the door slightly ajar he began to feel that he was being watched. He couldn't put his finger on it and there was nowhere obvious that there was a camera but as he scanned the room he felt a gaze upon him. He was just about thinking of pouring himself another coffee when in walked Anwar and Jeff quickly withdrew his hand abruptly from the saucer of biscuits.

"I'm afraid it doesn't look like we have Mr Sharma's records. Are you sure he was a client of the day centre?"

"Well I was told he was. No matter. Could you look for some others? Perhaps Mr Reece and Miss Halliday please."

"Any more? There are quite a few locks?"

"No I think that should be the lot."

Once more Anwar went out for a few minutes and once again he returned empty handed and embarrassed.

"We don't appear to have any records for those names either. Are you sure it's this day centre?"

"I must be misinformed."

"I'm sorry I can't help you."

Jeff was about to give up but then had another thought.

"Well Anwar – do you have any basic electronic records of the clients who visit your day centre facilities?" He was determined Anwar wouldn't go on any walkabout and he was absolutely convinced now that Sue was still somewhere in the building.

"Yes I have some basic information."

"Say for instance I wanted to get some information like age, date of birth or sex of a client could you provide me with such details?"

"Yes we have those records on a spreadsheet."

"O.K can you open it up for me for just a second?"

"Yes I can do that but you'll have to ask me specific information.......O.K here we are what would you like me to search?"

"Can you tell me how many clients from The Orchard have come here in the last year?"

Anwar didn't even look at the screen he just looked back at Jeff quizzically, as though it was a trick question.

"What's wrong Anwar?"

"Well as far as I am aware we don't have anyone from The Orchard that comes to our day centre….. but let me check anyway."

He pressed the column marked for 'Homes' and scrolled down the list trying to help Jeff whilst appeasing Sue at the same time. *'Tell him nothing'* kept running through his head.

"No I'm afraid there's nothing there."

"Do you know why no-one from The Orchard comes here?"

"No I'm afraid I don't but I could get someone to ring you if you like." and he wiped the beads of sweat that were forming on his brow.

"O.K that will be great."

Jeff pulled out of the drive but couldn't work out the motive. *Surely this isn't all about fiddling the books for some extra cash – not a company this size. Perhaps Anwar's telling the truth and they don't come here at all but then where in the hell do they go and why?*

As he stopped at a t-junction a mile down the road all he heard was the gentle hum of a black Honda motorcycle that obscured his view of the road as it pulled alongside him, waiting to turn an alternate way out of the junction. Both men in black leather and black helmets looked forward. Jeff was admiring the bike but as it pulled away gently the man riding pillion leaned back to his right turning his body towards Jeff's car and suddenly bowled over his right arm. Jeff saw nothing leave his arm but the disintegration of the driver's window told another tale. At first all he heard was the noise and much too late raised his hands to his face. Then he saw the gaping hole where his window once was and glass splinters everywhere: on his jacket, on his trousers, all over the dash board and the passenger seat next to him. He checked his face with his hand first, gently pawing at his cheeks, which appeared to be clean but as he checked in the rear view mirror he could see a fragment of glass sticking out of his forehead. It was not much larger than a granule of sea salt but as he released it there was trickle of blood.

He looked up and saw the motorcycle had already turned right and was falling over to the left as it turned into a side road and was gone. He couldn't see the registration plate from that distance and knew a chase would be pointless. He checked the interior of the car for the missile. There on the floor well of the front passenger seat was a single steel tube with lids. He picked it up and immediately regretted it. Fingerprints he thought, but then again, no. If this was a deliberate attack and not just a couple of joy-riders then they were hardly likely to leave any evidence.

He looked into his rear view mirror, reversed forty yards back from the junction and switched on his hazard lights. He checked the rest of the car for any damage – there was none apart from a small dent just above the glove compartment. The steel container had rebounded off the casing and against the passenger seat before falling into the well. The pipe as he examined it was a 30cm piece of scaffold tube with two yellow protectors taped to each end. He was about to open it and thought better of it. It could be a device. It could contain anything. So he rang the only person he could trust.

## 44

*Poker*

*It was during a regular periodical respite following complete failure of one form of gambling or another, in this case roulette, that he would reconsider his options and look at other ways to find some action. As far as card games went he was a novice. Enthusiastic in any game as a child with his parents and as schoolboy, where he lost too many lunches, and occasionally at the seaside arcade where 5 card draw poker took his silver, he had henceforth turned his back on the game. Now stumbling across Youtube videos and marvelling at the great card players he saw where his future lay. Texas Holdem' was the game and his hero's bet hundreds of thousands at a time. Whilst any card game was subject to the usual randomness of luck, no-one could predict the next card, but as far as he could perceive in the bigger picture this was a game of artistry, over time and with patience, skill would prevail.*

*He read widely to begin with and tried to hone his game on the small stake tables. But the gambling addict crosses a bridge, a bridge where the neural networks in his brain are rewired and where no matter how hard you try deficiencies creep in and one of the first is patience and greed is the only resolution.*

*Over an hour on an online poker table he would only have to make a handful of key decisions and even if he made the right one every time he might still fail, although making the right ones was the key to success in the longer term. He was learning quickly and felt he had grasped the basics so it was time to move up with his stakes, playing tables that his budget couldn't afford and going against all money management advice that was freely administered by any of those who had played the game successfully. Within a week he was paralysed, losing a few unlucky draws and bemoaning his luck and often going 'on tilt.'*

*'Tilt' occurs when the anger of a bad card or run of luck becomes internalised. The gambler becomes became an agitated, machine gun toting maniac, firing off bullets left right and centre. With snipers waiting round the table he was easily picked off. His frustration exaggerated it was not long before he left the table still bemoaning the moment that had sent him firmly over the edge. This may have been the end of his poker career but gambling addicts never give up. Once across the small divide between rational and compulsion his addiction would never wane. He may stop for an hour, a day, a week, a year or a decade. He may be in recovery, he may in awe of his maker, he may be in the most beautiful relationship he could ever have imagined but the pilot light is always on. He may love himself, he may loathe himself, he may be content, he may be troubled but as soon as a trigger unleashes a spark then his world will light up and like a moth he will consumed by the flame.*

## 45

Detective Sergeant Richard Matthews pulled up about twenty-five minutes later.

"I wasn't sure if I should open it but my fingerprints are all over it." Pre-empted Jeff.

"How heavy is it?"

"At least a few kilos– it went through the glass like it wasn't there."

"To be honest I think I'd better bag it and take it straight to be analysed. At least they can look inside to see if there is anything else we should be worried about. How about the bike - any memories return on it?"

"I know it's a Honda but I didn't even get a hint of the registration."

"How about those on the bike - anything at all about their description?"

"Nothing really. I couldn't even guess their height but they looked fairly slim, even with all their leathers on."

"Alright. Not to worry – I'll see if there's any CCTV in the area but they won't pull out all the stops for a broken window. They'll just blame it on some overzealous joy-riders. I'll check if there's been any reporting of a bike matching the description being stolen in the last 48 hours…What have you been up to anyway? You shouldn't go round upsetting people."

"Just another one of my defects." He smiled weakly.

"Any injuries?"

"Not really – just the odd splinter."

"Do you need assistance with the car?"

"No…..no worries. I'll drive it home. The insurance are on it. I had to occupy my time whilst I waited for the police to turn up."

"You wanted a cabriolet anyway didn't you?" and Richard parted.


The neighbours curtains were twitching as he hoovered his car. He enjoyed the scuttling as each tiny fragment hurtled up the pipe and he imagined trapping

Octocare but he was still pondering on the why?  He cut, shaped and taped a piece of plywood across the window and let that be that for the evening.  He couldn't be bothered to cook so slipped round the chip shop for a take-away then as he settled on his sofa he ran through the advantages and disadvantages of telling Mia.

## 46

"Well it definitely wasn't joy-riders." were Richards first words as Jeff answered his mobile. "We x-rayed it before opening it but there was nothing that was going to do any physical harm to you but I don't know what you're going to make of the note inside."

"Go on."

"Well it was written with a black marker pen and I think they have tried to disguise the writer for some reason. It's been written in capital letters but we had a handwriting expert look at it via a photo and her preliminary guess is that it appears half of the words are completed by a right hand person and half of them by a left handed person. Either that or they're ambidextrous or just trying to be bloody clever."

"Sounds a bit weird." and he was starting to feel wary.

"Yeah I think you're right…..forgive the pun."

"None taken, but I'm left actually – what does it say?"

"Not much, 'PLAY BALL OR WE PLAY DIRTY.'"

"Any idea what it means?"

"No."

"Well there's not much I can help with."

"I know."

"Anything you want to tell me? Are you in any trouble? Borrowing money off the wrong sort?"

"Not a chance."

"Upset a family who didn't get the care they wanted?"

"I don't think so."

"Well you know I'm only a call away."

"Cheers Richard. Appreciate that. I'll let you know as soon as I do."

## PART 3

### Mid - December 2012

### 47

Richard's meeting with Rebecca and Mia couldn't be held in the hospital - the operation had to be as covert as possible. They met instead at a police video interview suite several miles away from the hospital. Mia hadn't exactly lied to Jeff as she was following up one of the clients that had recently left hospital and this offered her the best chance of some further insight about the thief but before she went there she drove to a detached house in a leafy suburb that would ordinarily go unnoticed on a residential street except for the fact that barely anyone went in and out. There was never anyone living there and the lights were nearly always off. Occasionally officers who booked the suite were assailed by neighbours with requests to cut the grass so as not to devalue the neighbourhood but in general life passed the house by.

Mia waited patiently for ten minutes but then not trusting herself went and rang the doorbell but received no answer but as she turned to return to he car Richard pulled in the drive. Inside dulled  salmon pink chairs filled the magnolia lounge and Mia could see the camera's; one facing one set of chairs, the other facing the adjacent set whilst a third, further back, had an overview of the whole lounge. The video control suite was upstairs in a bedroom. The kitchen was clean but last furnished probably when the house was built and contained only cupboards full of tea, coffee, biscuits, long-life milk and a fridge with nothing apart from a half empty packet of cream cheese.

"Right let's go over this." Richard began. "The first ring is made to look like a set of small diamonds over an engagement ring and contains a radio transmitter. The gold band is purely furnishing and is actually gold plate but heavy enough to fool any unsuspecting thief. Mia – You're to plant the rings at a convenient time amongst the belongings of the client. We don't need to know who that client is at the moment but it should be on a ward David is covering. It shouldn't be too obvious but must be in a position where a member of staff is likely to look as part of their duties. Once in place Mia telephone either Rebecca or myself. We both have devices that will be remotely activated by the rings. If the ring is moved more than five yards then a sensor will sound on our devices. This allows for the rings to be moved within the local vicinity but not if it's taken to the safe, which will eventually block the signal but we're hoping the staff won't be so diligent. In such circumstances you'll be on emergency call in the first instance and you'll have to make an excuse to go and visit the client. Here is a phone for you to carry that will only receive calls by one of us."

"Thanks. I've already asked admin to open up the client to me. The only issue is if I'm stuck with another client or family."

"This investigation will take priority over your other work. It is up to you how you make your excuses. David isn't due until the afternoon so the patients should be settled after lunch, most will nod off for the next hour or so, which is an ideal time for Mia to smuggle in the rings. Any movement of the rings will be tracked by GPS. Mia - you can cover the hospital, if we instruct you to do so, but one of us will be working locally for the next couple of days, maybe even in this suite, and we'll cover any movement outside the hospital. Mia you are at all times under instruction from either Rebecca or me. If the signal is activated you will not approach the assailant at any time, as he could be desperate. Please keep your phone on at all times both on ringtone and vibrate and make sure it is easily accessible; in fact the top pocket of your shirt is ideal. Let's see how much Gollum is attached to his precious."

## 48

Shortly after lunch Mia popped up to the ward. She was becoming well known amongst the nursing staff who found her fair if a little unconventional. She went to Mrs Pat Kelly's file and checked the notes and the bed she was in. There was still indecision about the view to operate but Pat was to be closely monitored. Her dementia could be an overriding factor, but the decision not to operate would leave her unable to walk for the rest of her life. Mia wondered what it was that anyone didn't understand about the young soul still inside the dilapidated shell they called their body. The need to push to the limits what was achievable even if that meant risk. Turn off the light of hope and you have surrendered your spirit and settled in for a long slow death where the only activity is that of your dreams or regrets. Mia couldn't imagine ever getting there.

She closed the file and sauntered over to Pat's bedside on Dickens ward but there was just an empty bed.
"They've just agreed to surgery. She's been moved to a single room at the end of the corridor." said the occupational therapist.

As Mia entered she could see Mrs Kelly was asleep. She looked on top of the set of drawers that housed all her worldly goods during her stay. A blue plastic beaker with her dentures, a comb, a jug of water and a plastic mug sat on the top. Mia wasn't sure if the mug was deliberately put as far as way as possible for concerns about spillage or was just another poor piece of practice she had become used to.

A single room had one disadvantage for the investigation because a camera couldn't be trained on the inside but Mia guessed that it didn't matter if the thief was caught red handed, or they had some picture of him walking into her room. On the other hand a single room also had advantages. It meant that there were a limited number of persons who used the room, it remained on David's ward and wasn't far from the nurses' station either. It also allowed the valuables to remain in the room and be private if she could place them where only a thief was going to look. The blue framed door with striped frosted front could also be shut and there was an individual blind for the window within the door so the lights near the nurses' station didn't glare into the room overnight.

Mia rummaged around the set of drawers where there were normally clothes, knick knacks, including sweets, fruit, and chocolate that had seen better days. Mrs Kelly only had a spare nightie and some incontinence pads but inside the bottom drawer was her perfect accomplice, a blue leather handbag with a silver clasp. She opened the handbag and found very little. A purse full of change, some wrapped mints, some tissues; many of which looked used, a small pocket mirror, an assortment of used lipsticks, a small bible and a couple of creased and grainy black and white photos. On each side of the inside of the bag was a flat zip, one smaller than the other. There was nothing in either except a perfumed bag that had lost its fragrance long ago. Mia's original plan was to leave the rings clearly visible in the top shelf of the drawer but now she knew the handbag would be the best option. *You'll have to fight for them you bastard!!*

She chose the smaller zip pocket. Even her petite fingers only just went inside scraping against the side. It certainly wasn't going to be easy. Rings weren't the only assets that had disappeared and Mia surmised that the thief, who must be desperate, would search everything.

She placed them in as carefully as she could and left the room quickly. She made an excuse to write a couple of sentences in the hospital file and signed her name, profession and time. She wanted to cover herself in all circumstances and usually a social services named contact was warmly accepted by health staff when anything outside their remit turned up; family disputes, pets, housing unfit for living all came under the banner and a whole lot more. She took her mobile from her breast pocket.

"Hi Richard. It's done. They're in her handbag."

"Thanks Mia. Let me just check for the signal. Just hold on a minute........It's a bar off maximum but will do. Game on."

Mia offered to work a couple of hours overtime that night, unpaid. She was still compiling reports thus far on her other cases. Jeff wouldn't begrudge her the time back when she needed it. She knew her way to his seemly side. In case anything happened this evening she wanted to be in on it and Richard wasn't going to be able to discourage her. All they could do now was wait.

## 49

Jeff didn't expect anything less of Mia's commitment and he was far too concerned about his date with Kath tonight and his trip to Rovaniemi in thirty six hours as an emergency stand-in for his cousin, Marie, whose broken ankle just two weeks earlier had ruined her chances of the twenty four hour Father Xmas experience. He was used to changing his plans at the last minute, perhaps the only one used to his fleeting change of heart. Kath had become his new provocateur but it was his first cousins, once removed, who he would fly with directly to the arctic circle along with planes full of Brits to experience snow, reindeers, huskies and Santa Claus in the flesh.

It was now 8pm and Mia started to have a mix of inquisitiveness and paranoia that came with her anticipation. *Was the device working? Was David the thief? Was it another and were they on shift and if so were they on the right ward? Was he even chosen to see the client? Was he aware of the trap? Had he found the rings and chosen to do nothing? Would he find the rings and hand them in?*

Richard had assured Mia that even if the bag moved a few metres there would be a signal. Mia should do nothing to alert anyone in health, including phoning to see if he was in. She certainly couldn't start ambling amongst the wards hoping to see where he was. The whole operation could be jeopardised with one false move and determined as she was to catch the thief, whoever it was, she had to sit still and wait and it could take days. This was not a state she was used to but she couldn't force herself away even with Oreo left alone. At 9pm she was pacing up and down the corridor. Richard and Rebecca on the other hand were relaxed, catching up on paperwork and trusting in their equipment, strategy and ability to move as soon as they needed to. Mia eventually rang Richard from home at 10.45pm. "Just making sure that the phone was working."

"I thought you'd be asleep by now. Rest up it could be a long wait."

But she didn't sleep until beyond 3am, tossing and turning, upsetting Oreo. She woke as a text message came in from Richard . 'No luck tonight. Can you check in and give me a ring later.' It was 7.30am. Mia gently eased Oreo off her, who had found his usual spot at the end of the bed, and always managed to be lying on her feet by the time she woke. She felt safe with Oreo, despite his having no real protection qualities, so she scooped him up, nuzzled him and then stroked him before she made her way to the shower.

Despite her lack of sleep Mia was energised by the pressurised shower and as she washed she closed her eyes to feel the full force of the water on her face and started to think about David, his life, the difficulties he would have to face, the journey he had taken to get to this point, and whatever hole he had dug himself. And then she began to breed the hate in her heart, to despise every cell in his body, to feel the anger rising within her. She then turned that anger onto herself. She turned the water to its hottest setting and through gritted teeth took the pain, thrusting her arms against the wall and the shower panel door, punishing herself and then switched and thrust the water onto cold. She relaxed, bowed her head and then dropped to her haunches. She began to press her hands against the enamel tray, and then she started to weep and for two minutes let her tears be washed away before she finally rose, left the shower, screamed into the warm towel awaiting her and then checked the mirror and wiped away the condensation and her pain, placed a kiss from her lips onto the mirror using her hand and whispered "I miss you." She then slipped into the bedroom to change and thirty five minutes later she was up on the ward.

"How's her night been?" Mia asked the Sister as she flicked open the file on Dickens Ward prior to the ward rounds by consultants and doctors and checked to see if David had written any notes.

"Not brilliant – she's become laboured in her breathing, she's obviously in a lot of pain. They've delayed the surgery."

"I'll just pop in if you don't mind."

The smell was the first thing that shook her. There was no window ajar and the blind was still drawn; the door had probably been shut all night. Mrs Kelly had a gray pallor and her lips were dry and her eyes shut. She appeared to be gasping, but Mia had seen this many times before and didn't underestimate Mrs Kelly's natural fight for life. The picture in front of her was one of struggle and decay but this belied Mrs Kelly's inner spirit, which drove her body to recovery and embraced life in all its splendour, be it limited in resourcefulness as she lay there.

For the second time that day she dropped to her haunches. She was able to confirm in seconds that the rings remained where they were. She was up again quickly and checked the water in the jug and beaker. It was empty but she had missed the drip line attached to Mrs Kelly, which consoled her. She opened the window.

As she returned to the station she couldn't help but ask the nurse on the desk.

"Hi, have you seen David around?"

"No, he'll be catching up with his sleep. He's back in at 2pm. He relies on the overtime with the wages they pay."

That was all she needed to know. On the way back to the office she gave her update to Richard. Jeff was sitting at his desk on her return looking tired and bedraggled.

"Look at the state of you. Was the night not so successful? Perhaps too much? Better get that coffee down you."

Jeff recognised her indignation.

"Trying to get away early today if I'm honest. Straight to Marie's so I can go direct from hers to the airport with the kids."

"You'd better get some sleep in tonight it's going to be a long 24 hours for you in Finland. It will be minus fifteen tomorrow."

Mia had already prepared him with a personal guide of what and what not to experience and see. She had also ordered several bags of liquorice sweets that Jeff could purchase through the duty free shop on the way back. She knew he would have an amazing time and unusually wished she was with him but her focus was on different matters and she quickly returned to her work.

"Jeff. I think we need to catch up about the investigation."

"Any leads yet? Any news on our chief suspect?"

"None at present."

"Ok. Well maybe we'll catch up later." And he didn't even lift his head from the screen in front of him.

"Don't worry I'll fill you in Thursday....if you make it back in time."

## 50

Mia left Jeff to his own world and instead she hastened through her work in the morning. She wanted her desk free for the afternoon shift.    David was due earlier at 1pm according to another source on the ward.  She opted for a sandwich from the trolley brought round by a member of the Friends of The Hospital, who on a Monday to Friday wheeled their way around the departments furthest from the canteen offering the usual fare of lightly filled sandwiches and baguettes that squeezed half their contents onto the wrappers that encased them as well as oat bars, and confectionary.  The two retired volunteers brought cheer to the deliveries and were scrupulous with their checks regarding payment.  First one checked the money and then the other.  The choice was limited so Mia chose the egg and cress, a reminder of her early school days in Northern Finland where the children were taught in a provincial school that attracted all those in a fifty kilometre radius.   Many parents endured forty five minutes journeys each way dropping and picking up their beloveds.  Cress was one of the few things that she ever saw grow in the classroom, the long winter months in the north grabbing the sun and hiding it under a cloak of snow.


She tried to stay out of Jeff's way and had foregone her daily free dive exercise on the grass between the wings or a walk around the perimeter of the trust land.  She gave it till 1.10pm before making her way to the ward. *Richard will be expecting an update.* She met one of the Filipino nurses who she remembered from the interview room just a week ago.

"Hi, I'm Mia from Social Services.  Can you tell me who's covering the ward this afternoon?" She expected the answer but wanted confirmation that everything was back on.

"That will be me."

"Oh, why's that?"

"David isn't in."

"Oh I was hoping to meet him in regard to a client. Do you know what time he's in next?"

"I'm not sure he'll be back. Can anyone else help you?"

Mia pretended to stay calm but inside she was frantic.

"No, it's David I really needed to see – is he O.K?"

"I'm not sure, I saw him leaving his flat with all he could carry about thirty minutes ago. He caught a cab. No-one knows where."

"Thanks – I'll come back and talk to one of the sister's later."


And then she was running, running between the Doctors and the support staff as she fled the wards towards the ramp holding her mobile to her ear as she did so.

"He's run….he's run!!"

"Who's run?" answered Richard?

"David of course."

"What do you mean he's run?"

"I've just spoken to a Filipino Nurse." She couldn't remember her name and thought that sounded awful. "He's cleared out his flat half an hour or so ago. She's covering his shift. I'm off to his flat now."

"O.K but no going in until we arrive and make sure you're wearing some gloves."

"Don't worry I've got some in my pocket. See you in a mo."


She went quickly through security before reaching the top of the ramp. She didn't know why she was running anymore. In essence it was too late, but she persisted in walking, running, jogging, walking, running. The fresh air and cool wind hit her as she past the automatic door at the bottom. She turned immediately right and followed the road. The residential block was only 200 yards away. She could see the balconies; towels and bedsheets breathing in the wind, the odd satellite dish, and as she approached the first block the bass beat of a stereo.

Mia had the address, J1 – 08. It was the first floor then. She followed the signs, as difficult as they were to read. As she approached J block, she thought she might have some trouble. She recognised the key code system. Traders were sometimes allowed in before 11am but anything after 12am was a distinctive non-starter. But then she had some luck - she caught the eye of a young woman by her car, first looking and then heading her way. She waited as she approached.
"Who are you after?"
"David."
"The whole world is after David."
For a moment she wasn't sure if it was a barbed jealous comment about David's sexual prowess. You couldn't deny he was attractive.
"I'm probably too late then." She joked.
"You're certainly that as she opened the door for her….there's a couple up there already."
She hopped up the stairs to the first floor landing and looked both ways. On the first occasion nothing, but on the second a tall portly man in his mid 40's who she recognised from security was exiting one of the flats carrying a cardboard box in both hands. He strode towards her.
"Stop!" she shouted, although she didn't know what she could do. He looked surprised and irritated at the same time. Mia didn't really know what else to say so thought on her feet.
"Don't remove anything this is a crime scene."
As she spoke Angela came out of the flat with a folder under her arm
"Angela, what are you doing? You can't remove anything from a potential crime scene?"

"And whose authority do you have."

"Mine." said Richard as he hurtled through the door at the top of the stairs.

"Please put down everything you have in your hands. This is now under my shout and will be regarded as a crime scene, although by the look of things you've tried to bloody ruin it. What's got into you Angela? And where the hell is my phone-call? David takes flight and it doesn't even warrant a phone-call. Mark, leave the box there please."

"Of course mate."

"Angela. What's in the folder?"

"Nothing really....look Richard, we needed to verify the nature of his leaving. I was going to ring you as soon as I could."

"After you take everything? Angela please spare me the bullshit just this once and give me the folder."

She handed it over reluctantly.

"I'll need to talk to you both as soon as I'm cleared up here and you'd better not compile some cock and ball story. How long have you been here?"

"We only found out 15 minutes ago. A call came from one of the ward sisters to say that David had left in a taxi with a suitcase and a couple of black bin bags. A nurse who knew he was on shift became concerned for his welfare and called in."

"Another one of your spies Angela?"

Mia was dumbstruck with the language that Richard was using. The chequered history between them was tangible and he wasn't hiding his feelings.

"We're only trying to help get to the bottom of things."

"Yes, you've just annihilated a crime scene. Where's your bloody gloves? God damn it Angela. Go. I want a statement written by you before I leave tonight exactly what you've been doing for the last fifteen minutes. Mark you wait here. Rebecca's on her way – she'll take your statement now."

"Shit." said Mark.

"Who's got the keys to the flat? This is now a no-go area. No-one goes in and out unless I know about it. If they do they'll be arrested. Understand.... Do you understand Angela?"

"Yes, yes, of course. Here have them."

"What about the master."

"You can't have that but I give you my word no-one will come in unless it's cleared through you."

"And not a word to anyone else."

"It's a bit late.........on all accounts." jibed Angela.

Richard was too wrapped up in his thoughts to take the bait. *What was David up to? Where was he going? Why run?* Richard handed the folder to Mia and picked up the box from next to Mark's feet. As he did so Rebecca came barging through the stairwell door.

"Oh Fuck!"

"We're too late. The trust couldn't keep their hands off. Mark?"

"Yep."

"Where are you going to be in 30 mins?"

"Office probably."

"Ok. Rebecca you take a quick statement now and then meet Mark later when we've finished up here."

"Will do."

"And then can you find the nurse who first saw him leave; we need a statement from her. Mia you stay with me - we need to look around."

In the folder that Angela had been carrying was an A4 pad with some scribbles, some certificates, a calendar, two blank CD's and a hospital pass. In the box were some novels, some old wage slips, some Durex, and the odd cd case.

There was no jewellery of any sort anywhere. The rest of the flat was clean and tidy and the sheets and duvet left neatly folded at the end of the bed, with a wet towel hanging over the door. The shower tray and the bathroom floor were both still wet. The wardrobes were empty but for his staff uniforms and the hangars. The kitchen shelves still had some unopened tins and jars. There was little in the fridge aside from a small drop of milk.

They were joined shortly by Rebecca with her laptop held by her side.

"Well what did he have to say for himself?" enquired Richard.

"Mark received a call about 12.45pm. He was, as had been requested by Angela, ready to have the cameras on David that afternoon and had drafted in an extra member of staff to do so. As soon as he had received the call he telephoned Angela who agreed to meet at the flat in five minutes. As they entered the property David's key was just inside on the floor. The door was self locking when closed so he didn't need the key when he left but he may have held onto it until he was happy he had everything in his possession. At, which point he returned the key through the letterbox. The flats are paid in advance so he's likely to lose his deposit as there should be a minimum of a month's notice. Angela asked Mark to go and speak to the nurse who raised the alarm and see if there was any more information that could be gleaned in regard to either the taxi details, colour, car make, or taxi-telephone number. Other than the colour, red, there was little else to go on. Mark also took it on himself to knock the immediate neighbours, one of whom is out, the other who heard nothing unusual. David wasn't a very loud person and would often have a pair of headphones on when he was in the flat. Getting an answer wasn't always easy. Outside the flat and with his headphones off he appeared to be particularly friendly, and a charming man. Angela had already packed the empty cardboard box, normally carrying hand towels for toilets, which nurses used for all types of shelving and storage as they were sturdy. That's about it."

There was little doubt that David's actions were suspicious and Richard was desperate to speak to him. Mia, Richard and Rebecca were conducting more door to door enquiries about David and finishing one last sweep of the flat when suddenly there was a continuous ringing. Mia who was in the shower room thought it might be a fire alarm but Richard's words soon changed that.

"He's on the move with the rings. Rebecca!"
Rebecca was already running back to the flat with her laptop.
"I'm on it." For her alarm had gone off simultaneously. She placed it on David's desk in front of all and clicked straight into the desk-top and up popped a map of Woking, which quickly became a map of the hospital site. She zoomed in and true enough a flashing star appeared to be on the move in the hospital.
"What's the signal like?" asked Richard.
"Pretty good."
"O.K. you stay here and monitor. You might need your car. Mia and I are off to the wards. Keep the channels open."
Richard knew the limitations of the signal they had. Whilst the rings remained in hospital the signal would be reduced and the map they followed wouldn't differentiate between the floors but if he fled Rebecca could follow him effortlessly.

Mia had a feeling of déjà vu, only this time in the opposite direction as she led Richard frantically back down the road and left onto The Ramp. As they reached the top of the incline Richard began to tire so he called Mia to hold on whilst he got an update from Rebecca.

"He's still in the main building. Somewhere to the right. He's probably grabbing all he can before he gets out of there. Mia. Get us to where it was planted first and we'll go from there."

Mia didn't bother waiting for the lift and flew up three flights of stairs. She narrowly missed a couple of occupational therapists descending but didn't have time to apologise. She reached the nurses' station panting – the door to Mrs K's room was still shut and the blind was down.

"Have you seen David?"

"No – I thought he wasn't coming in today."

"Mia hold on" as Richard followed behind in conversation.

"It's not here it's further on. What's behind that door?"

"Theatre"

"And behind that?"

"Staff quarters but you won't be able to go through theatre; you'll need to go back out and round."

They did so and saw the sign that said 'Private – Staff Only."

It opened with a key code so he banged on the door loudly shouting.

"Police open up."

He didn't wait to introduce himself as the door was opened by a shocked junior doctor. He followed the corridor past the lockers and the kitchen area into the larger rest room where his heart sank. Directly in front of him were two large windows, which had a view over the front end of the hospital. On the other side of them was only thin air.

"Shit – it's not on this level. What's above us?" Richard asked the doctor who had followed the commotion.

"Nothing – the roof. This is the highest point this far out."

What about underneath us?

"Well on the second you've got maternity, 1st floor is paediatrics then the ground floor leads to the canteen and the basement is where the stores are."

"Mia, you take the canteen – I'll go to the basement. If you find him don't approach just raise the alarm, phone me or come down and find me."

When Mia flew out of the entrance ahead of Richard she had to think about her bearings, just for a second. The stairs had gone one way and then another but she saw the sign for 'Exit' so she knew she was heading in the right direction. She slowed trying to keep an eye out for the handbag as well as for David because despite all of the evidence there was still no certainty it was him and to come back in for a couple of rings seemed desperate at the very least. Her eyes were everywhere, any trolley that came past, any bag on a shoulder, perhaps it was hidden. In fact as she thought about it, it was more than likely that whoever had taken them was almost certainly not going to have the handbag with them. This would be like looking for a needle in a haystack unless they could lock onto the ring. She decided to double back and hit the basement because there was no sign of David in the main corridor or the canteen but as she passed the toilets she ran straight into the gents  - barging in quickly and catching one man standing at the urinal.

"Excuse me." before crouching and checking to see if there was anyone in the cubicles.

When she came out she quickly popped into the ladies, which was empty, before running back to the stairs and down to the basement. As soon as she was there she called out for Richard but there was no answer. She headed for the stores. There was little traffic in the corridor she was now in and no natural light from the outside world. The artificial light was dimmer and the hairs on the back of her neck had already started to rise when she heard a crash come from the storeroom fifty yards in front of her. She was off again running to the double doors and pushing them open.

There in front of her was Richard lying on the floor holding his left arm with his right. Next to him was a large collection of bleach containers.

"Fuck it!" he muttered.

"What happened?" asked Mia.

"Nothing."

Mia helped him up with his good arm

"Is there definitely no-one else in this store area at the moment?"

Mia wondered who he was talking to but then an older gentleman with a full head of grey hair, a weathered and tanned face and a blue uniform adorning every other part of his body, gently strolled around the corner of the shelves. He shrugged his shoulders and opened his arms.

"No-one here."

"Becs."

"Yes."

"Is the signal still here?"

"It was but it's gone. The last live signal is where you are but we are no longer live."

Richard turned to the porter.

"Is there any chance someone could come through here and go on elsewhere?"

"Well there's the loading bay outside the door on the left but I'm sure that no-one's been in here for the last half an hour. Deliveries are all in the morning from 6am so once we tidied up after lunch that's about it for the day. The official closing time is 2.00pm but if we're done and dusted I let them go a little earlier right. I just stay to lock up. Looks like I'll need to tidy up again."

As they walked back to the stairs Richard explained.

"I crept into the stores entrance, hearing some noise, suddenly convinced that this was the way David got the rings out of hospital safely by depositing them in something that wouldn't attract anyone else's attention – for instance the rubbish bins where they can collect it once they leave. It makes perfect sense. Remember the thief doesn't know we are looking for him. I followed the noise and heard the footsteps double back as I crept along the shelving and as I turned to hide I knocked the metal shelving with my shoulder. The next thing I know something sharp but heavy hit me on the side of the head. It was in fact a cardboard box full of detergent. Fortunately the contents didn't spill but I ended up on my ass." Richard hit the button.

"Becs – any news?"

"I'm sorry Richard still no signal so it's either hidden away somewhere close or that is the last signal we received."

"O.K we'll wait" let's see if we can find it with the laptop in the building. Mia will meet you at the top of the ramp whilst I check I haven't done any permanent damage to myself. Do you mind Mia?"

Richard hadn't expected the ring to remain in the hospital and was hoping for a chase on the outside where he would have the advantage with technology and resources. He inspected his elbow in the nearest men's toilets on the next floor up but despite a throbbing pain and a small cut there didn't appear to be anything serious.

In a little while Rebecca and Mia arrived with the laptop. The reception wasn't the best in the world but Richard already had access to the hospital wireless facilities as a result of the staff interviews. Richard and Rebecca looked at the screen. It's definitely not the basement let's go up one floor at a time. They headed with the throng towards the canteen. Once again there didn't appear to be a definitive place that corresponded with the last known signal, just an empty table and chairs.

"Don't tell me this was all one big false alarm, let's go back to the starting point." said Richard.

They climbed the stairs again and Mia took them to the ward. The last known signal remained out in the corridor near the main lift but they needed to check on her bag. As they passed the nurses' station Mia turned and told the nurse.

"We're just checking in on Mrs Kelly."

"I'm afraid she passed away an hour ago."

"What? How?" Asked Mia.

"Not 100% sure yet but sometimes the trauma of injury in a frail person is just too much to bear."

"Where is she now?" said Rebecca.

"The morgue I guess."

"And where is that?"

"Back along the corridor, right, and last door on the left. Next to the service lift." She looked at her watch. "You won't be able to get in though. They're closed between 1.30 and 2.30 – you'll need someone from security. Let me ring for you......I'm getting engaged at the moment."

"Don't worry I'll go and grab someone." said Richard.

Rebecca and Mia went to wait at the morgue entrance whilst Richard went down with his badge at the ready to grab someone from security. His last words were

"Not a word to anyone. I'll do the talking when we come back up."

## 51

Richard regarded his entire training superior to that of Mark: *If you don't make police officer you make prison officer, if you don't make screw you make security.* He regarded the security in the hospital as slipshod. He knew he had only heard about the tip of the iceberg but even this was enough to have the alarm bells ringing. Assaults on staff were a major problem. Stolen items including cash, clothing, and electronic equipment seemed to be a regular occurrence. Almost none of it was recovered and too little paid out by the trust via insurance or a slush fund; the complaints just rumbled on.

Two weeks ago and much too late a trial staff entrance had been created including an archway metal detector. Staff were only allowed to use this entrance to come in and out of the building. Consultants had kicked up a fuss and were excluded, their complaint being that the entrance was some distance from the main body of the building and the car parking forcing them to run round in circles, especially those who visited more than once a day due to other private appointments. Mia had already received the wrath of Mark for slipping through fire doors to complete her breathing exercises.

There was a 'no jewellery policy' in the hospital unless registered and if you hadn't done so then security would hold onto it until the shift was completed. Anyone found going in and out of alternative entrances would face an initial warning and then disciplinary action. The monitoring of the system was one of irritation for Richard. The checks weren't secure enough and even when a search was completed too often medical objects were just passed round the detection screens to the other side. Every time he saw it he raised his objections but every time Mark and his work mates would shrug their shoulders and report that they were doing what they could within the resources at hand.

As Richard approached the security office Mark was facing his colleague chatting about the upcoming football and having the sort of unshackled conversation that if you came in halfway you wouldn't understand a word of it.

"Can I help you Richard?" as he reached out and opened up the window.

"I need you to unlock the morgue urgently, and before you ask we have tried the bell already and there's no answer."

"What do you expect it's two o'clock in the afternoon! Hold the fort Keith I'm just off to the fridge. I'll be back in a mo."

"Bring back a couple of beers then."

On the journey they spoke little and Richard strode purposefully ahead of Mark as if to make a point, whilst Mark, whose body couldn't refrain from swinging side to side followed nonchalantly.

"Hi you two. We haven't graduated to murder now have we?" joked Mark

But no one was in the mood for games.

"It's Mrs Kelly." said Richard "She died an hour ago we want to know if she had any valuables on her."

"All belongings and valuables are listed, bagged up and sealed until relatives or someone else confirms their identity and comes in to claim them."

"Can we have her bag please, we need to check something?"

"Anything I can help with?"

"Yes, have you got the camera action for Dickens Ward in the last hour or two?"

"Probably not. When I heard David had scarpered I pulled my man off. We've had some sickness........so I sent him over to A&E instead.... it's always manic there."

"The bag then please."

"O.K well I'll open the bag, if we have one, then I've got to nip down to the stores so I'll give you five or ten minutes and then I'll need to reseal with a different number and you can be my witnesses."

As soon as Mark had opened the morgue door and the office door inside that they identified the bag, which he handed immediately to Richard and closed the door. Richard emptied the large polythene yellow bag onto the shiny tiled floor and started to rummage through the items. The handbag was soon identified.

"Where are the rings?" Richard asked Mia even though he had been told the previous day but he wanted some assurance.

"Inside the smaller of the two zipped pockets."

Richard could barely get one of his fingers in the small pocket especially with his cream latex gloves so instead he patted the outside. There was nothing so he patted the other side but that didn't stop him checking the inside of the larger pocket although he knew the answer. So he vigorously shook the contents onto the floor until everything was out and looked in any creases in the leather, especially in the corners but still nothing.

"Help me, check every bit of clothing, every piece of equipment, they must be here somewhere."

They were all crouched on their knees now, flapping clothing, unravelling tissues, undoing anything they could including boxes of medication. Even the polythene bag was turned inside out. Still nothing.

"Becs – can you check you're sure this is the last registered site." said David

"This map is within five metres of the last registered site, although I can't confirm this level."

"So they've got to be here and whoever was in here or who has access to it has taken it."

"Say she's actually wearing them." said Rebecca.

"I'm not sure that's feasible." replied Mia.

"Becs. I want a list of everyone who has access to the morgue including our good friends in security and make sure that this is treated in the utmost confidence."

Mark ambled back in.

"We need to see the body Mark."

## 52

*Casino*

*There are numerous stories that arise in any Gamblers Anonymous room about what drew a gambler into the lair and often you will hear about the 'big win.' It is this payout, this reward for little effort that the gambler senses is an opportunity. Whilst this may not be the exact turning point of addiction the die are loaded as they struggle continuously to repeat the feat that promises glory on Idle Street.*

*He drove to the casino on a dark autumnal evening straight from work eager to pit his wits in a live weekly Texas Holdem cash tournament with a small £25 entry fee and over 40 players that would ensure the prize money would exceed £2000 once players had re-bought entries if they had lost their poker chips in the first hour.*

*He breezed through the early stages of the tournament, playing loose, getting the right cards at the right time, and benefitting from some very lose play from the other combatants. In the blink of an eye he had made the final table. He decided to maximise his prize money by playing only the best hands and whilst he lost the chip lead before long he was suddenly one of two remaining. At 2am in the morning they broke up for ten minutes and moved to another table to play heads up for the winner.*

*Simon was his nemesis, a regular poker player for a decade, and he quickly realised he was like a field mouse cornered by a cat in a barn that he had visited for the first time. Simon read his every move, never once taking his eyes of the prize. He was bemused into surrender and the cat played with him like a rag doll in the hands of a child, controlled by one paw. He, having understood his fate, knew that only outside interference would save him, but there wasn't any and this mouse, caught in the dazzling gaze of his predator, wilted slowly to his demise.*

*In time he would learn that you play an opponent and not necessarily the cards and this could be as lucrative as any other form. Yet right now he knew he had just been given a lesson and even in that 40 minutes of play he had learnt more about tactics, more about strategy, more about himself, more about the game than in the previous two months.  Internally he was grateful and the teacher and student became friends and would look out for each other in future games.  He had lost the psychological battle by telling him his own history as they had played and his honesty had been his downfall.  And for all that he was £893 better off for the privilege and drove off into the night satisfied that he could make something of this game.*

## 53

Jeff arrived at work on the Thursday morning still tired from his exertions in Rovaniemi with commotion all around him. The hospital was on red alert and floundering. Angela had already been down to visit once and wanted an immediate call as soon as he was in place. It was 8.50am but the corridors and the wards were abuzz with activity. His usual daily meeting was at 9.30 am and he wasn't considering ringing Angela prior to the meeting when she strode into his office and shut the door.

"We've got a serious blockage in the system." and he knew that a light hearted quip wasn't going to be the order of the day. Instead the stock reply.

"Where can we help?"

The morning disappeared under an avalanche of phone calls and emergency meetings and Jeff had to apply pressure on not only his team but a collection of external agencies to start clearing the beds. By lunchtime he could sense the team was on top of it so he cleared his desk, grabbed the list of The Orchard and sat to do the work he had hoped to begin three hours earlier.

For those funded by social services he went through the lists. This was easily obtained by a search engine within the social services register. He included those who had died in the last six months. He checked whether any of the clients had any major health issues other than dementia. Dementia could just be a screen for a number of health issues particularly in regard to physical deterioration. He cross referenced names with those who may have been private funders and once again he came across little information. He was beginning to lose the will to fight. He thought of medical records, and then thought again as he knew the bureaucracy he would face. And as he leaned back in his seat, the answer came to him.

"Kath speaking."

"Hi Kath, Jeff. Sorry Kath, this is professional." her blush began to fade.

"Yeah, O.K shoot but promise I get the full story about Finland tonight."

"Sure. I need a favour – it's about those clients I was concerned about. If I send you a list of names by e-mail and a date of birth can you just check to see if there are any links in their health records? I'm just interested in any general health background – major issues – who's treating them. I don't need it urgently, but the quicker the better."

"On this occasion O.K but it better not become a habit" – and then she whispered. "I can't have you taking advantage of my good nature now can I. What time tonight?"

"How about 7pm and thanks Kath." and he was gone.

## 54

Richard hated Heathrow. His younger detective days had cemented that opinion. He was also aware that if he dredged up the past there would be some unpleasant memories; actions he regretted, a disregard of the rule book, even some violence but things had moved on. The world had become more aware of its rights and he was expecting a tough time over the next few hours. He had incorporated a thirty minute delay into the itinerary for the inevitable log jam on the M25 and commuter traffic hadn't disappointed him.

The unexpected call came late on Wednesday night. He'd expected David to lie low, hide amongst friends in the community, and perhaps even pay for alternative identification. He had seen it all in the past. What he didn't expect was David to book a chartered flight; an open return to his native Trinidad, and with a large suitcase and hand luggage wander into Heathrow three hours before departure to be met by an excited immigration officer who like most red flags expected a run of the mill overstay and not 'a live one.' *They had to have their own little interrogation didn't they – why couldn't they just follow the instructions under the arrest warrant.* David had eventually mentioned Richard's name and unusually waived his right to a solicitor for the time being.

David's night had been uncomfortable. There was always the one detainee, whether it was drugs, a mental health problem, or the insecurity that capture brings, who hadn't wanted to sleep for the night and kept everyone else up, including the officers, with his constant yelling, shouting and smashing of the holding cell door with the soles of his feet. Nothing would placate him and everyone else suffered.

Richard entered the custody suite at 7.30am. He accepted a cup of coffee and read the initial report of the late evening's detention. David had duplicated his answers from his informal interview willingly accepting Bryan's offer for swapping roles. He loved the interactions with the patients and his paperwork had never really been up to the standards required by the trust. He had trouble with some of his spelling and his vocabulary and although he hadn't been formally diagnosed he expected he had a form of dyslexia. To make up for his inability to perform written duties he had tried to go the extra mile when assisting clients. He believed that he had succeeded in the main and enjoyed the work with patients on the ward, particularly with the elderly, who he always treated with respect and habitually used the term 'sir' or 'mam.' He loved their 'little ways', their attention to details that were important to them and their daily discussions about all things to do with life, their openness and care not to offend, their banter as they toyed with David, and used his height and colour and stereotyping to their merriment. It was true he had heard the other side, the occasional slur, the request not to be assisted by 'one of those' or 'his sort,' or as one gentleman put it "you can't trust em once they've got a tan.' But he never took it personally and in the main forged some beautiful short friendships, even though he knew it would hurt that little bit more if they passed away. If this was to be their last resting place on earth then he wanted it to be a positive one.

He had heard the rumour about the missing jewellery and money early on, probably much earlier than a lot of others and had tried to keep an eye on those older people who came in wearing jewellery. He had told the officer that if he checked the patients files then there would be plenty of evidence to support the number of times he had reported that rings needed to be taken into security, some of which had failed, and, in turn, had put the spotlight back on him.

He had heard that most of the staff in the wards near him were being interviewed and that the police were also due to interview him after returning from a weekend in Birmingham but he had never regarded himself as a suspect. He had always been wary of Angela and had deliberately tried to stay out of her way. Yes he had smoked weed in and around the residence but then who hadn't. There were a lot of parties. He had enjoyed the company of some of the nurses – but there was never any controlling aspect to his relationship. He admitted he'd been angry during his previous interview, the concept that he himself could be accused of being the perpetrator had never entered his head. He saw the impact in the eyes of some of his patients when things went missing and he just couldn't hurt them like that.

Richard entered the room where David was sat alone, head bowed and seemingly relaxed but as soon as David saw Richard he sat up straight, raised his hands and uttered words that Richard had heard a thousand times.

"I didn't do it."

It was still only 8.00am but Richard had the impression he was going to be in for a long day.

Generally, whenever Richard had heard the exclamation, he let the charged person give him their version of events and then bit by bit he would start to unpick, unravel, contradict, defy and then finally expose the liar before charging them. In the case of David  he expected an early hearing and a request for remand in custody particularly as the suspect had already made an effort to flee the country. He started with the obvious

"So why run?"

"Look I'm going to be completely honest with you. It was all about Mrs Priddy. She liked a drink. Sometimes we turn a blind eye to the patient because a small drop a day for 'constitutional purposes' was O.K. But Mrs Priddy, had regular visitors to help her and had taken it too far on occasions, ending up ranting and raving for most of one unfortunate afternoon. A decision on the ward was taken to withdraw her alcohol intake, but in the short term it made it worse. That night she had asked for 'just a few drops' to help her sleep so I did as she asked and borrowed the bottle hidden underneath the nurses' station and poured some in a medication pot, to give her a little to rest at night. She was very grateful at the time and then everything went wrong. When I checked on her a couple of hours later she was totally lifeless so I started to panic. I ran to the staff rest room to give me time to think. I knew I had put myself in a difficult position. If I needed any medication to arouse her at that time of night I would have to get it signed off. I tried to think of what I could do to maybe bring her round. As I sat in the staff room I remembered my locker. I'd twinged a muscle the week before so I'd bought some Deep Heat. I squeezed it onto some tissue paper and took it back to her to see if she would respond. It had the reaction I hoped for. She coughed and spluttered so like a coward I left the ward, and decided to keep out of her way for the rest of the night. I thought that was the end of it and felt sure that she'd be fine in the early morning but then one of the security guards couldn't help but make a comment. 'It's amazing what you see when you follow a member of staff for an evening isn't it big guy? I'd be seriously questioning your career choice. Get back to that beach big man.'

I didn't sleep the other night. I thought I was being set up and had no place to go. Then I made my decision to leave so I wrote a resignation letter about a family member being ill. But I swear none of the thefts are down to me.

If I had been caught on camera then my career was over anyway because of the alcohol and endangering life. I knew Angela wouldn't need any excuses to get rid of me so I thought it better to resign and go home to begin with and give it another go in a few months time once the dust had settled. Please go and check my locker - you'll find the Deep Heat."

Richard was one step in front of him. He checked the resource inventory for David's locker and there it was, fourth on the list.

"What about her Mrs Priddy's jewellery?"

"If you ask anyone they'll say Mrs Priddy didn't have anything. She used to fabricate a lot. But go and speak to the other staff. She'd make up stories every day. I think you'll find that she came in with very little, as most drinkers do. I'm often asked to hand over handbags, go in handbags. I don't deny the opportunity is there but it's more than my job is worth.......... although I realise that I've blown it now. God what a mess. You have to believe me I didn't take any jewellery. Please do your checks. I made a mistake, a stupid mistake that I can't take back now."

"Let me ask you something – would you believe you?"

"Probably not – I know how it looks."

"O.K If it wasn't you who was it?"

"I don't think it is any of the nursing staff. I'd notice that. I've been thinking - trying to piece something together. There's only one other department that has that kind of access you need but it's going to sound like sour grapes."

"Security you mean."

"Yeah" and he bowed his head.

"Where were you at 1.30pm yesterday ?"

"1.30pm......I can tell you exactly – on my way to Egham to pick up a ticket home. I know a friend of a friend in the business. I was in luck despite the start of the season. Go check through my things. There will be a receipt in there. Ring the travel agent. I'm sure Julie will remember me. She served me. There can't be too many like me who run into a travel agent looking for an urgent flight out of here. God I've even missed my flight home now."

He was an accomplished actor or he looked totally dejected Richard thought.

"Stay Here."

An hour passed and then another before Richard walked back in with two steaming cups of tea and a folder under his arm.

"It seems a lot of what you said adds up."

"I swear man – I didn't take the jewellery."

"I'm going to need to ask you a few more questions."

Rejuvenated by the tea David picked up. The questions were only ancillary, those that Richard felt might help his investigation. His mind had moved on. Anyone could see that David wasn't the thief. Half an hour later and Richard ended David's agony.

"You're free to go."

"Free to go where?"

"Home."

"I don't think I am now. My money's spent and I'm certainly out of work."


It was true Angela had already had the acceptance of resignation letter typed and pushed back through the letterbox of David's flat, even though everyone knew he wouldn't be returning. That they had received a letter of resignation also meant they were able to cancel any payments in lieu of his notice period - Angela never missed a trick when it came to staff. There was also a note that 'the trust may need to discuss with him again, if the opportunity prevailed, outstanding areas of investigation.'


"I can't help you with work but I hope you've learnt your lesson.......You're on the passenger list for tonight's flight. They've got all your details and personal belongings at the desk outside.  Here's your new boarding pass.  You've got a 10 hour wait until you board.  I've chucked in a couple of meal vouchers. Have a safe journey."

David couldn't hold the emotion any longer.  Richard accepted the handshake, the tearful eyes and the bucket hand on his shoulder.

## 55

*Discipline*

*He was used to discipline as a child. His parents' generation had known that to fall out of line as a child was to expect a heavy hand at the minimum, scarring for life at the wrong end; tales of abuse they didn't repeat in front of their own children. There lingered inside his parents a reverberation and this echo of discontent would transfer generation to generation accepted by a society who viewed physical punishment as the norm. He knew the rules and had to accept the results: a verbal dressing down or a bellowing in the face, a hand, a slipper, a stick to painfully remind him not to stray too far from the path of godliness. It had the desired effect in that he became a servant to their demands but there was a force inside of him that reminded him daily that there was another way, another world. This was the world of secrets: tell no-one, admit to no-one and enjoy the fruits of your own labour.*

*Unknowingly his secret world had made him a kleptomaniac - a compulsive thief, alongside his gambling addiction. There were signs: if he wanted something he took it and there was no stopping the ingenuity to which he did so. If it was fruit out of the bowl, a note out of the wallet, or a pair of designer sunglasses out of the department store he was always the same; he may have been educated by others but now he worked on his own, he covered his tracks, he lied, and he told no-one less they find out about his secret world. There was discipline in stealing.*

*In time the apples became credit cards, the notes became loans and the sunglasses became other people's property. He remortgaged his house not once but twice, not over a few years but over a few hours as his online applications for credit became more daring. It wasn't his fault if the appropriate checks weren't made. He had drawn the line with other people's money since his childhood although his parents always remained fair game but slowly and surely he had run out of options. There wasn't enough money to pay the loans, let alone live, and his credit had been maxed out but still he hadn't crossed the one line he held firmly. Work would remain work and there was no way he would put his livelihood at risk……..yet.*

## 56

Within the hour Jeff received the e-mail in his 'Inbox' that he was hoping for. Wow she's efficient. Attached to the email was a spreadsheet and a short message. 'Here you go. Hope this is enough…are you picking on someone?'

The spreadsheet was sorted alphabetically by patient name. Jeff had chosen admittances into The Orchard in the last year only. The list included 'Date of Birth', 'Hospital Admission', 'Nature of Stay', and 'Length of stay'. The first thing he noticed was there were several instances where two or sometimes even three of the patients had admittances across one week. This was unusual but there didn't seem to be any other pattern and he became disconcerted. He was about to ring Kath when he realised he hadn't been viewing the whole spreadsheet. As he scrolled to the right he also had 'Ward' and 'Consultant'. He thought at first there may be a typing error. Every single client who had been admitted whether self funder or social services was down as under the same consultant, Dr Patel and when he scrolled further the ward had been replaced by one word 'Octocare.'

He immediately returned to his computer and cross checked Mr Reece and Mr Sharma. They both had the same dates for the day centre visit as they did for their operation. It seemed to be falling into place *but what were they doing in the private hospital, to what end and who was gaining.* Jeff had no jurisdiction there unless he could tie it in with the vulnerable adult investigation. The information he had taken from Kath was illegal. He would need to request their medical files in an official capacity but that could take forever.

His memory clicked back to the man falling on the ramp. *A man running away from the private wing but why? A bogus operation could be used to withdraw monies from their private funds. If they already had private health insurance that would make it easier and why were they just transferred over to this mysterious consultant? Body parts could be sold on - not that anyone with dementia would have anything to offer in terms of organ donation but he couldn't rule it out. Perhaps Angela would know more about them. And what was Sue's role in all this? Should I confront her?* He felt his arm again. *Who can I go to with my concerns? There's no real evidence other than someone messed up the dates in the client's files at 'The Orchard' and this could easily explained away with the state of the home.* These and many other questions flew around in his head. He wasn't going to be able to answer them all now so he opened the e-mail for a second time, this time on his laptop, downloaded the spreadsheet and started to formulate the questions.

## 57

Richard drove back from Heathrow bemused. He had, despite initial reservations, been convinced that David was the thief. The evidence as it had been presented to him appeared sound but he now knew that David had told him the truth. No one had seen David on the trust premises after he fled. The travel agent confirmed David in person had visited them, backed up by their photocopy of his passport and a verbal report that he wasn't the type of man that you might confuse with someone else. Mrs Priddy was everything David purported her to be, his records on file were accurate, even if he hadn't written them. Back to square one he asked himself? He rang Angela on her mobile.

"Hi Angela."

"Richard."

"Can you tell me about the video evidence you received regarding David. Had you instructed them to specifically target him and when did you hear about it?"

"I'd asked Mark to concentrate on the wards where the stealing was most active. It was David's work pattern on the wards that had alerted him in the first place."

"Are you in your office?"

"Yes."

"See you in twenty minutes."

It was lunchtime. Time for Angela to catch-up on paperwork and close the door. Richard had free reign.

"Can you go into David's work pattern for the last three months?"

"Yes .....ok fire away."

"Apart from the recent spell how much time off has he had?"

Angela scrolled down. "It looks like he's only had another three days off. Two Sundays and a Wednesday. Obviously needed the money."

"Does anyone else have access to the morgue other than those who work in it and security."

"Only the porters but they would still need someone to let them in. Any news on David?"

"Nothing yet."

For sure he didn't want Angela to know, neither did he want her to spread the news around the hospital. If David had worked almost every day he was sure to be in the firing line for the thefts. As David wasn't the thief and the thief didn't know the inner workings of the rings that had been planted then there was still a slight chance that another signal would be received at a later date or he could set another trap.

Richard felt that there was only one other possibility as to the perpetrator. It had to be someone who knew the workings of the hospital and how do you catch those who are there to safeguard others?

## 58

*The Line*

*The money nestled loosely in the bottom of her bag; several hundred pounds in twenty pound notes alongside her one and only debit card. The patient, whose name was long forgotten, had asked him simply as a favour to check the card was there as she couldn't remember following the rush from the house to the hospital. She was one of the many who had woken in her own home confused and alarmed that she was unable to move herself about in her own flat. In the end she had sat on the floor rather than attempt to walk and crawled to her red alarm lead. She remembered it was men who had put her in the ambulance and she had clutched at her red handbag throughout her journey but she couldn't remember whether the card was in it.*

*Now the card was incidental. Here was a small chance just to get him back in the game; nothing extravagant, nothing obvious, just a few notes to build on. The battle in his soul began to take hold.*

**No! Don't be ridiculous. You can't start this. You know where it will lead. There must be another way.**

*There is no other way. This is the only way. She won't miss them. You can replace them in the morning.*

**But this is the line you never cross. Your job is at stake. You know it will only go one way. Just stop.**

*Stop? Stop? You're doing her a favour you idiot. What would she spend it on? If you don't take it someone else will. You can build on this. Here's your chance. You're back. Come on. Let's get to it.*

**I'm not sure I can do this. It's just too much.**

*Look. Just think for a minute. Sometimes you just have to push a bit further. Sometimes you need to think of the long game. If you're not back in how can you help anyone? Give them 20% of whatever you make on top. Here's the moment.*

**But what if I lose?**

*You won't lose and if you don't give it a go you're a loser anyway and so is everyone else. Is this the end of the dream or the start of it?*

**But she'll know.**

*Of course she won't. She won't notice anything. Just take a few. Come on. Now!*

*The crisp purple notes were a magnet and drew his hand closer and closer and as he turned to her triumphantly holding the debit card in his right hand his left hand clawed a few of the notes and pushed them into his back pocket pulling his sweater down afterwards so even the indentation in his pocket couldn't be seen.*

## 59

Jeff was still puzzled when Mia passed his office doorway.

" Mia. Come in and sit down. How are you doing?"

"Good, a little tired, the heat is on - it's been non-stop from first thing this morning. How was your trip?"

"Amazing thanks. Only two hours sleep mind. I'll need to have a catch up with you about it but I need to check your grey matter first."

"Go for it." Mia was already firing memories of their past but Jeff cut her short.

"You remember the guy who had a fall, the one outside the offices?"

"Yeah you mentioned him."

"I didn't have a name for him did I?"

"I'm not sure. I don't think you did."

"Pity."

"Why?" But he ignored her question.

"Did anybody say anything else about the incident?"

"There were a few stories about why he was running." She broke out into a smile. "Some of the usual, the food was good, the nurses too attractive, and the healthcare top quality."

Jeff limped a smirk but let Mia continue.

"Well he was on Dickens ward for a few weeks before he went to 'The Orchard'. He was a private funder if I remember correctly. Following his transfer to 'The Orchard' he somehow ended up in the private wing for further treatment.....to repair the previous probably."

It was a low shot, a jibe that only surfaced when Mia was rattled and she had been pushed from ward to ward in the morning with seemingly every Sister after her to help clear the backlog.

"How come we didn't review him or have him on the list at 'The Orchard'?"

"Oh, he died following his fall. Actually I think I have it."

"Have what?"

"His name. I thought about the sand timer, about how we all have a time to die; we just don't know when."

"I don't get it."

"It's Sands. That's his name. Mr Sands."

## 60

Richard had a gnawing thought as he descended several flights of steps and waited in a small queue of staff near the security window so started making mental notes. The security team were proud of their work. They had an on/off duty system where their silver plaques were slotted into the board for the day. On a large board behind them were the names of all the staff who worked in the department, twenty four in all. He'd already discreetly taken down nearly all names on his notebook, memorising four at a time, when he realised that he was at the front of the queue.

"Can I help?"

"Is Mark available?"

"He's not in the main office so I'm not sure where he is?"

"Can you tell him to ring me back as I need to make a full tour of the premises."

"Sure. I'll message him now. You can get a map from reception."

"No. I'll need something more detailed than that, a map of every door in the building."

The guard went off to his supervisor to see if he could obtain one and whilst he did Richard continued to finish writing down all the names he hadn't managed to include thus far.

"I haven't got an up to date map at present but Mark should be back in within the next 30 minutes. You can wait here or the canteen is just round the corner."


Richard had an expresso - he knew it was good. His first call at the canteen was to Alison, an old colleague who had moved upwards rather than sideways or out in the most recent reshuffle. Now in a department with greater clout he asked for a favour, information she had available was deeper than anything he could find. He was lucky, she was in the office so would run a quick search.

Fifteen minutes later and she was back. There were only two that came up with anything out of the ordinary. Ken Simmond's credit history was poor. He had outstanding fees on several parking tickets, was a member of the BNP and had legal action currently underway. Mark Cricklewood had previous for tax fraud, with a six month suspended, and there was a note on the system 'gambler.'

Richard had never been remotely interested in gambling himself and didn't even flutter on the lottery. *Losers the lot of them.* Yet his experience of gamblers' was twofold. Some drug dealers who were regularly in and out of her majesty's prisons would use gambling as an excuse to hide assets and just take the punishment knowing full well that on their return to the community the money would waiting for them. Yet he had also known gambling addicts and the destructive nature of the problem; more questions than answers over their sudden fall, several of whom he had put in jail. The one thing he noticed about the majority of them was that when there was no further places to hide their defences dropped like a sheet of glass shattered on the floor. Once uncovered all pretence gave way. Instead their life story tumbled out of them glad to rid themselves of the castle of lies they had constructed. He remembered one who was so wracked with guilt that he'd even chased Richard as he left the police station to get him to take his confession. Amongst all the addictions it seemed the most psychological. Yes, there were problems with anger and violence but in interview there was timidity and shame. Worst of all were the suicides, usually messy and catastrophic for the families who were often completely unaware of the other side of their loved ones character.

Gambling was certainly a motive for stealing and white collar crime was on the up, particularly in times of austerity and the end of almost insatiable amounts of credit that had been accessible. Mark didn't seem the sort, but then he clearly hadn't known the other gamblers that had appeared out of nowhere and slipped seamlessly back into obscurity when all was concluded. He decided there and then if he put enough pressure on him during the tour he might just get the clue he needed. He waited patiently and as he did so Jeff wandered into the canteen.

"Top up – busy day today." as he raised a pretend cup. Do you fancy another?"
"No thanks."
"How's the investigation? I hope Mia's been a help."
"Yeah – she's been brilliant thanks – I think she'd be able to play for the opposition."
"She's the best I've got. Don't you dare steal her."
"I think there's been enough stealing around here don't you?"
"Yeah – I heard David's done a runner – Angela is adamant that he's the man – she told the board earlier about 'her investigation.' Could I ask a question?"
"Yeah, sure."
"Have you heard anything out of the ordinary regarding Dr Patel from Octocare. He's a consultant on the private wing?"
"The name doesn't ring a bell but I can send out a feeler if you like."
"No, it's alright. I'm hoping to go and see him myself later on this afternoon."
"O.K Just shout if you need anything."
"Will do."
"Oh, and tell Mia I'll be in touch later. I'll hopefully have some developments by then."

## 61

*Anger*

*He pushed his hands through his hair. His card hand was beaten not because he had played it badly, on the contrary, he had played it exactly as he had meant to but the poker gods do not reward exactness in the short term. The screen stared back at him and mocked him as the chips slid across the online card table to his opponent. He had never been an angry man but his world of lies was closing in. In the next hand he did play badly and the result was a clenched fist smashing the small wooden table, part of a nest of three. By the end of the hour he had closed his laptop and hurled it into the sofa.*

*Day by day a little more anger entered his bloodstream, seeping into arteries that were close to bursting. He couldn't contain it and his friends and colleagues started to notice the difference even though he had distanced himself from them. He had started to swear; even the smallest memory of his inadequacy was a trigger for a vulgar tantrum. He initially targeted himself. "You fucking idiot." How can you be so fucking stupid?" "Don't you ever bloody learn?" "What the hell are you doing?" "For fucks sake you idiot."*

*This was only a prelude to seeing the faults of everyone else. They were all entirely to blame. If he didn't have so many distractions then he could concentrate on his game. Why don't they stay out of my life? He didn't want phone-calls, he didn't want conversations. He didn't want to know about the bloody weather. He didn't want to know what they had for dinner last night. He didn't want to know if you were sick or why you couldn't do your job. Just leave me alone and stay the fuck away.*

As *a result the split in his personality became complete. Agitation, indifference, hatred and immorality on the inside, attentiveness, empathy, enthusiasm and energy on the outside. But he didn't hear their words, he faked his concern, he couldn't give a shit about their lives and his motivation for anything was to return to his other world - a world of peace, a world where his future was the brightest star, a world he thought he could control, a world that devoured his soul.*

*If he wasn't gambling he was watching gamblers. If he wasn't watching gamblers he was watching pornography. Masturbation replaced meditation. Biscuits and fast food replaced a balanced diet, lounging on a sofa replaced exercise. Money became a series of figures that had no worth or meaning. It wasn't the money he was chasing it was the dream; the dream that would take away the hurt and the pain. The immortal ally, that is love, had vanished and he was left with just a mirage.*

*His only friends were imaginary, his fellow online gamblers with their quirky aliases. The professional players were his heroes. Hour upon hour he'd watch Hellmuth, Ferguson. Ivy, Fahar, Negranu: breathing in their bluffs, examining their calls, questioning their raises, admiring their wit, yearning for their camaraderie, understanding their blow outs, imbibing the madness of it all.*

*He couldn't face the hand of fate any longer as failure after failure piled up. Now he would cover the screen with his hands as the last cards fell into place; afraid to win, afraid to lose, afraid to admit he was beaten. He was drowning in an ocean of despair; a fast route to the abyss where the light would no longer find him.*

## 62

Mark didn't keep Richard waiting long and it wasn't long before they had made their way to Austen Ward.

"I'm just trying to go through some scenarios about jewellery being taken out of the hospital so I thought I would start where the action is."

"Let's face it Richard, you can get anything in and out of here if you really wanted to. There's no end of opportunities. If you worked in the kitchens, stores, any delivery entrance for that matter. Jewellery is easy to hide almost anywhere. You could probably send it by post if you really wanted to. There's a post box at the front entrance and staff send all manner of items through the system. You can't go and open everything up – there's simply not enough man-power."

"But how could David get if off the ward safely? Aren't the nurses scrutinised a little bit more than any other staff?"

"The way I see it he's got an accomplice. He could pass anything to anyone. He wouldn't even have to put them in his own locker – he could already arrange for one of the other agency workers to be the postman. With the amount of jewellery and cash disappearing there could be a whole gang of them."

"I appreciate that but they must be pretty desperate to take such risks. Surely one of the patients is going to be able to remember how their rings were removed?"

"I guess the nurses are in the best position for that, they can identify the highest risk. The patients are probably sedated in the first place. Even if it is mild who is going to know?"

It was clear that Mark had thought about the issues so Richard thought he'd throw in a curve ball.

"What about stealing from the dead?"

"Well that's a possibility but the dead patient is signed off by a nurse and a Doctor with a member of the morgue team so if there is any jewellery on the body it will be accounted for on a quad form and removed."

"Quad form?"

"Quadruplicate"

"And where would I find a copy of the forms?"

"Well one should be held by the nurse to add onto the patient's medical records, one held by the morgue and the last two would be added into the bag of their valuables."

"Where do the valuables go in the end?"

"Property services. They're just along the corridor from us and they will be signed out by either family members, who must provide I.D or they'll be signed off by a bod in Finance who deals with all unclaimed items and will have links to the Guardianship Office or the Coroner if there's no family. You can probably go through either channel though I reckon your best bet is through the property office."

"Is there any other department that has licence or access to go everywhere?"

"Is there anybody that doesn't?" but he had caught his drift as Richard continued to look directly at him.  "Of course we have access to everywhere but I'm bloody sure it isn't one of my lads."

"What about problems, anyone under stress at the moment?"

"What's this all about?  I thought it was David who was our chief suspect here. You should be out there looking for him."

Richard wondered if he had said chief because he was aware that there could be other suspects.

"Don't worry we are but some things don't add up."

"Like what?"

"Like he wasn't under any financial pressure, he doesn't appear to have any relationship problems."

"But he legged it for Christ's sake. That's not the actions of an innocent man."

"You do have a point but there may be other reasons. He got a lot of stick here. From your own department especially I believe."

"If you've got a problem with one of my lads, or me, then you'd better just bloody well come out with it."

"Your department seems a little bit well.......let's put it this way. You're all white and you're all male."

"We don't actively need to promote ethnic minorities in this hospital. Just look around you. Anyway it's about trust and we all trust each other."

"What about women?"

"Yeah – we've had the odd one but they tend to move on. A few have ended up where the David's of this world belong." He could see that Richard wasn't getting it. "As prisons officers."

"So how would you do it?"

"Do what?"

"Steal something out of here."

"What do you mean?"

"Don't tell me you haven't thought about it."

"We try to cover the bleedin' obvious. There's an easy route through the private wing for those who know the ground well."

"I don't get it."

"Well the private hospital doesn't have to undergo the stringent checks that we have here in the trust. 'We're not the same animals' was their Matron's comments when it was introduced at the board meeting. There's more than one entrance but there are a couple of stairwells, mainly used as a fire escape, that aren't covered. If you could arrange to get the stolen whatever through to them then you've got no chance of stopping them. Or they might be getting rid of them some other way and not carrying them on their person. Because of the randomness of our security checking system we would have surely stumbled across it at some point just through the laws of averages."

"What about trusting someone? Is there anyone who gets away with it, who doesn't have the same stringency of checks?"

"No Angela was adamant about that. Everyone has to be open to spot checks on occasions."

"Who checks the checkers?"

"Look, I know who you're aiming at but we have a strict rota which ensures that the parings and numbers on duty are constantly shifting. We also have random checks that Angela will supervise and no-one gets away with it and I mean bloody no-one."

"Is the metal detector any good? Can all items be x-rayed if necessary? I've seen some items go through in the past: briefcases, medical equipment."

"Yes I'll admit that we weren't as tight as we should have been but now we can double check through the x-ray? Not everything of course."

"Does the x-ray damage any equipment when it goes through?" Richard was thinking about the rings. He couldn't work out how the signal would have been lost. Was it deliberate damage, was it uncovered? If it was security then he would expect an ending to the thefts even if he didn't catch him red handed because he'd shown his hand.

"No the precious metal lights up pretty well. It's also picked up on the body scanner. We have had some very embarrassing moments when newer members of staff have forgotten to remove certain rings. We had one..... Well it's best left to the imagination. We get nipple and stomach earrings all of the time but this other ring caused particular embarrassment especially when she had to remove it in the cubicle. on the way home. She refused to shake hands with the officer though. The CCTV is quite hi-tech, not only can we manipulate it, that's how we caught David, but we're also able to make sure that regular visitors that come into the hospital are visitors, so if they don't register, which they all have to on the wards, then we're onto them.    And if they are registered well we won't be expecting them back in when their relatives aren't around will we. The reduction in visiting hours has also helped."

"Well it sounds like you're on the ball."

"We like to think so but some bastard got away with it."

"I know.  Can you show me the entrances that you talked about?"

"Sure – this way – I'll give you a little history lesson on the way."

Jeff had only visited the private hospital once as part of his induction tour. He did remember signing off some services to private hospital patients as social services no longer discriminated against self funders as they used to but in reality he was on virgin territory. He was a little hesitant as he reached the doorway. He recognised the insignia again and just for a second he thought better of entering but this was going to be the only way to push on and face up to the burgeoning knot that was tightening in his stomach.

He went to the reception with a forced smile and automatically signed the visitor register.

"I'm sorry. I haven't made an appointment but I wondered whether I could see Dr Patel?"

"Unfortunately he's not in practice here today but is there anyone else who could help you?"

"I'm afraid not."

"Well what is it in connection with?"

"I'm Jeff, the Manager of Social Services I just wanted to catch up really. I've never had a chance since I've been here."

"I could book you in for an appointment, it would be after Christmas now." as the pleasant twenty something tapped away at the keyboard in front of her.

He was about to walk away but had a sudden change of heart.

"How about the most senior member of staff?"

"Can I give them any reason?"

"Yes it's about an ongoing strategy meeting regarding a home that has links with you here?"

"The Orchard?"

"Yes that's it."

"Take a seat and I'll get someone to see you."

It wasn't long before he was offered a cup of tea, which he politely refused in his nervousness. As he sat down his attention was immediately caught by a young nurse of twenty five, with a short blonde blob of hair, a delicate frame and watery eyes, as though emotion was to flood out of them at any given moment.

"Hi. I'm Jeff the Manager from Social Services."

"Dawn." and they shook hands.

"Do you remember Mr Sands?"

"Of course."

"Can you tell me a little bit about him, we're just trying to fill in the gaps for our records as part of the review?"

Dawn was flattered by the attention and spoke enthusiastically of Mr Sands despite his recent demise.

"We all loved Mr Sands. He was really engaging at certain times of the day, normally first thing in the morning and last thing at night. He would regularly share some of his stories with us. They were always delivered with a cheeky grin. The sparkle seemed to switch itself off and on so that when he was tired he became irritable. He did have some inappropriate actions, which we were warned about, particularly the younger nurses who learned not to turn their back to him. He was also prone to hallucinations and would wander around the room. He seemed certain to be seeing things in front of him but when he did his 'sleepwalking' he would say things that weren't there were and wasn't seeing the things that were there, hence his falling."

"Had he made attempts to leave before?"

"No that's what's so strange. He occasionally got out of his room but would head to reception or mingle in the main foyer."

"What was his job?"

"He was in the navy. Submarines I think. Come to think of it that was one thing we were all jealous of."

"Travel the world did he?"

"No his hearing. Said he could hear an ant fart at fifty metres. We had to be careful what we said around him. He said we were all conspiring against him."

Dawn looked up and became conscious that she was being watched by other nurses on the ward so made her excuses to move on.


Jeff was surprised by the amount of fond memories for Mr Sands. He continued to wait another ten minutes and was beginning to get restless so he went back to the receptionist again who cut him off before he had time to ask.

"She'll be with you in a minute. She's on her way."

He sat patiently and picked up a six month old copy of a science magazine and was reading an article on string theory when he was interrupted.

"We meet again Jeff."

Jeff could scarcely believe that Sue was standing to the side of him. He had heard the double doors behind him and felt the breeze come through but he had chosen the seat facing the ward so that he could keep an eye on the behaviour of the nurses and patients.

"I didn't expect to see you here." as he lifted himself from the chair and offered out a hand. "You're not Matron here as well are you?"

"No but in my role I guess I cover a whole range of the groups' interests. It's best to have some consistency whenever these little issues pop-up don't you think?"

Jeff could feel his indignation rise so he got straight to the point.

"It's regarding Mr Sands  I was just wondering if you had some information on him as I realised he was a client at The Orchard and a patient here. I'm trying to find out what happened to him.  We were aware of a nasty fall outside our offices you see."

"I'm sorry to report that Mr Sands succumbed to his injuries and died within a short time of his fall."

"And what were his injuries exactly?"

"A fractured skull and a broken hip. He was a very fragile man."

"Have you any idea why he was trying to run away from the ward. It doesn't seem the type of place you'd make that kind of effort."

"Well I don't think he was running, more disorientated. We take great measures to make sure they are not at risk but it looks like Mr Sands slipped through the net. It's only when we went to check on him after Doctors rounds that a staff member noticed he wasn't in his room. It was one of the other patients that alerted us that someone had left the ward in a shuffling motion through the door to the main wing. Of course, our staff went out to find him but it was too late. We've written a full report as well as future recommendations that head office are ratifying. I'm sure I can get you a copy in the next few days."

"That would be useful. What about his family?"

"He didn't appear to have any next of kin. We're getting our solicitors onto it now to see if we can locate someone as quickly as possible but obviously we can't delay the funeral indefinitely."

"Is he upstairs?"

"I'm sure his maker is looking after him."

"No – I mean is he here in the morgue."

"No we have our own funeral services we link into. I'm sure he's resting in peace there for the time being."

Jeff was interested in the term 'our' but inside he was fuming as much about his own deficiencies in not raising this whole episode as a possible alert in the first place as well as being tired of Sue's benevolent and patronising tone. He couldn't stop himself. "I suppose he went to the day centre as well?"

"Sometimes the odd record becomes muddled. Perhaps I should have said day surgery and not day centre. It's the staff that sometimes makes these mistakes. I've already asked them to go back and check the records of all clients in 'The Orchard' to make sure there are no others."

*I bet you have*

"Why was he here for surgery anyway?"

"He was having trouble with falling. We wondered whether it was his eyesight. It was more exploratory really."

"What about Mr Reece– was that exploratory as well?"

"I can't speak for other clients but I'll have a chat with the Dr Patel and then I'm sure he or I can give you a fuller explanation."

Jeff muttered his doubts under his breath.

"I believe Mr Sands stayed in room 8. Can I have a look?"

"Who told you that?"

"One of my staff mentioned it when they came to check on him a couple of weeks ago."

"I didn't realise your department was involved. Unfortunately Room 8 is occupied by someone at present. Would you like to look at another?"

"No it's O.K."

"Is there anything else I can help you with?"

"If we need access to his records for the investigation I hope you'll be able to help me."

"Certainly, we'll do our very best to make sure you have everything to complete all your enquiries. Please don't hesitate to ask. Is there a number I can get hold of you on?"

Jeff was going to give his mobile number but changed his mind.

"Here's my card with my extension number in the hospital." and with that he turned and left but as he did so he smiled at Dawn on his way out and she returned this small gesture, which didn't go unnoticed by Sue.

*How smooth is she?* Jeff headed back towards the office. He'd never met anyone so slippery before, even with Angela in the same building, and so quick to provide an alternative solution. It was the monotony of her sweet sickly charm, the presentation of the professional persona to those who wanted more than that; those who wanted a quarrel within a sentence, a debate within a response. Where was the life force in her? She wouldn't bare her soul to anyone.

Jeff threw his file and jacket down on his office desk and was just about to open up the screen when the phone rang. The receptionist bore him bad news - Angela had been hunting for him. There was 'an issue' where the care manager appeared to be working against the rest of the multidisciplinary team. There was currently a meeting going on, attended by relatives in the small meeting room next to physiotherapy on the first floor. Can you join immediately on your return. It wasn't a question. Jeff recognised the case name and knew who it was and that the care manager would be no match for Angela. So he threw back on his jacket and headed off.

*Radiators*

*When a child burns itself against the radiator for the first time it receives a nasty shock. After a second time the child realises that radiators not only provide heat, warmth and pleasure but also pain and scars if they get too close to it. Addicts get pains and scars on a daily basis only they can't be without radiators because in their winter they increasingly rely upon them and forget all the other ways that a person can get pleasure and warmth. The closer they get to the radiator the happier they are. As long as there are opportunities to find a radiator the addict will seek them out. It doesn't matter how many scars they have because after a while they get used to the pain and it becomes a part of their daily living. The only way to start the recovery in the first place is to take their dependence on radiators away....but how do you do that?*

Just a minute later and Mia came out of her room next door and headed straight for Jeff's. She was just about to step through the open doorway when the receptionist reported Jeff's change of schedule.

"That's a shame, I've got some good news for a change."

Mia was on a natural high, pleased with a result that had gone the way of social services rather than health and the rest of the team were in congratulatory mood as they all revelled in the boost and felt that they had rightfully got one over the opposition.

Spying Jeff's empty desk Mia sat in his comfortable, all singing and dancing, leather chair. She helped herself to a couple of biscuits from a never ending packet that was always next to the tissues and started to swing from side to side but as she did so the sleeve of her arm brushed against his flask which began to wobble on the indentation Jeff had caused in his anger. The coffee spilled out onto the table and she grabbed some tissues quickly and immediately mopped up the mess as it started to flow towards the end of the desk, becoming aware that the coffee was stone cold. Only then did she investigate the rest of the flask which lay on its side and had an obstruction that stalled the little coffee that was left. She peered into the flask but could barely see anything even after trying to hold it angled to the light above but as she returned it to the vertical there was a little grating noise. There was definitely something in there so she emptied the flask into Jeff's mug and tried to catch whatever was left in the flask. In the end she gave in to her curiosity and tipped and shook the flask vertically. A few more drops of coffee fell to the desk and on top of them a stained swab of cotton wool.

As she started to pull away at the clump of wool metal started to appear as an anchor does, gradually freeing itself from seaweed other obstacles from the murky depths. Like a small child unwrapping a present with the tips of her fingers her initial investigations began to get more frantic as the rings finally revealed themselves? She reeled away and her whole body was suddenly filled with nausea. And then she started to struggle breathing again. She rested her hand back on the table and started to lurch over it.

*But it can't be. How can it be? Why would he?* She picked up another tissue and cleaned both the rings and held them in her hand heading towards the window to see them in the best light. No doubt about it, they were definitely the rings that she had placed in Mrs Kelly's handbag.

If this wasn't enough to deal with her phone in her top pocket started to ring and vibrate. She was woken from her preoccupation in disgust and horror and started weighing up the options.

"Mia."

"It's Richard. Are you able to talk?"

"Yes. Go ahead."

"We're back in the game the rings have just started to kick into gear again. We're just pinpointing them now. Becs what have you got?"

Rebecca was on the other side of the room at the station.

"Richard." –Mia whispered, but he wasn't listening.

"Hold on - Hold on –It's off the Ramp."

"Richard."

"Yes."

"I have them in front of me. I've just taken them out of a flask. It's been handed into social services. They've used a coffee flask to contain and mask the rings."

She was sounding very flat not excited as Richard would have expected with such a dramatic development.

"You said you opened it?"

"Yes."

"Were you wearing gloves?" She had to rethink

"I'm afraid I wasn't. A person rang the buzzer on the door and left it outside saying it was for me."

*I need time to confront Jeff before Richard gets his claws into him.*

"The receptionist picked it up and left it on my desk. Neither of us has been wearing gloves as we didn't think it was suspicious. We just felt it was a flask being returned. ......Richard."

"Yes."

"I'm holding the rings in front of me – they were in the container hidden in tissue in some coffee. I think between myself and the receptionist we've probably destroyed any evidence."

"What about the receptionist – can I have a chat with her? I need a description and the timings."

"I'm afraid she's gone already." Mia lied again. "She only works till 3pm three days a week – she'll be back in tomorrow morning. I can bring the rings over to you or we can meet later."

"What about the flask – what colour was it?"

"Metallic Red."

"O.K – I'm going to get security now to scan the hospital CCTV for anyone who was carrying a metallic red flask."

Mia was being backed into a corner.

"Richard."

"Yes."

"Don't bother.....I know who it is. I need to talk to them first. Can you let me do that. I'll meet you in 10 minutes at the canteen."

"Mia – you've got to tell me who it is."

"I can't Richard. I'll see you in ten minutes." and she rang off.

Mia left the flask standing on Jeff's desk and started the long uphill climb to the meeting room with the weight of the world on her shoulders. She didn't know how he had done it but he'd have the perfect opportunity. As a manager of Social Services there was little doubt that Jeff had the authority, knowledge and the requisite opportunity to take advantage of those he was supposed to serve. But she couldn't understand why. *He hasn't reporting having any financial problems. His salary is good, well that is what he used to report. He isn't a drug user or a heavy drinker.* She didn't let her mind consider his generosity when around women. *I loved him. I let him take me. How could he possibly betray all that? Who can I believe any more? How can I trust anyone? Was my transfer to the team all part of his grand plan? My God I've had shared everything him. Why didn't he say something?* It was if a piece of her was being ripped out each stride she took towards him.

The tears were falling down her cheeks now as she climbed the stairs and walked down the corridor to the meeting room. She wiped her eyes and tried to stop the sobbing. As she peered through the window slit she saw him sitting with her back to her, opposite Angela, with another care manager, members of the multidisciplinary and the family forming a small circle between them. She checked the physiotherapy room next door, it was clear.

She knocked and everyone in the room turned to face her as she said
"I'm sorry to interrupt you but I need to speak to Jeff urgently."
"Is there anything I can do to help?" asked Angela, eager that Jeff wouldn't have an opportunity to leave in the middle of the argument.
"No I'm afraid it's really urgent."

Jeff looked at Mia who wasn't returning eye contact and appeared to be looking out of the window opposite.

"I'll be with you in just a minute Mia."

"That's fine - I'll be next door." And with that she was gone and Jeff heard the click of the door as it closed behind him and the whine and click of the door next door as it open and shut.

Jeff quickly apologised to the meeting but resolved to raise a number of action points, which would have been the same outcome once everyone had had their say. It was important for everyone to have their opportunity to speak but such was his experience that he had already devised a plan within a few minutes amongst them. He ended by instructing Angela and the Care Manager that he would be with them just as soon as he had finished with the pressing matter at hand.

Over the previous three months there had been the odd occasion where Jeff had felt a chill breeze across his soul when called into see someone, with the knowledge that his whole world might soon come crashing down, but this occasion was not one of them so that when he went into the room next door he had no idea what he was stepping into.

Richard was panicking and was hurriedly making his way back to the hospital keeping an eye on the tracker. After his tour from Mark had concluded he had left to return to his office and was just sitting down when the alarm went off. He checked with Rebecca, who not to be outdone, was also on her way. He had her on the radio as she was still carrying the laptop in the passenger seat. Against Mia's wishes he had already contacted security at the hospital – and required them to bleep Mark as a matter of urgency. He did not want them to detain anybody but wanted a CCTV check. But before Mark had rung back it had come to him. He had been trying to picture the metallic red flask and was sure he had seen it but it was so in front of his eyes that his brain had barely allowed him to recognise it. And then slowly through flashbacks it began to drip through and make more sense but this time he was only worried about Mia.

"Shit........shit shit shit shit shit" as he banged his hand against the steering wheel. Who knew what a desperate man would do confronted with the truth?

Mia was facing away from Jeff as he entered. As she turned he was horrified. Tears streamed from her face. Her mascara was pushed outwards towards her temples and her expression suffered like he had never witnessed before; the skin seem to fall away from her face, clinging at the edge of her jaw. She walked towards him.

"Your hand."

He was about to hug her realising her distress but instead her left hand pushed out towards his right shoulder and with her right hand she took his right hand and slipped the rings in his palm closing his fingers around them. Before he had a chance to view them properly he was being propelled backwards. Both her hands pushed into his upper chest. One, two, three on the fourth he caught her hands. She screamed.

"How could you?"

In the absurdity of the situation Jeff was suddenly more concerned about the impact of her booming voice infiltrating next door.

"Shhhh."

"Don't you tell me to be quiet you bastard."

"Mia, stop, stop, stop it." His voice rising with each instruction. He was already formulating the lie. "You don't understand. There are things going on that you don't understand."

"I don't understand. Are you insane? I understand. I understand that you're a thief, a low life fucking thief. Can't you see what you've done? How can you steal off the dead?"

"Look. I was signing off a death certificate. I just got caught in the hallway. They said they needed someone official. I'm sorry about the rings. I'm truly sorry but this is bigger than you think."

"Can't you stop? Stop making fucking excuses." And she was screaming again and he knew he had no place to go.

"O.K, O.K – I know I've lost everything but there are other things going on here. "Look." And he started to roll up his right sleeve. He pointed to the scar on his forearm. "See this? I need you to trust me."

But she didn't understand.

"How can I trust you? You're a liar and a thief." and she started to withdraw away from him.

"I know. You don't have to tell me I know, but I need some time, please give me some time to explain."

"I can't."

"What do you mean?"

"I can't, Richard is on his way here already you idiot....The rings."

"What about them?"

"They're bugged, they've got a tracker."

"Oh God – I need some time."

"He's on his way."

"God, I must go. I'm sorry Mia I must go. I'll let you have all you need to know in 24 hours – I promise. I know I said I'll never make you any promises but you must believe me. Just 24 hours. I'm sorry. Truly I'm sorry."

He walked towards her and passed back the two rings. With that Jeff left Mia standing crestfallen in the centre of the physiotherapy room. He hurried quickly out of the door and was gone.

As Richard ran through the front entrance Jeff was striding into his own office. He picked up the red flask and hurled it in the bin. He collected his laptop and turned to walk out for the last time. As he began to do so the receptionist called him.

"The whole world seems to be after you. There's a note here for you and I've got a strange message from a Mrs Latif. I couldn't quite understand her but it's got something to do with bird's. I didn't know you were into birds of the feathered kind."

He took both pieces of paper, the former being a twice folded A4 piece of paper with a staple in the centre. He didn't have time to open them so just shoved it into his jacket pocket and as he headed out of the door he turned and with a gentle wave he said.

"I've got to go. I'll catch up tomorrow."

Richard saw figures so sensed this was the meeting place as instructed by Jeff's secretary but as he opened the door without knocking he realised neither Mia or Jeff were sitting in it so abruptly apologised and closed it. He thought better the second time and looked through the window of the adjacent door. Catching a glimpse of Mia at one end of the room he entered.

Mia was sitting astride a large blue gym-ball, gently motioning forwards and backwards with her face looking directly at the floor. She didn't even look up until he had spoken.

"Are you O.K?"

"Not really."

"Did he hurt you?" as he approached her.

She shrugged.

"He hasn't touched me if that's what you mean."

As he came close she started to cry again.

Richard pulled her up towards him and hugged her for a few seconds that seemed an eternity. As he withdrew she knew the question was coming.

"Where's Jeff?"

"I don't know, he just left. He said he needed time. He said it's part of something bigger. He showed me a scar on his arm."

"Did he mention anything at all about where he was going?"

"No ... but he gave me back the rings."

"What all of them?"

She laughed and wiped a tear almost in relief.

"No, just the two that I put in his hand."

And with that she showed Richard the two rings as she released her fingers from their grasp so tight that the tops and the middle of the palm were imprinted with their shape.

"Where does he live?" and for the next two minutes Richard teased as much information as he could from Mia including Jeff's address, his car details, even part of his registration.

"You seem to know a lot about him."

"Obviously not enough........but I did live with him for over a year."

"How come I didn't know that?....... Sorry."

"I didn't want you to."

At that moment Rebecca charged into the room and seeing the scene in front of her.

"Fuck."


Richard walked back with Mia to the Social Services Office then told her to go home, and try not to worry too much but that if Jeff did get in touch to try and persuade him to talk to him to see if he could help whatever the problem was. Richard would try and catch up with him but he would be in touch with Senior Managers at the Council and Angela. There was no question of that.


Rebecca was already putting out a a bulletin in the local area for Jeff's car. She'd already managed to attain the full registration of the vehicle from Mark at security, who was full of questions but had to wait a little while for answers. Then she headed back to Jeff's office to conduct a thorough search.


Richard headed to Jeff's house to try and catch up with him. Whatever it was it sounded desperate and despite his professional friendship he had a job to do and a job to finish. A colleague stealing under his nose wouldn't be seen as a success, whatever the outcome.

He reluctantly had to inform Angela and Mark after a hastily arranged private meeting and requested that any sighting of Jeff should be reported immediately but the broader details should be retained with as few as possible until he was in contact with Jeff. Knowing how the hospital worked though and envisaging that word would be round the wards in no time he believed that it would act as its own reconnaissance.

## 70

As Jeff approached home he already had a plan. Richard would come after him so he didn't park the car at home but drove to the local G.P surgery where parking was available out of sight, and, at least for the evening, the car would be safe. He didn't expect to be hanging around in the morning. He made one last call.

"Hello Mrs Latif. It's Jeff from Social Services."

"Ah Good. I just wanted you to know Jeff that I rang the home to see if any belongings needed picking up but they said there was nothing of consequence so then I rang the solicitors to see if there was anything I could do to help. They said Mr Sharma was no longer a client. He'd been transferred to another solicitors just a month after his original stroke. Hold on I've got their name........ Devlin and Coombes with an office in London. I can't understand why they would change solicitors at that stage? He'd been with them for so long. They'd tried to talk to the new firm but were being run ragged. They reported it to the Ombudsman but haven't heard back. What's really strange is that he never told me. I had his absolute trust and this is so out of character. I'm going to follow it up myself but I thought you should know."

"Thank you very much Mrs Latif. I've got to go now but can I ring you at the start of next week just to go over a few details?"

"Of course. You have my number. Speak soon."


He turned off his phone and left it in the glove compartment but took out the SIM card and put it in his pocket. As he did so he felt the folded paper again but didn't have time to look at it right now. He wondered what saucy message Kath may have written. He grabbed his laptop and walked a longer route that would not put him on any major pedestrian routes or in view of the countless CCTV cameras that were dotted around the estate as a result of drug dealing and anti-social behaviour in the local area.

He swiftly entered his property through the front door but didn't turn any lights on and left the curtains as they were. He took some chilled pies from the fridge and a bottle of lemonade and climbed the stairs to the bedrooms. He opened the attic hatch and allowed the ladder to fall at the ready if necessary. He placed a mirror in his bedroom at an angle that would allow him to see his front drive and the road outside and he opened the small upstairs window ever so slightly before opening his laptop and setting to work sitting at the base of his bed.

As he untangled his jacket he habitually checked his pockets and felt the folded paper He withdrew the staple without ripping the paper and opened it gently. Inside were a couple of short sentences in female handwriting.
'Some more information for you.
Chapel Fri 6.45am
Dawn.'

## 71

Mia, as usual, was welcomed enthusiastically by Oreo as she turned the key. She scooped him up with one hand and gripped hold of him as she collapsed on the sofa. She immediately cancelled her evening out with ex-work colleagues for a bite to eat and a film at the local cinema. Oreo, feeling her tension, jumped from the sofa and started to rummage around with a rubber jingle ball. This normally instigated a game between them where Mia would take the ball and pass it round her neck, back, side and legs as Oreo scrambled after it but this time to no avail. Instead, following a large deep breath, Mia hauled herself from the sofa and went to the kitchen cupboard to get some food.

The thought of what she would normally be doing reminded her about Jeff's forearm. She had received scratches from Oreo during the game but none had left a scar like Jeff's. She didn't know whether to believe that someone else had caused it. She tried to remember her times living with him. *Have I missed the signs of depression? He was always so bubbly around me. Admittedly he had become a little withdrawn near the end of the relationship but he blamed it on the pressure of work – he was always on his laptop doing something.*

She racked her brains about his motive but didn't get anywhere other than it must be financial. *What the hell had he got himself into?* She rung his phone number and wasn't surprised it went dead.

Mia had an idea of going over to him at his home but knew Richard would already be there. She felt completely hopeless. *Have I treated him too harshly? Am I going to regret my words?* She started to well up again and Oreo jumped onto the kitchen work-top opposite via a chair eager to jump into her arms and comfort her.

"Where would I be without my Ori?" and she threw open her arms and hugged him tightly before dropping him to his bowl where a larger feast than normal was waiting.

## 72

Richard tried in vain to ring Jeff several times. The next 24 hours was vital, any outcome could be likely. In honesty he worried for Jeff's life; suicides were often hatched at the moment of discovery. The soul's exposure to the inner turmoil as the delusional shell had been cracked and discarded prompted thoughts like no others. For some it would be the fulfilling of months of secret planning, the straw that broke the camel's back. For others it was the sudden realisation that they were done, lost and frightened in the new world they had suddenly found themselves in, where they they were naked and defenceless, like a new born, but without a mother to cherish and protect them. Shame and guilt was the driving force, butchering a schism through family, friendships, neighbours, and society.

Jeff had no time for shame at present. His time was dedicated to detailing his concerns and he poured over the information and dates he had collected thus far in order to provide a theory for those in authority and for the only person he could trust to continue the task ahead - Mia.

Jeff's first interruption to his thoughts was the slamming shut of a door. He peered at the mirror and saw Richard approaching. He had missed the car pull up. He shut the laptop, pulled the mirror of the shelf and threw it under the bed, and crawled through the bedroom door, pulling it slightly to him as he exited onto the landing. He then climbed the attic ladder, pulled it up behind him and made his way to the very back of the attic, where he crawled behind the chimney breast that lay in direct alignment with the ladder to the trap door and there he waited in the stillness.

Richard was going to ring Jeff one more time but thought better of it. The bell was clearly disabled so he knocked combatively on the front door several times and then shouted through the letter box. He didn't expect anything but held his ear to the gap in the door waiting for the slightest detection of noise from inside. He walked to the back door through a side gate, continuing to listen for any sound. But the only the movement was a stray cat on the back fence and a rustling from behind a fence as neighbours cleared some leaves in their gardens. The door didn't budge so he returned to the front door and dialled Mia.

"Sorry Mia, quick question. Did Jeff ever leave a spare key around?"
"Yes....I think so anyway. If you go to the alleyway there are some hooks to hold a ladder. If he had one he would leave it on top of that hook. Actually thinking about it I may have one myself if you need it."
"Thanks. I'll come back to you....by the way we didn't just have this conversation."
"Ok. Please let me know if you find him."
"Will do. Bye."
Jeff was aghast. How could he have been so stupid? He could clearly hear the call. The attic had no insulation and the sound rose straight through the eaves to where he was sitting pensively.

Within ten seconds Richard was standing in the small entrance hall, with another set of nitrile gloves. On the floor was some unopened post and circulars. He picked them up but it appeared like a few credit card bills.

He closed the front door behind him and decided to give one more call to see if Jeff would come out of his own accord. No answer. He started downstairs, firstly for clues about Jeff, secondly for any paperwork that he might come across - he didn't expect to find any jewellery. The lounge was sparse apart from a nest of tables, a 42 inch flat-screen television on the wall, a few books on shelves and two sofas. He checked the sides and the bottoms to see if there were any hidden objects tucked away, especially in the lining at the bottom. He's lost count of the number of unimaginative hoarders of drugs and accessories he'd found in such obvious places, but on this occasion nothing.

In the kitchen he checked the fridge, the cooker, all the washing appliances, kitchen drawers, kitchen cupboards, containers etc. The kettle was cold. The fridge whirred into action when he opened it but there was little in there. The heating was on a timer above the dishwasher, he checked – the hot water was due on shortly for two hours, ready to heat the shower for Jeff's ordinary time to return to the flat. The whole of the downstairs floor was tiled and solid even with the occasional crack in the tile there appeared no hiding place in the flooring.

The kitchen surfaces were dry. The high shelf above the appliances and cupboards attracted the usual Knick-knacks – electrical leads, wine boxes, string, empty shoe boxes etc. He checked the bin but nothing. In the recycle bin above the sink were the used coffee grounds from the percolator that was placed upturned on the sink, a present from Finland by Mia. There was a distinct lack of photographs anywhere, and just some cheap art that were copies you could find in any high street picture shop.

In the conservatory was a stereo, a couple of easy chairs and a magazine rack but they were all well worn, in fact nothing was modern. Eyeing a key in the lock of the back door he withdrew it and placed it in his pocket.

He returned to the entrance hall and the mermaid, who, as always, struck those who witnessed her beauty. He then climbed the creaking wooden stairs to the two bedrooms and the toilet.  He checked the side of the bath but it was solid.  The toilet cistern was empty but he flushed it none-the-less just to make sure.

He systematically went through the two bedrooms, mattresses, drawers etc and found little.  The hanging wardrobes were clearly Scandinavian in build and design.  He did find a bundle of old photos at the bottom of one of them; none were of Jeff and Mia.  In the second bedroom was a large collection of folders, which he flicked through:  bank statements, bills, insurance, loans, mortgage information, credit card statements, and lots of them.  Checking one of the more recent bank statements he quickly scanned some of Jeff's expenditure, transfer after transfer to an anonymous site, probably a casino. The carpets were all clean in the rooms and the vinyl floor was clear in the bathroom so as he was about to return downstairs he noticed some flakes of paint on the landing flooring.

He looked up and saw some peeling paintwork on the hatch to the attic.  He took a chair from one of the rooms and standing upon it pushed up the attic hatch and pulled the aluminium ladder towards him. As he climbed he took out his small LED torch and soon located a switch on his right hand side just alongside the well of the entrance but before he switched it on he climbed to the top of entrance to the attic and using his torch to direct him leant forward and checked the temperature of the fluorescent light above his head.  It was cold, so he crouched and returned to the switch and turned it on.  The attic was full of junk including numerous boxes of books in large clear plastic box containers, piles of electrical leads and gadgets that had outdone their usefulness.  There were several empty rucksacks and one suitcase, two large rolls of fibrous insulation, cardboard boxes full of outdated magazines and another full of vinyl LP's and twelve inches.  Behind him was the antiquated boiler system and the myriad of pipes that fed the hot water and heating system.  He couldn't see a single free space around him to make any type of journey around it and past inspections had told him you're only one step away from putting your foot through the ceiling, especially with the frailty of the plasterboard below him. As he took a step backwards there was a sudden rattling of the pipes and gurgling in the water tank as the heating system kicked in. His heart fluttered a little and the hairs rose on the back of his neck, so he crouched down again, switched off the light and returned to the landing. He closed the attic lid and made his way to the bottom of the stairs. As he reached the entrance hall next to the door he dialled Mia's number whilst Jeff listened intently from above against the murmuring feed of the hot water through the system, only the odd car dampening his antenna as the conversation was transmitted.

"Hi Mia, no sign of him here. Can I ask you a couple of questions?"

"Yes. Of course."

"Were there any issues other than his own investigation that you were aware of, particularly financial?"

"No. I can't understand it. The more I think about what has happened the less I can work out what he's been up to."

"What about his general mood?"

"Nothing, he seems the same as he always has, except for the early days. Why would he do it? Do you think he's in trouble?"

"I'm not sure but he must be desperate. He could be a danger to himself."

"What do you mean?"

"Desperate situations sometimes call for desperate measures."

Mia didn't say a word but understood. Richard brought her back

"What about hiding places here?"

"None that I know of other than for the key. He kept things pretty sparse in the house. Not a great collection of anything. Do you think he'll go to prison?"

"It's early days but if it is him then the scale of thefts and length of time this has been happening means a custodial sentence is likely."

"This is unreal. Could it be someone else and he's just covering for them?"

"Who knows? But we need to find him before it escalates. I don't want to call the heavy mob in. Do me a favour. If you get any contact and I mean ANY then please let me know immediately."

"I will Richard. I will. I just wish I could help."

Mia ended the call and sighed. *Where was he? Where the hell was he? And why hasn't he called?* She tried Jeff's number again. Still dead.

Richard wondered if he had gone too far with Mia. He needed her to face reality; away from her past relationship, the triumphs, the misgivings, and was fairly blunt in spelling out the possible danger Jeff was in. Here was a man who was committed to helping others and who, for whatever reason, had ended up abusing them. Did Mia understand the pressure that would put on his conscience? He'd seen bigger men fall.

## 73

After Richard left Jeff climbed out of the attic and returned to his work. It was going to be an arduous night but he was determined to get as much of his evidence and thoughts down on paper. He had all the information he felt he required at least to take it to the next stage and he drew up a document. If Mia wasn't willing to involve herself she could at least pass it to some of the higher Managers in the Safeguarding Adults Team. He didn't even consider that his reputation could never be salvaged.

It took until 3am to complete the dossier after which he went onto the personal. He drafted two letters; one for Kath and one for Mia. He envisaged that his arrest was imminent and wrote accordingly. He wasn't worried about Kath. Whilst she was warm, kind, and understanding and their relationship had been intimate physically it had also been fun and without a lot of what he regarded as baggage that came with building a longer term relationship. The vibrancy within the relationship was linked to their freedom without unnecessary weight anchoring them. Their ground was the seas and they bobbed around playfully in the shallows without being tempted into deeper water. He believed Kath would soon move on. The only downside was that the rest of the hospital might learn about them, especially if Angela had got hold of it, so there might be some comeback to Kath on a professional level. Jeff didn't think about himself and what future lay ahead of him. He was immune to the catastrophic circumstances that he had created, emotionally bereft of the feelings of others and completely deluded as to his part in all of it. Instead he focused solely on the work that he must do to remedy the other issues that had dominated his thoughts.

He left Mia till last. As he started to reflect on the rationale for her assistance he began to realise the damage he had inflicted. He couldn't comprehend that he might have lost her trust for ever, which was contradictory to his needs now as he had never needed her more.

Mia sat on the sofa alone. Oreo was locked in the kitchen and no amount of scratching would tempt Mia to release him. Over and over in her head Mia replayed the events of the day but still nothing made sense. She phoned Richard again and talked to him about Kath but to her surprise he already knew. Richard wanted other addresses or places that Jeff might find solace. Mia gave all the names and occasional addresses that she remembered as well as all those in her phone book. She had been fastidious in her recording of information about acquaintances that she had met through Jeff, such was her desire to integrate her life with him. Asked about other sanctuaries she reeled off favourite pubs and restaurants and B&B's that had held a special place in their hearts. Richard wanted more but Mia was spent and couldn't provide anything else so he reassured her that they would find him and she was not to venture out of her home. If anything Richard reported that he wouldn't be surprised if Jeff turned up at Mia's and so he would be having someone sweep Mia's area throughout the night. Mia knew who that sweep would be; she sometimes thought that Richard never slept.

Richard had been to Kath's house and disclosed the minimum of details. Kath didn't know of his whereabouts and too had no luck with her calls to Jeff. She was actually expecting the knock at the door to be him. She was shocked more than upset and questioned whether they were sure they had the right person. It threw her off kilter and all she could report was the pubs and restaurants they had used and the weekend hotel on the coast. Richard made the same urgent appeal for information if she heard anything and then decided not to delay any longer. There had already been a plethora of calls made to other known close friends and acquaintances so later that evening he decided to personally follow up on some places that Mia had mentioned several hours earlier.

As Jeff finished rereading his letter to Mia he knew his words were as honest as he could imagine them to be in his current state. He had written how he regretted the way he had behaved, the lost opportunities, and how he managed to allow himself to distance from the person he admired the most. He tried to set out and almost excuse himself from the behaviour that had taken him to the brink and was still hopeful that his plea for support would not fall on deaf ears. Lastly, he left her some clues to hidden messages knowing that if he wasn't around to tell the story he could at least hope to salvage something from his miserable existence, underestimating the tenacity of those who preferred his investigation to be buried. Several times during the night he considered ringing Mia to ease the pain in his soul but knew he couldn't - Richard would be all over it. He resolved to post both letters on his way to work that morning.

For the last hour, bereft of sleep, and in a sudden attack of lucidity and self consciousness Jeff considered several forms of suicide. It wouldn't be a train, despite the certainty of death. He had read many failures about the use of pills and certainly didn't want to leave himself a drain on society if he didn't complete the job wholly. He did consider devising an accident so that in his warped mind there was honour in his death. He believed the whole time that death would reduce the suffering of those left behind without even considering that all anyone would want would be to have a chance, however small, to save his life from its own destruction and to help find that part of his soul that was pure, that wasn't tainted by the rigours of life. Facing the abyss he was unaware of the love that poured over him, unseen to the naked eye but abundant in the universe He forgot about the true victims of suicide; those who were left behind - distraught, helpless, rejected and leaving a scar so deep that they might spend the rest of their lives trying to recover from it.

Jeff's thoughts switched to Dawn and their meeting. *I should record any evidence.* He had his phone and dummy pen that would record everything and right now he could use the additional evidence to back his case. *Will anyone anyone believe me? A thief charged with neglecting those he was supposed to protect suddenly has a case against others. It couldn't look any worse.* He was worried about Dawn and the courage it takes to speak out as well as the security he would have to face at the hospital. She probably started work at 7am. Maybe he could ask her to get some more information for him. She had been very willing to assist him in the first place. She may just be the key to unlocking the whole puzzle. The chapel was safe but would it be open, then again, patients don't die between nine to five. He was also worried that it wasn't only Richard that was after him but in twelve hours he knew he would be either in a police cell or in a place no-one could get to him.

Jeff used some wet wipes he had in the bathroom drawer to clean himself and put on a change of clothes. After hiding his laptop beneath his mermaid he took his phone, wallet and keys and went to the back door noticing the spare keys were no longer there. He opened it with his main set, locked it again as he left and slipped quietly to the back fence where he climbed onto a disused chair and jumped over it into the children's park behind. He slipped away taking the same route back to the car.

## 76

The waxing moon had all but disappeared and the cloud cover aided him as he moved closer to the hospital from his car parked half a mile away, conveniently near a post box, unaware that as soon as he had posted his letters and left the area a tall lean looking forty something woman had too pulled over to the post box and using a key out of her boot retrieved both letters he had just posted.

The chapel was near the main delivery area and he was convinced this was the best way in. Here the laundry hosted another smaller ramp fifty yards long, where the large metal crates full of clean and dirty linen were pushed endlessly up and down and out onto the main corridor to service the wards. It wasn't an official entrance and once in a while the odd e-mail would fly around the departments from Mark and Angela warning staff not to use the entrance otherwise disciplinary action would follow, but the unwritten rule was that management could occasionally be get away with it and their stand out orange necklaces that held their security cards were a different colour to the rest of their subordinates who were kept a closer eye on. Jeff was well known and was hoping to avoid having to talk to anyone and as expected, even at just after 6.45am it was rush hour for this department.

The scent of clean linen pervaded the entire area and the whirring of the enormous machines in the large rooms that led off the ramp made any normal conversation quite difficult. Two private laundry vans were already parked outside the loading bay and as Jeff walked through no-one took a blind bit of notice. After reaching the end of the ramp and now ground level to the wards Jeff passed through an entrance where large dirtied plastic strips hung from the ceiling in disarray, some shorn away through use, and others shredded at the sides. No two pieces were the same length. The dilapidation resembled the state of the hospital he thought, battered and bruised by successive governments promising much and delivering little except more body blows.

The chapel was a right turn and then a short corridor before an immediate left. He checked his watch. It was 6.47am. The chapel was dimly lit and empty as he entered and when the door shut behind him it was surprisingly quiet. He was nervous and felt it in the pit of his stomach so he sat down on a seat at the central edge of one of the aisles, stretching his legs out as he did so but not long afterwards felt that this was inappropriate with only his maker as a witness.

No light came through the stain glass windows, of which there were a dozen, that in just a couple of hours would dazzle in multicoloured luminosity. When Dawn turned up he wanted to present an aura of authority and calmness to try and glean as much information as he could in the short time they had available so he didn't sit for long and was soon standing and then hugging the walls as he moved clockwise around the chapel following the story of the Crucifixion.

He heard the door open behind him but was immediately disappointed. A stocky man with short hair wearing jeans, long sleeve shirt and trainers went straight down the central aisle to the altar and fell to his knees. He was still but Jeff sensed effort in his prayer. He hadn't even acknowledged Jeff being there and his head remained bowed as it was when he had entered and as it stayed all the time Jeff's inquisitive eyes were fixed on him. Jeff eventually felt he was intruding and therefore moved back towards the rear of the chapel closer to the entrance.

Jeff wasn't religious but neither was he one of the new breed of atheists. He couldn't even regard himself as an agnostic, because quite blatantly he wasn't the least bit interested. He was, like, many others his age, brought up with at least a weekly dose religious instruction at school. In his formative years he had been led through some New Age enquiry, easily led by the girlfriend he was dating at the time. Yet in spite of this he did have some empathy for the reverence the gentleman was showing in the face of his maker. His thoughts were interrupted and the silence shattered as a voice he recognised addressed him from the doorway behind him.

"Do you believe in God Jeff?"

He was wearing a white overall this time, buttoned at the front and without a badge and underneath some tracksuit bottoms and trainers. Jeff's heart sank. He had heard perfectly but couldn't help himself.

"What?"

"Do you believe in God?"

Jeff didn't answer and thought only of Mia and the words he had just compiled in his letter.

The alarm was raised at 8.17am. The screams were easily heard in the laundry and before long a crowd had quickly gathered at the entrance with one member of management blocking the way. Security and Angela had been informed immediately and Richard was already on his way to the hospital, after receiving, on this rare occasion, an early call.

A cleaner had walked into the chapel and witnessed the desecration. The altar measuring 6 ft x 3 ft was constructed above a carved panel in pine, with the base supported by steel struts for legs. Two large candle sticks with half burnt tapers, each about twelve inches in height stood a further 2 yards to the side and Jeff's jacket hung from one of them. Behind him was the cross on the wall.

Jeff's body was splayed, back down, on the altar. There were blood stains on the drape and on the floor. His head and torso remained on the granite surface but his legs were at least part hanging over the side and he was still wearing his shoes with his laces tied. His shirt top was ripped open with several buttons lying on his right hand side and another two on the floor and his hands still gripped and covered the instrument of his death that was plunged into his chest?

Richard and Mark were soon amongst the throng and barged their way to the chapel entrance. Mark had his colleague clear the entire corridor and placed a temporary barrier in the form of 'cleaning in progress' signs and two mops and buckets. The distraught cleaner was already taken back to security and Angela was her caring and curious comforter.

As Richard approached Jeff's body out of habit he went to his inside pocket and pulled out a pair of gloves. He looked at the floor but didn't see anything remarkable aside from a couple of buttons. The chairs remained uniform and tidy, the flowers in front arranged perfectly. Even as he approached the grotesque image in front of him the stained cloth seemed unruffled, perfectly set with the creases remaining starched and the lifeless body on top.

He felt for a pulse in Jeff's aorta but knew he wouldn't find one. Then, like Jeff, he walked the perimeter of the room looking for anything, any clue. He heard the commotion a little further outside and by the voice and language knew what was coming. He was ready for her as she pushed away security and tore through the double doors to the entrance. He was the last physical barrier between her and her ex lover and he could see the pain in her eyes. He raised his hands and copied her moves as she tried to side-step him.

"Hold on, Hold on." And then she was in his arms sobbing. After a while, as he held her tightly and gestured with his hand to Mark to report everything was O.K, she lifted her head slightly and muffled imploring him.

"I have to see him."

"It's perhaps better you didn't."

"I don't care…I have to see him."

He realised his efforts would be futile.

"I can't let you touch him. Come with me." and he led her gently holding her shoulders with his hands, whilst her left hand wiped away the tears with the back of her wrist. As they stepped onto the raised platform he stood behind her ready to catch her and his anticipation was accurate for in just a few seconds she was buckling. He held her and then led her away quietly. At this moment her welfare was paramount, he couldn't do anything for Jeff. As they headed out onto the corridor they were engulfed by blue uniformed officers and men in suits. He spoke to the one in authority and reported briefly what he had found.

Without knowing how they had arrived there Mia was conscious that she was sitting in Angela's office and a cup of coffee was placed in front of her. She heard voices about her but was lost deep in her own thoughts. She became conscious that Richard was sitting opposite her and it was she who spoke the first words.

"I can't face it again."

## 78

The chapel and laundry area was sealed off for the day and it was well into the afternoon before forensics were happy to have the body removed and the exact cause of death confirmed, although the sharp sedated knife embedded in his heart left little to the imagination. The police presence was enormous and the Conference Room became a hastily built ad-hoc control centre within the hospital. The security team was besieged with requests for every camera recording throughout the hospital as well as immediate logs of everyone who had signed in and out in the last 24 hours although it didn't escape just Angela that it was known, despite stricter working practices, that some junior doctors found solace and slept in the hospital where they could use the available showers and toilets to freshen up before heading onto the next shift.

The social work team were interviewed individually and then given the rest of the day off. The team was instead run by a skeleton staff on a duty basis by members of other senior colleagues and management who were drafted in from other hospital and community teams. Angela took advantage knowing that there wouldn't be so many hoops to jump through and got several pressing cases on their way out as there were enough managers around to secure funding.

Aside from Richard the whole hospital was in shock. No-one knew why anyone would want to harm him. As rumours emerged of Jeff's involvement in the rings and that the events earlier that day were a possible suicide there were again shouts of dismay that Jeff was, in any way, a candidate for either action.

The body was moved upstairs to the morgue for pathology to get their hands on. The press were all over the place hunting for the merest whiff of scandal and it wasn't long before they got their noses into the investigation for a series of stolen rings and a 'Murder in the Chapel.'

The camera footage showed up nothing unusual and all visitors were accounted for apart from one; a short stocky man, with little hair and a paper in his hand, who, from the moment he entered the hospital to the moment he exited, had kept his head bowed. He had used the main entrance on exit as well and was seen walking away casually and was finally lost between road cameras.

## 79

It was mid afternoon and Richard had volunteered to take charge of a search of Jeff's property being that he already knew the layout. The murder squad would control anything that occurred in the hospital environment. Against Richard's better judgement Mia insisted on joining him declaring that she could identify any areas that he might have missed. Once again Richard started downstairs and with Mia's help hunted for anything to identify a change in Jeff's state of mind or a suicide note. There were two things that bothered Richard and Mia. Firstly, where was Jeff's laptop? He hadn't walked into the chapel carrying it and he was clearly on his own as he had done so. Secondly; where was Jeff's car? He had his wallet in his trouser pocket but no car keys. A man fitting his description was eventually caught on camera walking into the hospital site from the local area at 6.30am but a search of the local area within a 2 km radius had revealed nothing at all.

At Jeff's home Mia had suggested looking under carpets upstairs but Richard had checked that on the original night in the darkness and in several places he had ripped up the corners.

As they climbed the stairs Mia noted.

"You know there's a lot of crap in the attic."

"I know, I've already been up there once." But as he reached the top of the landing he stopped and closed his eyes.

"He's been here....or someone else has."

"How do you know?"

"The floor."

"What's happened to it?"

"Well when I left last night there were bits of paintwork all over the carpet but now they're gone."

"But why would anyone go to the point of cleaning up the landing."

"There's two answers...." and with that he covered his eyes with his right palm and his fingers wrestled with his brow. "And both of them aren't good. Either someone has come in and is scared of leaving any prints or......."

But he didn't want to voice the alternative. If Jeff had been here then he probably heard everything he said – he started to feel sickly.

"We're going to have to stop now – I'll need to make some calls and get the team in."

They both returned downstairs and as Richard prepared to exit the property to make some calls Mia couldn't help herself.

"I know this will sound weird, but do you mind if I take a couple of CD's with me. I saw them in the kitchen. Only..."

Richard understood that mementos were important, in whatever form they took and he wasn't going to deny her that. He interrupted her.

"Yes, but put some gloves on." and he handed her a pair from his inside pocket.

"You're like a magician with them..... I wish you could magic him back." And a tear rolled down her right cheek but Richard was already out of the front door.

Mia picked up the CD's and as she returned to the front door she saw the mermaid. She stooped as she always had done and blew on the glass. But as she did so a mark caught her eye so she blew again a little further down and then around the whole area, and there were more marks which revealed themselves. She found two distinct arrows pointing downwards to the floor.

Her head dropped and was almost horizontal to the floor as she searched for something, she just didn't know what. The tiles were firm and didn't give . There certainly wasn't anything under the sofa but she checked again, just for the sake of it. And then she spotted the gleam off a bright silver screw on each side. She stood up quickly and checked against the rest of the door and received her confirmation – only small black tacks were used everywhere else. She rushed back to the kitchen and opened the fourth drawer down where the odds and sods of screws, screwdrivers and tape-measures were kept. With a small Phillips' screwdriver she unscrewed the two silver screws firstly on the left and then on the right. As the second one loosened there was a slide and the plastic cover on the laptop hit the tiled floor. She pulled the flap of the doorway ajar and reached in to slide the lap-top horizontally to the right edge of the door. She took it out and quickly sealed the door again, keeping an eye on Richard who had walked up to the top of the driveway to get the best mobile signal. She returned the screwdriver to the kitchen with the laptop and then, obscured from the front door, opened up the laptop.

She tried the old password of his even though she thought she was being conceited. 'MyMermald' worked instantaneously and she was immediately alert. She closed the laptop shoved it in the rear of her trousers and covered it with her jacket and exited the property with a small piece of hope in her heart, completely unaware that every movement she now made was being watched intently.

The End

## Acknowledgements

There are always too numerous people to thank when writing a book but without Hannah and her faith in a broken man alongside her patience, wisdom, forgiveness and abundance of love to help mend me this book would never have come to fruition. Each day with you is priceless.

I'd like to thank Catherine Burnham who inspected and edited the very early draft of this book and helped me sail in the write direction. All future errors herein are wholly mine.

I am also grateful to Scott Moles for his artwork and for his permission to use the painting for the front cover for this book. Facebook Scott Moles Creations.

A big thanks to Victor from Nairobi on pexels.com for back cover photo.

Thanks to the entire GA Community. Honesty works and your love, compassion and encouragement never ceases to make a difference to me and to all those who find solace within your walls.

My children, Ossi, Aatu and India, as you can imagine, have been put the mill and have achieved so much in circumstances that would have been greatly improved without an addict in the family. I carry their strength with me and hope I can become the father they deserved.

I can only apologise to Outi for never having the courage to speak out and share my inner turmoil. Her honesty and trust in me was abused throughout our time together. Her bravery in the most trying circumstances is truly admirable.

My mother and father have always been there for support in the most disadvantageous and distressing moments and without it my recovery may never have had started. It is testament to them that I am actually still alive to write this trilogy.

## About David Joyce

At aged sixteen, on the back of some very poor exam results, I landed my dream job - to work in a bank just a stones throw from my home. The only problem was I was already a compulsive gambler and had been since the age of eleven. You can guess the rest. At aged forty six I finished my prison sentence for fraud and my life started again. My compulsion to gamble, like any compulsive gambler, was an insidious disease that not only wrecked my life but also the lives of family, friends, work colleagues and victims of my warped character and errant behaviour. Yet there had always been help available and if only I'd had the courage to tell just one person then my impact on society could have been so different.

With the help of family, friends, and new acquaintances, some of whom endured my worst traits, as well as the rooms of Gambler's Anonymous and God I began to turn my life around and to write this trilogy, the first of which centres around the secret world of a gambler's mind.

Compulsive gambling doesn't have to end in tragedy. If you recognise any of the traits of a compulsive gambler or live with its side effects on a daily basis then there is help. I have provided a brief list of organisations who support problem gamblers and their loved ones. There are also a number of links to tools that may help compulsive gamblers on their road to recovery.

For anyone with a gambling problem.

Gamblers Anonymous: www.gamblersanonymous.org.uk. Tel 0330094032

GA Scotland: www.gascotland.org/

Gam-Anon: www.gamanon.org.uk for families friends and loved ones of

problem gamblers.

GA Gamblers Anonymous International: www.gamblersanonymous.org/ga/

Gamstop - gamstop.co.uk - controlling your ability to gamble online

Gamban - gamban.com - controlling your ability to gamble online

Gamcare  www.Gamcare.org.uk gambling support around numerous issues.

Big Deal.  Gamcare website for young gamblers.  www.bigdeal.org.uk

The Samaritans - www.Samaritans.org   Tel 116123

The National Gambling Helpline. 0808 802 0133

Gambling Commission www.gamblingcommission.gov.uk

Counselling -   www.counselling-directory.org.uk

   www.bacp.co.uk

Financial. - www.stepchange.org

   www.citizensadvice.co.uk

   Christians against poverty  www.capuk.org

Further excellent information regarding support organisations country wide as well as governmental organisations, counselling, employment and financial support can be found at www.gamcare.org.uk/selfhelp/links-to-other-support-agencies and gamblersanonymous.org.uk

Printed in Great Britain
by Amazon

11352429R00157